"Sheild sets up the perfect storm in his grandfather-grandson road trip adventure. An archaeologist on the hunt for fabled artifacts and the bad guys who are willing to use deadly force to take easy pickings will have American western history buffs turning pages. Elegantly told, this fast-paced thriller set a generation earlier uses the magnificent prairies and haunting remnants of powerful nations as a backdrop. Secrets abound, justice may or may not be served, but when new friendships are forged, anything is possible. Past and present collide on multiple fronts as two cultures must work together to salvage peace."

-Lisa Lickel, author of the *Buried Treasure* cozy mystery series

"Join Dr. Colby Phillips and his grandson, Jimmy, on an archaeological dig that will change both their lives forever. On the journey to what could prove to be the biggest discovery of his professional life, Colby is forced to reckon with the misdeeds of his past and consider the legacy he wants to leave for Jimmy. The story includes many (earned) twists and turns, and the author paints a convincing portrait of the grandfather-grandson relationship. Readers will feel as if they have been dropped smack into the middle of a dig site in 1969 South Dakota. With a strong sense of place and time, this book grabs the reader and doesn't let go."

-Kim Suhr, author of *Nothing to Lose* (Cornerstone Press) and director of Red Oak Writing.

"*Bad Medicine* was a fast-paced story with a unique premise and a fresh take on the classic treasure hunter story. I love a good setting, and Sheild's vivid descriptions made me feel like I was right there in 1960s South Dakota."

-Amanda Waters, author *You Again*

"...an adventurous, engaging page-turner."

-Lee Whittlesey, National Park Service Historian & author of eight books, including *Storytelling in Yellowstone*

"Life is like a treasure hunt. We are doing our best to follow the correct path, hoping to find health, wealth, and ultimately happiness. What starts out as a bonding journey for a grandfather and grandson, turns into a race against the clock and more. They take us along on the treasure hunt of a lifetime, into ancient burials to find what was thought to bring ultimate happiness.

At a time when I needed the perfect distraction, Sheild pulled me in, and I couldn't turn away."

-Lauren Guelig, author of *Wish Me A Rainbow*

BAD MEDICINE

A Novel

PETE SHEILD

Author of *Sermons From Thy Father*

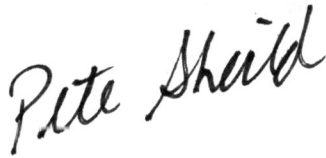

www.ten16press.com - Waukesha, WI

Bad Medicine
Copyright © 2021 Pete Sheild
ISBN 9781645383611
First Edition

Bad Medicine
by Pete Sheild

Cover design by Kaeley Dunteman

All Rights Reserved. Written permission must be secured from the publisher to use or reproduce any part of this book, except for brief quotations in critical reviews or articles.

For information, please contact:

Ten|16
PRESS

www.ten16press.com
Waukesha, WI

This book is a work of fiction. Names, characters, places and incidents are the product of the author's imagination or are used fictitiously. Characters in this book have no relation to anyone bearing the same name and are not based on anyone known or unknown to the author. Any resemblance to actual businesses or companies, events, locales, or persons, living or dead, is coincidental.

For Dan
1960-2020

AUTHOR'S NOTE

Human history can be unflattering and reprehensible—even in books of historical fiction based on facts. The reader should be aware that this book depicts sensitive scenes that could be deemed offensive. But they did happen—endorsed by private and public entities for decades. I have tried to convey those scenes in the most dignified manner possible. Additionally, I have used the term Indian, as opposed to Native American or Indigenous People, as the descriptor because it is historically accurate for the time period in which the book takes place.

I have the utmost respect, admiration, and affinity for the peoples indigenous to North America and their descendants. Exhaustive research of their history and lives only deepened these feelings. May this book provide the reader the opportunity for a similar appreciation.

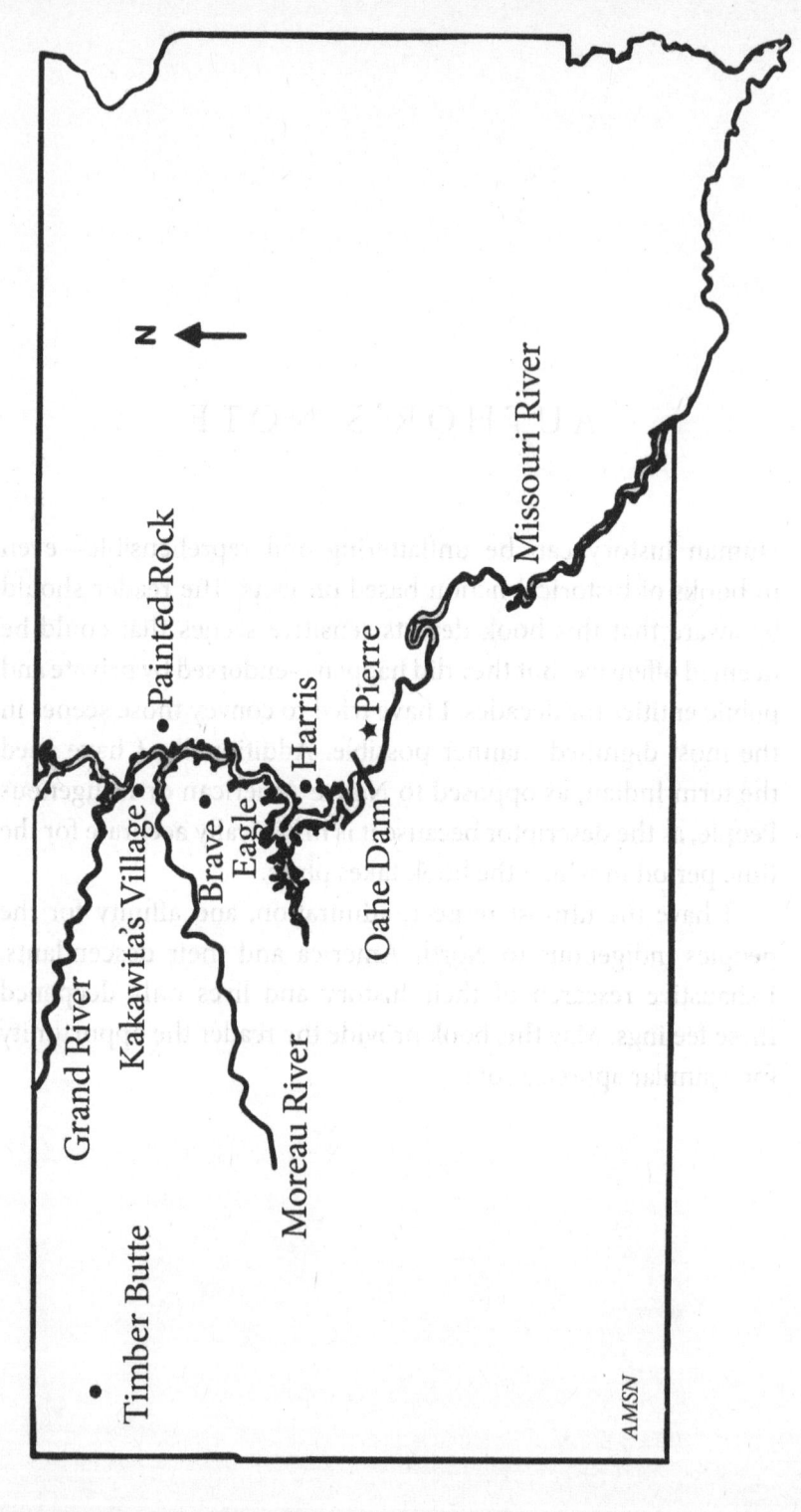

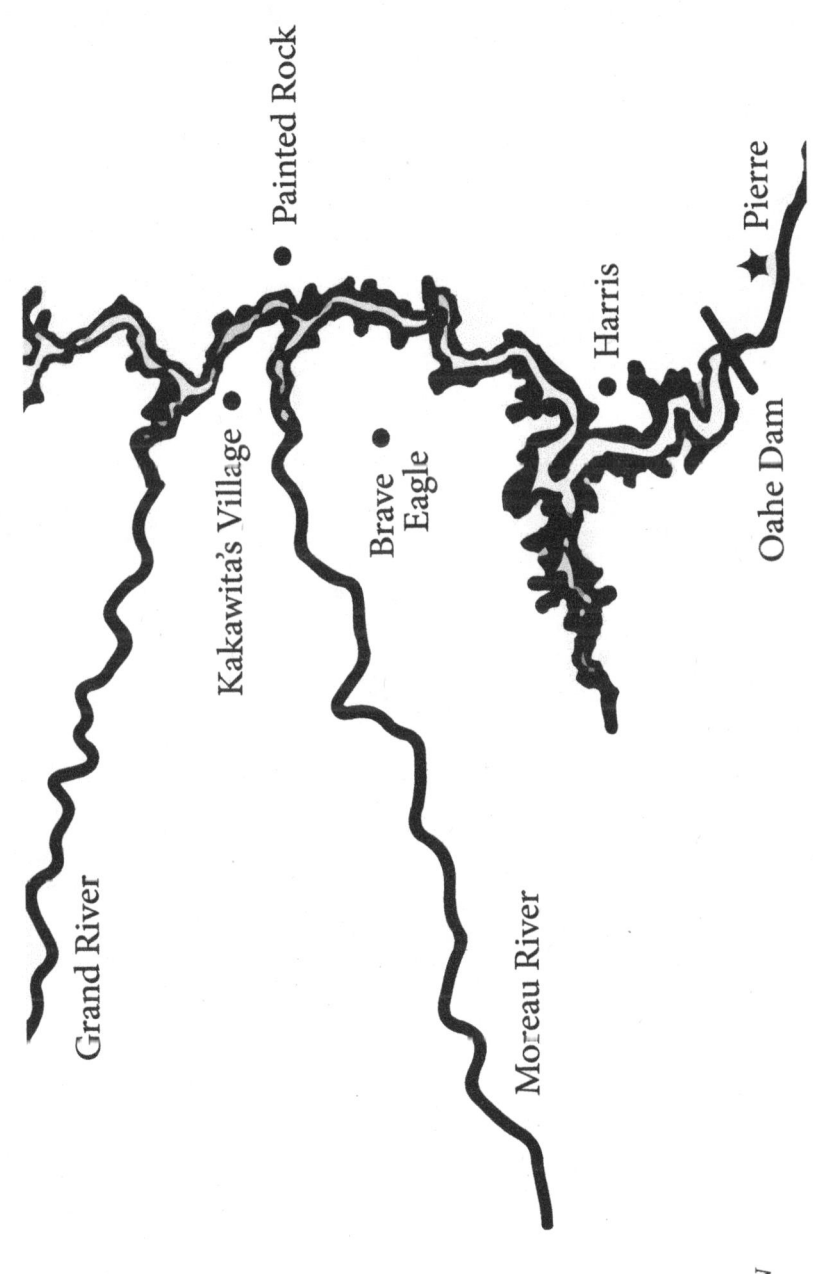

1

SOUTH DAKOTA

July 1969

The ribbon of asphalt stretched over hills and dales for miles, around fallow meadows overgrown with multicolored wildflowers and through sloughs ringed in cattails, guiding Dr. Colby Phillips and his nineteen-year-old grandson, Jimmy, ever closer to their destination. Past the abandoned farmhouses, surrounded by fields dotted with ebony Black Angus cattle. Through the acres of sunflowers, that accentuated the vastness of the South Dakota prairie, saluting them as they rumbled on in his University of Kansas issued 1965 International Harvester Scout. As the Scout sped past the green wheat fields, they swayed and bowed like a subservient worshipping royalty. Redwinged blackbirds darted across the highway from telephone wire to telephone wire busy collecting insects.

Despite his white t shirt being uncomfortably stuck to the

vinyl seat, Dr. Colby Phillips sat relaxed behind the wheel, window open, arm resting comfortably against the door, fresh air rushing past his ample white hair. His sunglasses softened the glaring Dakota sun blanketing the landscape. Colby liked everything about this trip. Why wouldn't he? Despite his getting along in years, he was still at the top of his game. He was the best in the cultural archeology field most recently documenting seven ancient Indian villages and burial sites for the state of South Dakota.

The road widened into two lanes as they approached one of the last hills before Painted Rock. Colby slid over to the slow lane in case other cars wanted to pass. Simultaneously, a mud caked pickup truck blasted past them, horn blaring, as the driver yelled an obscenity at the slow-moving Scout. Colby leaned forward squinting hard to read the license plate. Wasn't a South Dakota tag.

"Indian Nation tag," mumbled Colby.

Jimmy perked up. "Jeez, what's the rush?"

This trip would be his grandson's first archeological dig of burials, and Colby hoped it would be emotionally cleansing for Jimmy. Colby's daughter, Mary, Jimmy's mother, had died four years earlier of breast cancer, and it had hit Jimmy hard. It was obvious to Colby that his grandson was still processing the loss. Colby had set aside his own sorrow over the years trying to help Jimmy cope with his grief, which had become challenging at times during his young life. On more than one occasion, depression and anger had led to self-destructive behavior for Jimmy. Colby chose to comfort and heal rather than shame and judge. In doing so, the two had grown closer than ever before.

"Hey, I read about you and your work last summer in a *Life* magazine article," said Jimmy.

"Oh, yeah? I never read it. They interviewed me for over

an hour on the phone. I musta answered a hundred questions. What'd it say?" replied Colby.

"It talked about the largest earthen dam on the Missouri River located north of Pierre, finished around ten years ago to dam the river for power, irrigation, and recreation. The major impact on the economy. Then it went into your dig last summer when you traveled with a crew of six volunteer undergrads to an Indian village northwest of Painted Rock where you were excavating burials before the Oahe Reservoir could cover the site with rising water because of the dam. Stuff like that." Jimmy continued, "Hang on. I brought it. It's in my duffle bag, let me grab it." Jimmy crawled between the bucket seats to locate his brown canvas bag, withdrawing the magazine with folk singer Judy Collins on the cover.

"Just so you know, I had a lot of interest from students to come with me on this trip to finish excavating the burials," Colby explained following Jimmy's movements by glancing in the rear-view mirror. "I turned them all down. I want you to know that I'm looking forward to spending time together and excited to have you along. I'm not getting any younger, you know. This trip, just you and me," Colby said pointing with his thumb to Jimmy, then to himself, "is long overdue."

"I agree, Grandpa. Loooong overdue." Jimmy's face widened into a smile as he looked at Colby in the rear-view mirror. This trip was to be the last hurrah of summer for Jimmy. His sophomore year at the University of Kansas would start soon. He would be missing the first couple of days of classes, which made the trip even more worthwhile. "Yeah, I'm excited, too, but I didn't realize until I read the article that we were going to dig burials. I mean, I thought we were just going to dig in the village," Jimmy said as he made his way forward.

Colby slid his left hand to the top of the steering wheel and tapped his right index finger on the dash for emphasis. "Nope, we are excavating the burials. Other less experienced colleagues of mine can deal with the villages themselves, but me Jimmy... by God I am going to focus on the Indian burial grounds themselves. *Particularly* this site we are going to. Know why?"

"No idea, Grandpa." Jimmy's face reflected bewilderment as he settled back into his seat.

"Well, first off, this is a village I have researched heavily over the years for a reason I'll get to in a minute. Second, we are in a race against time due to the fact that down south they have had heavy rains all summer that have forced the Corps of Engineers to close the flood gates preventing any more water from going downstream. That, in turn, has caused the river to rise at an extremely rapid rate." Colby used hand gestures to demonstrate down and up. "By my estimation, the burial grounds of the village we are headed to will be covered within a week or two. All my research on this site will be for naught. A timeless piece of history, something I've been looking for most of my career, will be gone forever. At that point, I might as well quit."

Jimmy's jaw dropped.

"No, I'm serious. This could be the trip that finally gets me the recognition from a lot of different people in my life that I've been waiting for. It is, perhaps, the rarest and most sought-after treasure in the Cultural Anthropology world. We are talking chapters in history books about our find...my career...all of it...if I find it. Deserved recognition, interviews—I will be mentioned with the other great explorers of this century. I'm talking about finally receiving the Exemplary Service to Anthropology Lifetime Award or maybe even the Gold Medal Award for Distinguished Archeological Achievement. You will be famous, too, Jimmy. What do ya think of that?"

"I guess that'd be pretty cool."

Colby laughed, "Pretty cool?" Colby tilted his chin down as his brow raised, "That is a major understatement." He let out another chuckle. "But I digress. You asked why the burials, specifically. Because the burials often tell the story of life, death, and the hierarchal value of the deceased within the tribe. That is all far too important to let someone else do what I have been gifted to do. That's why private donors support my work, and the National Science Foundation awards me very generous grants."

"So ya going to tell me what this sought-after treasured piece of history is?"

Colby's thoughts drifted to how completed he would feel, personally and professionally, when he found the medal. "Yeah but read me the article first."

"Alright. Let me read some of it. It starts…"

Colby interrupted Jimmy, "Did they get into when President Kennedy dedicated the dam in 1962, he signed into law the Indian Cultural Preservation Act designed to salvage a portion of Indian heritage?"

"Yep, and it mentioned you were at the ceremony." Jimmy opened the magazine using the folded corner he had made to mark the article. He started, "Dr. Phillips' crew meticulously records, excavates, and then catalogues the countless Indian villages in the flood plain before the villages are overtaken by the ever-climbing waters of 'progress'. Colby, as he is known to his colleagues, has been given carte blanche by the Corps of Engineers, the South Dakota State Historical Society, and the University of Kansas to go where he needs to go and do what is necessary to preserve our native culture and heritage at the village burial sites." Jimmy laughed with eyes of adoration as he glanced at Colby, "Basically, you didn't need permission. Nobody questions Dr. Colby Phillips!"

Colby shrugged his shoulders, "What can I say?"

Jimmy continued. "An anonymous colleague describes him as self-absorbed, egotistical, but the most powerful force in our field. Without his background, his knowledge, and his desire, the history that is told in the burials would be lost for all of time." Jimmy looked up. "I'm not going to read the whole article. Let me get to the ending. Here…" He paused to turn to the last paragraph and continued. "Without Dr. Phillips' work future generations would never know the Arikara people. An entire tribe, their customs, their way of life, their story—gone." He closed the magazine.

"Not bad, huh? Thanks for bringing it with."

Traveling north from Kansas offered Colby the opportunity to connect with his grandson beyond the times spent fishing, hunting, going to University of Kansas football games, or just hanging out, talking about life. Hopefully, Colby surmised, this trip would help Jimmy's struggle to get over the emotional hump of his mother's death. Over the course of their lives, they'd bonded and became best friends. What Colby hadn't shared with Jimmy was that his grandpa had bounced around in both the academic world and the world of women trying to stay one step ahead of their accusations of impropriety and paternity suits. Around the time of his daughter's death, Colby had pushed the limits with the university when he had been accused of, "a gross misappropriation of funds" from his department. Colby felt justified and considered it a "loan" from the university to help pay his daughter's medical bills. He did pay the funds back but not before his envious colleagues reported him. He considered himself fortunate that his years of work had garnered the university an enormous amount of money and that made him untouchable. The Trustees at KU had to have a scapegoat because they claimed their accounting evidence was overwhelming. The newspapers ran the story front page and above the fold for weeks. It was not good public relations for the university. Donations from alumni were beginning to decline in a big way. In the typical fashion of a college's back-room dealings, Trustees and alumni clamored for the university President to get the scandal off of the front page. Someone had to be held accountable, they pleaded, and it wasn't going to be the sacrosanct Dr. Colby Phillips. That left Associate Professor Earl Chavey, Colby's friend, and co-director on many digging trips, as the fall guy. After an expedited trial, he was convicted by a jury of his peers of embezzling and was currently serving time.

The Scout lumbered along, straining to top the repetitive inclines of the hilly landscape. "Hey," Colby said turning to Jimmy, "I've been meaning to ask you whatever happened to that steady girlfriend you had senior year in high school?" Colby looked at Jimmy with raised eyebrows. "She was a cutie. What was her name, again?"

"Jenny. Last summer, the day after our high school graduation, she said we should go out with other people. She broke up with me." Colby heard Jimmy's voice drop and saw the heartbreak in Jimmy's eyes before turning away to stare out the car window.

"Oh, man. I'm sorry to hear that, Jimmy."

Jimmy pivoted toward Colby. "It's really ok. She was going to some school out in Boston I'd never heard of. Plus, she partied too much. She probably smokes pot," he said with a hint of disgust.

"You don't want to get mixed up with that stuff. And I've been wondering about your studies. How did your freshman year at KU go?" questioned Colby with arched eyebrows.

"Good. Made the honor roll as an Ag Econ major." Jimmy had always gotten good grades. Through the years, teachers remarked on his report cards that he kept to himself, never caused any trouble, and had good manners for a young man. His parents had raised him as such.

"Well, congratulations. But did you have any fun?" Colby smiled at Jimmy because that's what he really wanted to know.

"Yeah, I dunno. Went to a few house parties. My roommate wanted me to pledge the Delts, but I wasn't really into the frat scene. I said no to the dorm touch football team, too." Colby knew Jimmy could be withdrawn, especially when it came to his social life. "I usually went back to help my dad on the weekends or picked up some hours bagging at the Red Owl. Always nice to have a couple of extra bucks in my pocket."

"I'm sure he appreciated the help."

"You know how it is, Grandpa. Livin' on the farm it's all about the work." While growing up on the farm, his mother and father had taught him all about hard work, doing things the right way, to love God. Jimmy's gangly frame measured six foot three and about 200 pounds but farm strong with muscles earned from never saying no.

The conversation faded and gave way to their minds immersed in the beauty of the panoramic landscape. *Growing up in the middle of Kansas wheat country, Jimmy probably found the hustle and bustle of college life a bit overwhelming. Of course he retreated to the farm. It was his sanctuary.* Because of the time he had spent with Jimmy over the years, Colby could tell that Jimmy knew he was different from his peers in many ways and Jimmy seemed to be okay with that. After all, no one Jimmy hung out with went digging Indian burials with their grandpa for a summer vacation.

To its occupants, it seemed like the Scout knew the way from Lawrence to Painted Rock. The beat-up truck had made the trip north dozens of times. The red of the Scout had faded to a dark pink, and rust was beginning to show around the wheel wells. White wall tires were worn almost completely through the tread. The AM radio was tuned to Colby's favorite local station, KOLW, with the Beatles' "Get Back" blaring above the din of the open road. Colby thought about the significance of Neil Armstrong's walk on the moon just six days earlier and the paradox of the future that achievement represented against his mission to dig in the past. How odd. He had conceded to himself that the world was changing rapidly, but he wasn't sure he could keep up—or if he wanted to, as long as his work and the plains could offer haven for him.

"How much longer to Painted Rock?" Jimmy asked.

"I'd guess around 25-26 miles. We'll gas up and get groceries before we cross the river. Get your boots on because I don't want to spend any more time there than we have to. We're running out of daylight as it is."

"I gotta pee really bad."

"Okay, you're just gonna have to hold it. Make a list of what we'll need for groceries so we can get through the Red Owl quickly. We'll need ice for the cooler. Don't let me forget…I've got the Coleman stove packed away under the shovels, so we will need to keep that accessible. It'll be dark when we set up camp."

They surveyed the endless terrain in quiet until Paul Harvey came on the radio.

"Hello, Americans! This is Paul Harvey…Stand by for…The Rest of the Story!"

"Listen up, Jimmy," Colby said turning the knob so that Paul

Harvey could be heard above the drone of the warm wind whipping through the Scout. He checked his watch. 4:15, right on time. Colby loved Harvey's resonating deep voice, the stories he told with pauses for effect. It was always a beautiful blend of forgotten history and little-known biography only to reveal the subject's identity at the end. "I used to listen to Paul Harvey with your mom when she was your age. Let's see if we can guess who it is." The countryside became a blur as ears listened to the legendary radio newscaster and storyteller beginning to spin another web of mystery...

"*His daily walk to the three-story mint located at the corner of 7th and Filbert Street in Philadelphia was only 15 minutes. He was accompanied along the way by the sounds of the clip clop of horses and the hubbub of people hurriedly going off to the market or work. The stench of horse droppings, and the city itself, rose from the gutters alongside bustling cobblestone thoroughfares. The smokestacks of the textile mills reminded him of the pipe organ at his Lutheran church back in Uslar, in present day West Germany. He was 25 years old and had immigrated to our country three years earlier, in the year 1800.*"

Colby turned to Jimmy, "Who do you think it is?"

"Ha. No idea," Jimmy said, shrugging his broad shoulders.

He had started at the mint doing menial jobs just to make ends meet. No one knew he had come to the US as a skilled artisan engraver, or "die sinker." He rose to Second Engraver rapidly and was introduced, by the old and crotchety Head Engraver, Robert Scot, to President Thomas Jefferson who admired the German immigrant's work.

The "die sinker" was a bundle of nerves as he pulled out the chair and sat down in front of Mr. Scot who said to him, "The President indicates in his note to the director of the mint that he wants YOU to design and cast a medal, I guess a peace medal or whatever you want to call it, for an upcoming journey by explorers of land west of the Mississippi River. President Jefferson just bought a large tract of land from France," Robert paused, coughed, and took a deep breath. "These medals will be used as trade goods with Indians or fur trappers or whoever else- they encounter on their journey to the Pacific Ocean. You have three months to get it done."

"Can I put on some music?" asked Jimmy.

"Shhh. No way! Wait till it's over." responded Colby. He hadn't heard "The Rest of the Story" in a while but thought it fortuitous and gratifying that he would be introducing the radio legend to Jimmy, just as he had to his daughter. Jimmy let out a sigh of boredom, slumping in his seat. Colby turned the radio up to make his point. "This is a good one."

Immediately, the talented immigrant began to carve the plaster casts. It took an entire week just to get an outline of Jefferson's profile using carvers, spatulas, and double-ended picks. The following week, he withdrew another plaster cast from the shelving next to his desk. He was itching to create the back side of the medal knowing that the medal would have to be created in two halves and somehow joined. Using a rasp and small chisel, he started with the hands - one an outstretched Indian hand, the other an outstretched hand of a military officer, clasped in a handshake.

Ninety Jefferson profiles and ninety handshake sides were stamped out one side at a time. The tight time frame did not allow for every piece to be inspected. Unknown to anyone working on the stamping, the die of Jefferson's face began to deteriorate toward the end of the process, leaving some marred. Circular rings were then punched out to join the two halves of the medal into one piece. Once cast and polished, the finished product shined with originality and artistry.

Colby couldn't believe the irony and timing of what he was

listening to. He was sure to tell the narrative, on the certainly forthcoming banquet circuit, of how on the ride out he listened to Paul Harvey talk on the radio about the history of the Thomas Jefferson Peace Medal and then he actually found that very medal. "I've got something I want to tell you that will add to the story when Paul Harvey is done," Colby said to Jimmy. Jimmy nodded in return.

"Gentlemen, gentlemen! Quiet please. Quiet down." Robert Scot's hands padded the air in a downward motion for silence as he spoke to all the employees of the mint. The chosen craftsman stood toward the back of the assembled group. He wasn't much for attention. "President Jefferson's Corps of Discovery Expedition, as it is to be known, will be led by Captain Meriwether Lewis and Second Lieutenant William Clark. They will lead a group of volunteers and stake our claim to the territory before the British or some other treacherous country does. Undoubtedly, their journey will be fraught with peril and uncertainty. This small medal will serve as a gesture of peace and friendship with those they encounter along their route up the Missouri River from the city of St. Louis to the Pacific and back. We wish them Godspeed. May our work live for generations in the possession of those with whom we have made peace and found favor. Thank you all for your diligence and your allegiance to our country."

A jubilant cheer combined with a loud applause went up from the assembled employees. The unassuming German immigrant slung the knapsack over his shoulder and followed his co-workers out into the Philadelphia evening, proud of his work.

Robert placed the medal into the pocket of his vest for a keepsake as he headed upstairs to his office where he placed it on his desk. It served as a reminder that he should have been the one commissioned to create it. He was not sure the angst he felt would ever go away. Two men, vastly different backgrounds, one chosen, the other passed by. Forever linked by their work.

Unbeknownst to them was the twisted tale the Jefferson medal would weave through the centuries in the lives of explorers, Indian tribes, mountain men, and historians.

His name? The German immigrant chosen by our third President to design the Thomas Jefferson Peace Medal for Lewis and Clark...his name was Johann Reich."

"And now you know...the rest of the story...Paul Harvey.... Good day!"

Colby turned the radio down. "That's what we are after Jimmy!" Colby exclaimed. "That's the timeless piece of history I mentioned earlier. The Thomas Jefferson Peace medal. Some call it the Lewis and Clark medal. That's why we are headed to the Indian burials at the village west of Painted Rock."

"Have you ever found one?"

Colby laughed out loud. "You're kidding right?" Colby saw the blank expression on Jimmy's face and knew he wasn't kidding. "No, I haven't found one, but like I said, I have put decades of research into circling this village as a strong possibility of producing a medal.

"Hey, can we put some music on now?"

"Yeah, sure. Be my guest."

Jimmy turned the tuner knob trolling through the garbled words, whistling static, screeching interference, and three noted songs on the AM dial until he found a station playing Creedence Clearwater Revival's, "Bad Moon Rising."

The sun was looping toward the horizon as they crested the hill. There before them lay a picture postcard. The town of Painted Rock in a perfect grid of streets and avenues with the Missouri River wrapping around it like a mother wraps her arms around a child. Indian lore said an Arikara warrior courted a beautiful Indian maiden by asking the Great Spirit to paint all the rocks in the valley the colors of the rainbow to win her heart. The settlers who came to the area heard this tale, which had been passed down for generations. They thought Painted Rock appropriate, so the name stuck. In the distance the far side of the wide river offered randomly scattered mesas, eye catching taupe buttes contrasting the charcoal-colored shale bluffs, and a generally untouched landscape. The unevenly spaced draws along the river were filled with a mixture of shimmering green ash and cottonwood trees, emerald and olive in color. The blue sky reflected off the river with a glint of silvery radiance. The railroad had started this town when it was the farthest point west the Milwaukee Road went. A little less than a century earlier, cattle had been herded from all over the western expanse beyond the river to ferry across on steamboats. From there they were herded on rail cars for their trip east to the slaughterhouses and dinner tables. Since that time, the railroad had pushed farther west and expanded in every direction. Now it only went through Painted Rock once every other day carrying either grain or coal. It was no longer the hub of commerce it had once been. The town had diminished to a drive-in theater, gas station, a Methodist church, two taverns, an empty grain elevator, a grocery store, a bank, an insurance agency with apartments above, a hotel, and Chubby's drive in. The stockyards had fallen into disrepair, and the rodeo tour had long since stopped coming.

"Let's get gas first, then grocery shop," relayed Colby. "You go to the bathroom, and I'll get the windows."

"Okay. I need something to munch on, too. I'm starving!"

They pulled into the Sinclair gas station greeted by the double ding of the welcome hose and were acknowledged by Gus, the owner of the station. He was a portly balding man, wearing blue coveralls, who looked to be in his mid-sixties. Colby had met Gus the year before when his radiator hose had blown just east of town. He shuffled forward from under the big bay door of his garage with a red oil rag hanging from his right back pocket to meet Colby and Jimmy near the pump as heat radiated from the concrete. His head was oversized for his short body. He offered a welcoming smile that revealed a couple of broken front teeth.

"Filler up sir?" Gus took a closer look. "Hey wait. You look familiar. Yeah…didn't you pass through last year about this time? He stood close enough to Colby so he could be heard over the noisy passing of the semi-trucks carrying combines west or livestock east on Grand Street, as the highway was known, within town limits. "I recognized the University of Kansas written on the door."

"Yes, I did," Colby acknowledged. "Good to see you. Thanks again for your help. Fill 'er all the way to the brim, Gus. And check the oil, too. I'll do the windows. Seems like you folks had an insect hatch overnight. I can't see out my windshield!"

Gus went about filling up the tank while Colby cleaned the windshield of colorful insects and butterflies -- twice. They danced and jostled awkwardly around each other as Gus reached through the grill to unlatch the hood so he could check the oil. Colby finished the windows, put the squeegee back in the bucket, and headed inside to settle up. Jimmy was waiting by the cash register as Colby and Gus sauntered in. "Heartbreak Hotel" filled the small entryway.

"Put the salted nut rolls on the tab, as well. What's the river elevation above sea level at these days, Gus?"

"Last I heard it was 1,586 feet and coming up fast. You might know the river, 'er the lake I mean, oh the hell, the reservoir, is full at 1620. Until then they won't let any water out. Been a wet summer down south. Why do you ask?"

Colby could feel the blood drain from his face as the knots in his stomach twisted hard. He knew the consequences of the rising water. In a matter of days not weeks, at 1,593, the burial field would be covered. *How ironic, over one hundred and sixty years in the ground, forty years of research and searching, but it comes down to some pencil pushers sitting behind a desk at the Corps of Engineers? Time is everything now.*

"Oh, no reason. Just curious."

Colby remembered that Gus had asked what all the odd assortment of equipment and camping gear in the back of the Scout were for. "Research work for the university," Colby had said. That ended the conversation. On previous trips, Colby had learned that folks in these parts never asked a lot of questions. Their collective nature – live and let live. Best not to ask if you don't want to hear the answer. Gus's thick fingers hit the cash register and the bell tolled at $2.70. Gus waited as Colby dug into his right hip pocket for his wallet. Colby gave Gus a five-dollar bill, received his change, and out the door they went.

"Jimmy, you should know that this trip has some added importance attached with it," confided Colby.

"What's that?"

"I got a call from the White House yesterday as I was loading up the truck. Guy by the name of Haldeman somebody or other. I guess he's President Nixon's Chief of Staff."

"C'mon, really?"

"Yep, really. He said in no uncertain terms President Nixon thinks our work as the river is rising has national cultural and historic importance beyond anything else since the early 1900's.

President Kennedy had a similar message for the Egyptians in 1961 when they were building the Aswan Dam to flood the Nile. So many cultural and educational opportunities would have been lost without America's support along with the U.N. He said President Nixon put my work on that scale of importance."

"Huh. No pressure, right?" Jimmy answered. "Well, I guess we've got to get to work."

They left the gas station with a bump and a clunk as the back end hit the pavement of the curb. The Red Owl was up ahead on the left. They parked diagonally on the street and walked across the broad thoroughfare. As they entered the grocery store, the rush of air-conditioning met them. They split up for efficiency, gathered their necessary supplies, checked out, and returned to the heat.

Outside the grocery store, they opened the chest freezer and took out a block of ice for their cooler. Colby paused at the curb while Jimmy, block of ice secured in a cardboard box, scampered across the road ahead of a dusty light blue pickup truck with Tennessee plates. Both the driver and his passenger turned and stared at Colby as they passed, their tired eyes set in dust-covered faces searing right through him. *Are they looking at me?* he wondered, as he crossed the street. Grandpa and grandson pulled out the shovels and Coleman stove and replaced the shovels with the stove on top. They crammed the groceries in the open nooks and crannies around and in between the sifters, potato forks, note pads, and tent stakes. The bologna, cheese, and ice went in the small cooler in the back seat. Colby and Jimmy resumed their traveling positions, and they backed out into traffic to continue heading west.

The river grew broad as they rounded the bend out of town heading for the mile-long bridge that would take them from the comfort of what they knew to the distress of searching for something that might not ever be found. By now the sun was cut in half by the horizon. Magnificent blues and soothing purples, filtered by billowing clouds and dust, filled the sky.

"Look at that sunset. Wow, I'll never get tired of seeing sunsets over the Missouri," Colby commented. "Don't like the look of those clouds building to the north, though." They rolled up their windows to fend off the evening's cooling temperatures. Colby felt content despite knowing they were racing against the river's rise. The trip up from Kansas had gone well so far, filled with anticipation, and the promise that tomorrow could bring. If it wasn't tomorrow, it could be the next day, or the day after that. Just so that promise was kept before the river overtook the burials. Colby saw that Jimmy's eyes were getting heavy, "Might as well rest your eyes, Jimmy." Grandson glanced at grandfather for reassurance, then leaned his head back. Colby sat rigid, focused, two hands on the wheel as his mind wandered to the one prized artifact he had never found but knew intuitively existed on the west side of the river.

Colby pulled the knob to turn on their headlights as they sped into the great unknown, the vault of darkness engulfing them.

2

TENNESSEE

July 1969

Early Evening

The three-story penitentiary stood in a heavily wooded lush valley in the rugged mountains of middle Tennessee. It was appropriately named Brushy Mountain State Penitentiary. The minimum-security prison sat in a remote clearing of a thick mixture of spruce and Douglas firs intermixed with towering hardwoods. Oaks, maples, dogwoods, and poplar were abundant. Thick underbrush completed the forest. A stranger traveling through the area might have mistaken the prison structure for a medieval castle as it sat majestically in a ravine of the Crab Orchard Mountains on the Cumberland Plateau. Built in 1896, the jail currently housed over 550 inmates. Most of them were small time repeat offenders.

Inmate number 031972 had been assigned to Billy Dalton. The presiding judge had given him the choice of joining the Army and going to Vietnam or doing time at Brushy Mountain. He had no beef with the Vietnamese. He chose time. With that choice came court mandated therapy sessions with the prison psychologist, Dr. Brittany Melrose.

"Little chill in the air on your walk over I bet," Dr. Melrose started, as they settled into their time together.

"Yes, ma'am," responded Billy. "Feelin' like fall is coming early this year."

"It sure does." She opened Billy's folder that contained his record. "Okay, Billy, since this is our first time together, I'd like to review a few things. You're in for petty theft, fourth offense. Huh," she paused, "each time it was for liquor or cigarettes?"

"Yeah, well the first couple of times, my pops said he'd beat me if I didn't go to the store and get him smokes. I didn't have no money, so I had to steal 'em."

"If my math is correct, you were twelve," Dr. Melrose said removing her bifocals. "That would make you twenty now." She quickly scribbled a couple notations in Billy's folder.

Billy tilted his head to the side, "'Bout right."

"Right. So, let's start with your childhood," the Doctor said, sitting in her brown and gray institution-issued desk chair four feet in front of him.

For Billy, counseling offered a break from his light gray colored prison cell that smelled like an outhouse. His fingers fidgeted as his lean torso slouched on the faded tan chaise lounge style sofa, left arm draped on the arm rest. "What do you want to know?" Billy responded, his sunken eyes darting around the room, annoyed. He rubbed a scar that ran from his left cheek bone to his chin, the result of a broken bottle to the face in a bar fight in Memphis. "I already went through all that with the last shrink."

"Tell me about your family and what it was like growing up in Morgan County."

"My pops worked in the coal mines. Most days he'd stop at The Garage Bar after work, come home drunk, and either beat my mom or me and my brother. Whoever looked at him wrong." Billy let out a big sigh. "My mom left us when I was about eight. She left with my younger brother to find work in Nashville or Knoxville, I can't 'member which, and they never came back." Billy shifted on the couch trying to get comfortable. He hated it when he had to tell people his mom left them.

Eyes forward, Billy thought Dr. Melrose looked attractive with her flipped bob hairstyle and brown polyester pants suit over a wide collared white blouse. "Sounds like you had a difficult childhood. How did you do in school?"

"Pretty much my report cards were C's and D's. 'Casionally, if I paid attention, you know, I'd make a B. I did enjoy history and math." He shifted in his seat again and rubbed his shaved head, feeling antsy. "I remember in 6th and 7th grade I was in the genealogy club."

"Interesting. Why did you sign up for genealogy club?"

Billy laughed, "Because I could stall from goin' home. I tell you what, though, that genealogy taught me a few things. I had first cousins that married each other, my grandpa on my mom's side was a bootlegger, had a relation that did a stint here in Brushy in the 20's. Let me just say this, Doc, no one ever worked for someone in my family." Billy's palms had become sweaty. "Sure, seemed like we were taken advantage of by people goin' way back."

"School sounds like it was a welcome relief from your home life. What did you do once you graduated from high school?"

"Well, tried to find steady work. I guess them beatings made me show no respect for my bosses 'cause I could never get along with them or take their direction. I kinda got a quick temper, too. Previous shrink said I have a violent temper." Billy rubbed his index finger across his razor thin mustache, his eyes cast downward. "I think mostly they didn't like my kind and that's why they fired me."

"What do you mean by 'my kind'?"

"Coal miner's kid grew up on the poor and forgotten side of the tracks." Billy's voice went up a few decibels because he felt the answer was obvious. "They said I had a chip on my shoulder."

Billy picked at his fingernails watching Dr. Melrose uncross her legs and re-crossed them, adjusting her belt in the process. "What happened after you got fired?"

"My old man kicked me out, so I was shackin' up on a friend's couch. Nobody was goin' to hire me. Hell, don't you know Morgan County is where dreams die slowly over time? I wasn't goin' nowhere, that's for damn sure. Weekends my guys did dog fighting. Betting on it gave me money for partyin' most nights." Billy sat up, excited to tell Brittany more. "The rush of watchin' pit bulls fight till one of 'em died or bled out got to be better than any of them drugs we was doin'. I didn't even mind gettin' to shoot the loser in the head."

"Wow, that's a very strong message. I'm wondering how it made you feel to shoot those dogs." It looked to Billy that Dr. Melrose was writing 'sociopath' in capital letters in her notebook. "Is it possible that shooting the dogs made you feel powerful?"

"I dunno. I mean, I guess killin 'em or watchin' 'em in pain- I liked it. Yeah, made me feel powerful. Doesn't make me weird or anything if that's what you're gettin' at." Billy's face showed no emotion as he slid into a slouch again.

Billy and Dr. Melrose held eye contact in silence. She adjusted her bifocals and with pursed lips said, "Alright then, your previous counselor, Dr. Irma, has in her notes, and I quote, 'His face masks the fact that his mind is always active. Billy is shrewd in his thinking but keeps his emotions in check. He carries a blank look on his face which often conceals his true intentions as he has done his best to not make waves by keeping a low profile within the prison population. He has never been in favor of the race integration that is currently taking place across the country. Billy states he can relate to the poverty experienced by most of the negroes he knew. Because of this, he feels well-liked by his fellow inmates and tolerated by the guards,' end quote. Would you agree with that assessment, Billy?"

Leaning forward Billy nodded, "Yeah, sure, I reckon that's 'bout right." Billy had gotten good at telling people what they wanted to hear.

Billy stared out the window. Dr. Melrose made some notes as the afternoon crept into dusk. Gusts of wind rattled the three nine-pane windows of her office. The setting sun, partially obscured by a passing bank of clouds, cast dancing shadows of darkness into the room.

Dr. Melrose set her notepad and pen down as she stood. "That's all the time we have for today, Billy. I have to cut our session short because I have a family matter to tend to."

Billy's tense facial expression relaxed.

"It feels like you are starting to understand more about yourself. I think you are making a lot of progress. Same time next week?"

"Yes, ma'am." Billy bolted off the couch. "I definitely feel like we had a breakthrough session." Billy nodded toward Dr. Melrose, "You can count on seein' me next week."

Billy strutted out of Dr. Melrose's office with a big smile on his face. Heading back to his cell block, he crossed paths in the yard with Earl Chavey.

"Hey, Billy," Earl monotoned as the two stood facing each other. "You good with the info I got you and what you gotta do for me?"

"Yeah, I'm good." Billy casually scanned the yard to see if anyone was watching.

"The deal has to go down tonight, tomorrow at the latest. My wife told me during contact visitation today that her sister, Colby Phillips' secretary, said Phillips left for Painted Rock today. Remember what I told you. I'm good for the money. Just do your job." Earl moved a step closer but kept his hands in his pants pockets. His lips tightened and his eyebrows scrunched together. "Make your relatives, you know…the ones I traced back for you, remember? You coulda been a part of the medal's story, a part of American history. Make 'em proud…for you." Earl paused and pointed a finger at Billy, "You get Colby Phillips for me."

"Got it. You already made clear what's up. I know Phillips' kind. I'm aiming to settle your score, and I'll enjoy doin' it," Billy smiled. "Don't you worry 'bout me. You just make sure your wife gets the money in my account when I get that token, or whatever, to our drop spot."

Earl Chavey turned and walked away. Over his shoulder he said, "Have a nice night."

Billy mirrored Chavey's departure, mumbling to himself, "Plannin' on it."

Tonight, it is, he thought. Eight months into his eighteen-month sentence, he was already tired of all the rules and structure. Everything had been meticulously schemed out for his escape. Months of planning had gone into this evening. For his liberation, he had constructed his ladder over the last 6 months. Fortunately for him, the social worker at the prison had bought his story of rehabilitation through an electrician apprenticeship. He had schmoozed his way to be the foreman's assistant of the electrical shop. That gave him access to the storeroom and the ability to smuggle 12-inch sections of conduit along with various lengths of electrical wire out of the shop. He accumulated enough to build his ladder of deliverance. An oak forest, lowlands and a small marsh were all that separated Billy from his freedom. He knew if he got on the other side of the wall, they'd never catch him.

His cousin, Charles Ray Dalton, would be waiting with his pickup truck idling a mile away. Charles Ray and Billy had grown up hunting squirrels, catching bass, skipping school, and getting into trouble. Often, when they were younger, they'd picked fights against the bigger boys at school and always won. They never needed a reason, they just liked to fight. Sometimes it was a fight over lunch money, sometimes over a girl, sometimes they fought just to see the other guy bleed. Nobody messed with the Dalton cousins. They were cousins by blood, but brothers in arms. Always.

Once back from Vietnam, Charles Ray felt he didn't fit into society anymore. It was hard for Billy to see Charles Ray struggle with the headaches and flashbacks that forced him to go to the VA where they diagnosed him with "shell shock." Additionally, he had developed a twitch in his neck muscles that made his head jerk uncontrollably. His doctor told him it was a physical manifestation of shell shock brought on by stressful situations.

Alcohol proved to be the only elixir that cured the tic, the flashbacks, the headaches, the self-esteem. He drank too much whiskey with Billy one night at the Tip Top Tavern. Heated words were exchanged, and, in a rage, he beat some guy within an inch of his life using the butt of his Colt M1911 .45 pistol. Billy pulled him off the guy just in time. Then he stuck the pistol in the belly of the guy's pregnant wife and laughed. Witnesses said the guy was talking crap at the bar about the Dalton family. Billy said the other guy had provoked Charles Ray by jabbing his finger in Charles Ray's chest. Charles Ray swore he couldn't remember. The authorities said he'd done it. The judge pounded his gavel in agreement with the authorities. He served 24 months of a 36-month sentence and got released on good behavior. After talking with Earl, Billy phoned Charles Ray to pick him up along Valley Creek Road after lights out and head west to do a job. Easy money.

Lights out. Billy pulled off the vent cover in his cell to withdraw the makeshift ladder crafted from electrical conduit tied together with electrical wire. He worked quickly tying one end of the ladder to the bed frame. He wrapped his hand in pillowcases, smashed the window glass, and threw the ladder out the opening. The ladder unfurled into the darkness and landed with a clatter on top of the razor wire positioned atop of the twelve-foot chain link fence. He chipped the odd shaped pieces of glass still attached to the window frame and spun around to exit legs first. With his heart racing, sweat beginning to form on his brow, he scurried down the ladder like the athlete he used to be toward his freedom. As he reached the last rung, the rise and fall of the high pitched shrill from the prison alarm shattered the tranquility of the valley.

Whooop! Whooop! Whooop!

Bright search lights clicked on and began to comb the area around the prison at a frenetic pace. The clatter of boots running on pavement, keys jingling, men shouting, and doors slamming replaced the quiet hum of the fluorescent bulbs. The prison acted like a ravenous predator tracking down its quarry.

Without pausing he spun back around and leapt off the ladder and over the bulge of the razor wire. Airborne with arms outstretched to provide a balanced landing, he nevertheless hit the grassy embankment, tumbled, and fell forward awkwardly. He ended up face down, spread eagled, but intact. His left ankle throbbed. He bounced to his feet and took off running.

Twenty yards to the woods. His twisted ankle slowed his progress, but he fought through the pain. Behind him he heard the wail of the prison siren and dogs barking. He could hear himself breathing. Every muscle in his body flexed churning for the darkness and concealment the woods offered.

Eighty yards behind him, a dozen uniformed guards sprinted out the front gate toting rifles and shotguns. Out of the distance came a voice through a megaphone. "Halt or we'll shoot!" The prison's German Shepherds barked. The guards were probably releasing them right that moment. Billy was grateful to have a large lead on them.

Fifteen yards to liberty. In the murkiness of the evening, he processed all the noises of commotion as he scampered towards the woods ahead. He heard a bullet whistle past his ear followed by the crack of a rifle. With adrenaline coursing through his body, he was all legs and arms running efficiently racing toward the finish line he had envisioned for months.

Ten yards to independence. He stumbled forward but never lost his balance. A standard prison guard-issued .223 bullet tore through the flesh of his upper right arm and he felt an immediate searing pain. Blood began to soak his blue shirt. Charged with endorphins, he forgot the pain and entered the shadowed protection of the trees. The undergrowth was thick with sharp thorns and bramble. The terrain under foot contained uneven contours with an occasional rocky outcrop jutting out. He hopped and skidded right and left knowing it would slow the dogs just enough for him to get to the marsh. A couple more rifle cracks and a couple of bullets hit trees, one on his left and one on his right. He knew the guards were just shooting hoping to get lucky, pot shots really. Two blasts from a double-barreled shot gun peppered the trees above raining pellets on him. The lack of moonlight and the depth of the woods provided a welcome cover of darkness. Billy could barely see his way in the dark maze. He stumbled on the briar and logging slash, fell, and scrambled to his feet bleeding and determined.

Intermittent shotgun blasts were interrupted only by the barking of the dogs as he pushed on, knowing that the time he had spent running laps in the yard was paying off. The trees thinned as he crested a ridge. Ahead, the ground sloped down toward cattails and marsh reeds shrouded in fog. He stopped. Bullfrogs croaking in the distance. His feet and thighs felt heavy. Billy's shirt was completely soaked with perspiration as his heart pounded through his chest. He strained to see. *Where the hell am I?* He began to panic. He looked right. He looked left. He looked behind him. *This isn't how I remembered it from years ago.* Everything was a shade of gray or black. *Yes, this is the right place.* He bolted to his left for about thirty running paces through a babbling brook before his wet feet sank into the shallow marsh muck.

Plodding along through the dense bog as fast as his legs would carry him, he heard the hum of a V-8. He could smell the exhaust vapors from Charles Ray's pickup truck. Billy paused, listened, and looked. He could not hear the dogs, but he could hear the shrill of sirens departing the prison. With his arm throbbing, he scrambled through the remaining marsh rot. On the other side of the mire, he stripped down to just his underwear. A sudden chill went through his body as he hustled up the incline to the truck. The smell of cigarette smoke wafted above the vehicle. He grabbed the door handle and jumped into the front seat as Charles Ray put his shotgun on the floor, threw the car into drive, and did a U-turn.

"What took you so long, man?" smirked Charles Ray.

Clean clothes lay on the floor at his feet. He quickly put on his socks, t-shirt, jeans and laced up his boots. He grabbed Charles Ray's .45 caliber automatic pistol from the glove compartment and stuck it in his pants under his shirt.

"Had to stop and sign a few autographs," dead panned Billy with a sneer. "Time to get me the hell outta here!"

Charles Ray gunned the engine spitting gravel and squealing tires up and out of the valley. The cousins headed west, laughing all the way.

3

SOUTH DAKOTA

Three Years Earlier

October 1966

Colby spied the official looking car easing through the gate between pastures. It followed ruts that led it across the beaten landscape in the direction of the camp, located 12 miles west of Harris, South Dakota. Most of the prairie vegetation was in the midst of a color transition as fall had announced itself through fewer daylight hours and cooler temperatures. Overhead, a perfect V-formation of two dozen snow geese honked their way south.

Strutting like a peacock, apart from the dust and toil, hands clasped behind his back, surveying the entire burial dig site including the new arrivals, a man with vainglorious posture, Dr. Colby Phillips. In one trench, two females were packing up their excavating tools, notebooks, and cameras. Over a couple of trenches, a tandem of shirtless males, shoveled and sifted with a tail of brown dust drifting in the wind. Closer to the river, another group of three students were on their knees using trowels and brushes over an Indian burial. Colby wore his leather jacket embroidered with the University of Kansas emblem over his flannel shirt, work jeans, and sturdy boots. His cowboy hat held firm in the wind by braided leather stampede strings cinched under his chin completed his aura of machismo.

The driver of the car, with Department of Indian Properties superimposed over the outline of the state of South Dakota, parked near the cluster of pup tents. With long strides, he began to walk up the incline to the area where trenches had been cut. He was followed by a man, clearly his second. "Good afternoon! Mr. Phillips, is it?" The first shouted, approaching the crest of the hill. The man had broad shoulders tapered to a slender waist and beady eyes set in an angular face. His sidekick carried his ample pudginess around his waist, wore black rimmed eyeglasses with thick lenses, and had large jowls. In their mid-30's, they wore crew cuts and dressed in white shirts, black ties, and black suits under black trench coats. The high shine on their shoes seemed out of place, as did their JC Penney fedoras. A prairie chicken flushed ahead of them.

Colby turned toward the strangers, unmoved. "It's Doctor Phillips. What can I do for you?"

"We're Special Agents from the Department of Indian Properties out of Pierre. Name is Paul Gritzmacher, and this is Roger Calhoun." They flashed their silver badges and pocketed them all in one motion.

"Dr. Colby Phillips, University of Kansas, Chairman of Cultural Anthropology and Archeology. Is there a problem?"

"Oh, heavens, no, Doctor," Gritzmacher assured Colby. "Just a routine check of the site. We check all the ongoing excavations along the river for the State of South Dakota. Shouldn't take more than fifteen or twenty minutes."

Colby scrutinized the two special agents. "I've never been checked before. This seems highly unusual."

Gritzmacher shook his head, "Actually just a routine inspection. We'll start by setting up an inventory station over by the tents." Gritzmacher pointed toward their camp and the stand-alone blue tarp lean to with white boxes stacked neatly on top of each other.

Colby's chin jutted forward as he let out an exhalation of exacerbation at the two annoying intruders who had wandered into what Colby thought of as, "His Kingdom." "I guess there's no harm in that." The two Staties took their cue and began to walk back toward camp.

"Hey, Earl," Colby shouted to his right-hand man and Assistant Professor in the anthropology department, "Get everybody to wrap up their excavation with some photos." Earl had been one of Colby's best students and accompanied him on multiple digs in years past. Colby was grooming him to be his successor. "And get Bob, Ann, and Rob to carry those tools back to camp and put them in the back of the Scout. We won't be using them anymore." Colby put his index fingers in the corners of his mouth and let out a high-pitched whistle. "It's quittin' time!"

"Will do," Earl shouted back. Colby knew Earl looked up to him, not only as a mentor, but as a friend. Over the years, Colby had found that Earl was willing to do anything in the hopes of riding his coattails into a Chairmanship position at the university when Colby retired.

Colby met the Special Agents back at the blue tarp, where

Gritzmacher had begun opening boxes. Calhoun had laid out the artifacts on the box cover, efficiently taking pictures of the trove of Arikara artifacts collected upon excavation of the burials. Calhoun appeared to put something in his black suit coat pocket. "*What the—?*" Colby interrupted the clicking of the Canon camera. He stepped toward the boxes but ran into Gritzmacher's outstretched arm. "That's university property!"

"Relax," Gritzmacher snarled. "We just need a sample, so our boss knows we were here. It's just a rim shard of pottery. You probably have thousands of them."

Colby's eyebrows moved down and together. He backed off but kept a keen eye on every movement Calhoun made.

"While Roger is taking pictures, let's review your paperwork," deflected Gritzmacher.

"What paperwork? I filed everything with the State Historical Society and Corps of Engineers," Colby had his hands on his hips, his face contorted in anger as he stepped out of the shadow of the tarp and into the sunlight.

"I'm sure you did. Huh," Gritzmacher looked away, then his eyes returned to focus on Colby. "Well, the thing is, Dr. Phillips, we couldn't find any of it. I thought maybe you had a copy with you," Gritzmacher calmly replied.

"No," Colby yelled. He felt agitated at the incompetence of bureaucrats. He turned around and attempted to grab Calhoun's camera.

"What the heck are you—?" Calhoun fumbled the camera, glasses flying onto the hard prairie sod as Gritzmacher wrestled Colby into a one-armed head lock that put Colby's face within inches of his state-issued pistol.

"Let go of me!" Colby shouted, struggling to free himself from Gritzmacher's grip as his prized cowboy hat tumbled in the wind.

"Phillips, you're under arrest for obstruction of an investigation," Gritzmacher adjusted his hold, deftly reaching to get his handcuffs off his belt. He pulled both of Colby's arms behind his back to slap the cuffs on him. "Let's go. Time to take a drive."

Calhoun closed up the boxes, and they paraded Colby toward their vehicle just as the clan of his coworkers approached the camp. Colby could feel Gritzmacher and Calhoun's grip tighten as they marched at a brisk pace. "You have the right to remain—" Gritzmacher began.

"You're making a big mistake," Colby said attempting to twist away from the duo. "You can't do this to me. You have no cause, no warrant, and I'm Dr. Colby Phillips!" Colby spotted Earl leading the troop of understudies toward camp. They abruptly stopped wide eyed and open-mouthed when they saw the commotion. "Hey, Earl, get a hold of the AG's office in Pierre! They need our paperwork. The AG office has it." Digging his heels in the prairie, Colby turned to ask the Staties, "Where are you taking me?"

"There's a nice cell at the courthouse in Harris waiting for you," Gritzmacher wrenched Colby forward.

"They're taking me to Harris," Colby hollered over his shoulder to Earl, who had broken away from the pack and approached Colby's side.

"Okay, I'm on it," Earl said pivoting to the Scout. Back peddling, he cupped his hands to his mouth, "I'll get to town and make some calls. Meet you at the courthouse." Colby watched as Earl sped away toward Harris.

"Alright in the back seat you go," Gritzmacher ordered. He opened the door and unceremoniously pushed Colby into the back seat. Colby righted himself and looked in the direction of his group feeling like an animal on display at the zoo. He half smiled hoping to send a message of reassurance. The grim-faced university students continued to stand in shock as the sun ducked below the clouds, hit the horizon lighting up the sky in a kaleidoscope of colors.

In a show of power, Gritzmacher hit his lights and siren leaving with dust flying in his wake. Colby, not amused, endured Calhoun and Gritzmacher's laughter. A couple miles from the burial grounds and a mile from the county highway, Gritzmacher stopped the car, turned off the light and siren and got out.

He opened the rear driver's side door and scooted in next to Colby. "So, here's the deal. We can correct this terrible misunderstanding and," Gritzmacher smiled, raised his hands and rubbed his fingers together, "make us both some money. Such a deal, right?"

Colby stared at Gritzmacher with a seething glare. "How about we start by you taking these handcuffs off me?"

"Oh, we will. All in due time." Gritzmacher spoke with a reassuring tone, fluttering his right hand to calm the open space between them and the front seat. "Now, what we have is a mutually beneficial opportunity that we think you will be interested in. We know someone who will pay top dollar for those artifacts that are in those boxes back at camp," Gritzmacher tilted his head, his face softened, and he put his arm around Colby's shoulder. "Our proposal is that we split the proceeds, and should we, the three of us, think it best, move on to the next village, and so on. No one gets hurt, and everybody is a winner. And from what Calhoun and I hear, Doctor, you've got quite a reputation for finding valuable artifacts. Am I right?" Gritzmacher tilted his head to give Colby the look of a sincere car salesman closing the deal. "You like our proposal, right?"

"Are you outta your cotton-pickin' mind? Absolutely not.

Never." Colby shook his head. He turned to face Gritzmacher, "I have funders like the National Science Foundation that I have to show documentation, you know, for the journal papers I publish. I literally depend on them for financing my work. If I don't show results, they'll pull my funding. I've worked too hard to build my reputation to have it dragged through the mud for a few extra bucks. Ever hear of the word, integrity?"

"Now hang on," Gritzmacher took off his fedora and set it on his knee. "Wait 'til you hear the whole story. What about if you just took the good pieces and left some of the poorer quality ones for your report? Or supplement those boxes with stuff from other digs. Kinda recycle stuff."

"Look, if you're going to book me at the courthouse, let's get on with it," Colby replied. Blue veins popped along his neck. "And as soon as we get to Harris, I will call my attorney to report both of you for extortion. I will not compromise any of my Native American artifacts. They belong to the university, and I have too much integrity to go along with your crazy scheme." Colby turned away to look out the window.

Gritzmacher tapped Calhoun on the shoulder. "Roger, how much do think those boxes are worth back at camp?"

Calhoun paused to do the math in his head. "Ahh, by the looks of what I saw…I'd say about three-grand."

Gritzmacher turned to Colby with a cocked head, "So a poorly paid college professor couldn't use another fifteen hundred?"

Colby turned back to face Gritzmacher and laughed, "For fifteen hundred? Nope."

"Times three or four villages a year, Doctor."

"Still nope." Which Colby knew was a bit of a lie since he was still paying his daughter's medical bills even though she'd passed away a year earlier. A twinge of temptation bounced around inside his head. He admitted to himself that there was less and less left over from his paycheck. Despite that, he overpowered the thought knowing he couldn't do anything even remotely seen as illegal. If he ever lost funding, he'd be out of a job. No job, no paying his daughter's overdue medical bills. The debt scared him more than the extortion. No job, no searching for Kakawita's village, and no Thomas Jefferson Peace medal. *That* scared him more than the debt or extortion, combined.

"You're bluffing, Phillips," Gritzmacher's tone turned aggressive. "What about a poorly paid college professor that got an underage Indian girl pregnant? Oh, that would probably not help your reputation or help get you any more funding." Gritzmacher wagged his head from side to side while smiling.

"What the hell are you talking about? I never got an Indian girl pregnant!" Colby's face turned a deep red, his mouth dry. He took his shoulder and drove into Gritzmacher, with little effect.

"Alright calm down, Phillips." Gritzmacher leaned forward to catch Calhoun's attention. "I bet we could make up a juicy story 'bout the Doctor wandering onto the reservation after a hard day of digging. Brought some fire-water to a friend's house…" Gritzmacher looked away, his voice trailing off. "Your friend brought over some girls, some pot…the papers eat that kinda stuff up!" Gritzmacher's eyes and smile widened then narrowed with seriousness as he swiveled his head to look Colby right in the eyes. "Now listen, we can make all that potentially nasty alleged paternity suit go away if you just say yes."

"You've got quite an imagination. A ridiculous one at that. No one is going to believe you. It's too easy to disprove." Colby desperately wanted to gain control of the conversation. "Now, I think what's mutually beneficial is that I don't tell the authorities what you're trying to do, and you get the hell out of my life."

Colby leaned back as far as he could and quickly brought his legs up. In one motion he kicked the front seat, Calhoun's head hit the dashboard, and Colby's feet were back on the floor.

"Jeeeez," Calhoun lamented. He turned and glared at Colby, shaking his clenched fist.

Gritzmacher put his hand on the door handle, turning to Colby, "Alright, tough guy, can't say we didn't try. Let's put you in a cell. Maybe a night in jail will get your mind right."

"My answer will always be no."

As he turned to close the sedan door, Gritzmacher leaned back into the car. "You ever, I mean ever, discuss our proposal with anyone else and I find out about it.... you will wish a paternity suit was the worst thing I ever did to you. Are we clear?"

Colby didn't answer, eyes fixed forward, conflicted, yet firm in his resolve. Gritzmacher wriggled into the driver's seat and resumed the trek to Harris. Calhoun found a station on the AM dial with the Temptations telling all those willing to listen that they, "Ain't Too Proud to Beg". Gritzmacher and Calhoun sang along. Gritzmacher glanced in his rearview mirror to see Colby fuming, staring right back at him. The song ended as the gong of the top of the hour rang, and an ABC News Brief started:

"*The Baltimore Orioles have defeated the Los Angeles Dodgers to sweep the 1966 World Series for their first World Championship. Still no cause determined for the crash of a West Coast Airlines flight 956 in Oregon. Turning to the national economy, inflation continues to grow as part of the effect to fund the war in Vietnam. The upcoming Gemini 12 mission is reportedly still on schedule for launch for November. Astronauts Buzz Aldrin and James Lovell will be conducting several experiments during their four-day mission. I'm Frank Reynolds and this has been an ABC News Brief.*"

"By the way, how the heck did you hear of work being done at my site?" Colby asked.

Gritzmacher smiled, "A young Indian jeweler from the reservation keeps me informed of what goes on. I ran him about a year ago for trespassing on Corp of Engineers land. He had been duck hunting. Third offense so we came to an agreement. He helps me; I keep him out of jail. Seems to be a good arrangement for both of us." Gritzmacher chuckled, slapping the steering wheel.

They came off the prairie and hit the highway, rumbled alongside rail lines that connected grain elevators and small towns. Passed cars with occupants exchanging nervous glances as they roared around them. Past open spaces of pasture and harvested fields of corn that stretched for as far as the eye could see. America's heartland transitioning from green to brown, cloaked in a broad sky, split by a sliver of faded paving. The county seat of Glass County, Harris, had a population of 896. It offered the local folks the essentials: a movie theater, gas station, Congregational church, Catholic church, grocery store, community pool, Birch's clothing store, and the National Guard Armory. Upon their arrival to the brownstone courthouse, whose grounds took up an entire block, Earl was waiting for them. "I've got the AG's office working on it." Earl scurried across the gravel to join the three-person procession on the way to the jail entrance illuminated by the naked yellow bulb on the backside of the building. "Can't get anything done this late in the day. Secretary said she will send a courier from Pierre with the paperwork first thing in the morning. Don't worry Colby, I'll get this straightened out for ya." He got ahead of Gritzmacher and stood in his way with his chest puffed out. "And the AG is going to want to talk to you," he snapped poking a finger in Gritzmacher's direction.

"Good. I've got something he should know about. Isn't that right, Dr. Phillips?" Gritzmacher shot back with a smirk.

Colby ignored the comment. Instead, he turned to Earl, "Thanks Earl. Tell the others I'll be fine. This will be resolved tomorrow morning, and we can get on with our research. Pick me up at nine."

Calhoun opened the metal door, and Gritzmacher escorted Colby to the desk for processing. The officer on duty rose from his desk, shuffled up to the counter, handing Gritzmacher the clipboard containing the form to fill out. The intake officer stood at the counter, arms splayed, glancing at Colby, then Calhoun, then Gritzmacher. After a couple of minutes of filling out the paperwork, Gritzmacher signed the intake form, and Colby tried to get comfortable in his cell.

He leaned against the cold bars of the cell listening to the door close behind Gritzmacher and Calhoun. Colby pushed off the bars and sat down on the cot with his back on the cool cinderblock wall. He brought his knees up to his chest, touching the corners of his mouth as he surveyed his home for the next ten hours or so. The iron-stained porcelain sink sat idle waiting for another drip from the iron faucet. The blankets on the squeaky cot smelled musty and uninviting. *What the hell is wrong with them? I can only imagine what those bastards are up to now. I bet they are going back to the site to confiscate my artifacts for their profit. I'm sure their fence will be happy.* Colby clenched his teeth at the thought of the Staties trying to ruin him. He smashed his fist into the threadbare mattress. *Colby scooted forward, sitting on the edge of his bed. I'm pretty sure our paths will cross again, Agent Gritzmacher, and, when they do, I will make you pay for this stunt you're trying to pull.* Colby began to smile at the thought of exacting his revenge. The lights went out and quiet roamed the jail.

4

July 1969

Colby and Jimmy continued their trek on the west side of the river toward the Indian burial site. By now, the black curtain of night had been completely drawn around them only allowing illumination from their headlights and countless points of light overhead. Inside the Scout, backlighting from the dashboard cast dull amber warmth on the weary travelers from Kansas. At sunset, the Star-Spangled Banner had played on the radio and KOLW concluded their broadcasting for the day. By then, Jimmy had been fast asleep as Colby drove along the crest of a ridge that ran parallel to the river. The truck slowed as they veered off to the left transitioning from the asphalt to gravel road heading northwest. It proved slow going on the bumpy prairie.

The solitude turned his thoughts inward, backward, and reflective. Rebecca popped into his mind. Why, he hadn't a clue.

Oh yeah, this would have been our wedding anniversary.

She was the love of his life at the time they were married. Like a typical couple in love, they had shared their dreams, plans for a family, and their intentions of growing old together. Colby's mind travelled to a recognition dinner ten years earlier for the American Society of Cultural Anthropology and Archeology in Kansas City. A capstone event on his career. By then he was a tenured professor at the University of Kansas and there to receive the Viking Fund Medal for distinguishing research in the field of anthropology, along with the Rexford Monroe Award for Significant Publication in Cultural Anthropology and Archeology. Black tie, tuxes for the men, long gowns for the women, linen tablecloths, and crystal glassware. The smoke-filled room packed with 250 guests, the who's who in the field. Rebecca complained she did not feel well enough to attend another event honoring Colby. Again. An empty chair sat next to him on the dais all evening. This burned him on the inside to no end. As the room fell silent after prolonged applause from a worshipping crowd, he felt empty giving his acceptance speech, occasionally staring at her vacant chair. Driving home that night, after what should have been a joyous occasion for them both, Colby felt his jaws tighten and his grip on the steering wheel turning his knuckles white. Anger and disappointment consumed him. The night had ended up being hollow and meaningless without her being there.

Here I was to be recognized as a major player in my profession and she was not there to share in my glory. Don't you think she could have been there for her husband? Her presence, her acceptance of who I am, would have meant the world to me. I thought we were happy together. Somewhere along the way, she changed. I remember she stated in our divorce decree that one of the reasons for our divorce was that I had been constantly chasing the ghosts of success. What does that even mean? Often, she was dismissive and condescending toward my work. *I will admit, I enjoyed being busy and could be distant; however, I was always a good provider. C'mon, what more did I have to do? Damnit, I just wanted her to be proud of me! Just love me. For most, the price for memories is regrets, but not for me. No way. Memories like that are what push me even harder and why I'm here to find the medal. Finding it will validate my self-worth to her and others!*

A big bounce on the uneven terrain jarred him from the memory. After about a half of a mile, grandfather and grandson came to a steel gate for a pasture that was posted with a wooden, grey, worn, barely legible, hand-painted sign: "DANGER Buffalo Keep Out". Colby pointed the front end of the Scout at the padlock. He put the vehicle in park and gave Jimmy a nudge. "Jimmy. Jimmy, get the gate. Here's the key," Colby unclipped the key ring off his belt and handed it to Jimmy stirring in his seat, struggling to open his eyes. "Just leave the gate open. Ted will be here with the grader in the morning. I don't want to have to come back and let him in."

An orchestra of crickets and the hum of the engine filled the cab of the truck when Jimmy opened the door. The evening air that drifted in felt refreshing and had the familiar pleasant aroma of prairie flowers. Visible in the headlights, Jimmy waded through the thigh high fire weeds to reach the gate. Colby tapped his fingers on the steering wheel as Jimmy fumbled with the lock and key. Eventually he slotted and twisted the key hard to the right springing the lock open. He lifted the heavy metal frame of the gate, pivoting it on the opposite post and swung it in an arc toward the truck, giving Colby a 'thumbs up' as he passed. As Colby drove over an elevated set of railroad tracks, the truck bottomed out bouncing across the rails. He stopped on the other side waiting for Jimmy.

"Are there really buffalo here?" Jimmy asked, climbing back into the truck.

"From time to time the rancher brings them in to graze. Not sure why but we're going to want to keep an eye out for them," Colby responded. "You don't want to make them angry."

Their road ahead had turned into two well-worn ruts flanked by switch grass. The sound of dried weeds scratching the under carriage of the Scout filled the cab. It appeared as if someone had driven here recently. Colby briefly contemplated how that was possible. *The rancher must be using this for his cattle.* He thought no further. The trail followed a slight rise in elevation before it dipped down into a swale, followed by another rise and another swale.

The river came into view a short distance beyond a flat area where they would set up camp. Colby pulled over and let the engine idle with headlights on to aid with set up. They exited the truck circling to the back in unison to get out the stove along with the two-man green canvas pup tent. Colby paused, absorbed in his surroundings. From the silhouetted shadows on his left, the refuse mounds and circular depressions of the actual village transfigured the landscape. To the right, starting about 50 yards out, the gentle upward slope of the burial grounds. The smell of dew and prairie made Colby feel right at home.

"How hungry are you?" Colby asked swinging open the back door.

"More tired than hungry," responded Jimmy.

"Let's get the tent set up and you can grab a can of Chef-Boy-Ardee and open that if you are still hungry."

Reaching along the wheel well Colby handed Jimmy the machete, so he could knock down the yellow sweet clover and knee-high native prairie grasses that filled the camp site. "I'm gonna to let you set up the tent, and I'll get the tools organized," said Colby tossing the musty tent on the ground. The crack of the hammer on the tent stakes broke up the dull hum of the engine as the bivouac began to take shape. A coyote howl in the distance startled Colby as he began to assemble the sifter. He looked up to see Jimmy grab the tent poles and crawl inside the tent to place them upright at each end. Exiting the tent, Jimmy pulled tension on the guy ropes at each end and pounded a stake to hold them taut.

"Done. I'm going to bed. Food can wait till morning," Jimmy mumbled, dropping the hammer and driving the machete into the ground next to the tent.

Colby turned off the engine and slammed the doors shut, talking as he rounded the corner of the Scout. "Me, too. We have a big day tomorrow. The grader should be here by early in the morning," Colby pointed in the direction of the burial grounds, "I want to have the working plot where we are going to excavate staked out by the time he gets here."

Colby scooted into the tent, followed by Jimmy, bent to his knees to zip the outer canvas flaps, then the inside flaps of mosquito netting. Colby continued as he organized, "Time is money to those guys, and I don't want him here any longer than necessary. He's coming all the way from Campbell. I want him to get in and out in a half a day or, better yet, a couple of hours." The canvas, thinned by use and age, filtered the muted night sky to give a faint trace of illumination. By the time they got their suitcases, pillows, flashlight, water jug, and sleeping bags all arranged, they had a cozy abode. "You got enough room over there?" Colby asked.

"Yep. I'm excited for tomorrow," Jimmy unzipped his sleeping bag as he spoke. "It's going to be hot, but I'm anxious to get started on our adventure." Untying his boots, he put them at the foot of the bag and stripped down to his underwear and t-shirt.

"Not much wind in the forecast either," added Colby. "Either way, happy to be here with you." Colby smelled of sweat and fatigue as he stripped down to his white boxers. He put on a clean white t-shirt. His scalp tingled a bit as he scratched his head mussing his white locks. He would brush his teeth in the morning. They both were quiet for a moment as the soft sounds of the prairie courted them.

"Remember the Paul Harvey broadcast we listened to? I'm sure you already knew the story of Lewis and Clark, right?" Colby asked.

"Of course, yeah, I had. They went all the way from St. Louis to the Pacific and back in the early 1800's, didn't they?" Jimmy said with eyes closed.

"Did you know they came right up the Missouri? Right by where we are right now. They stopped at villages along here documenting plants, wildlife, and the natives. They also traded goods and tokens of goodwill along the way. You heard the story. President Jefferson charged Lewis and Clark with diplomacy by offering Peace Medals and American flags to Indian Chiefs they'd meet along the way. There's literature that suggests that at one of these villages along this stretch of the river…I think it was this one…they gave a Thomas Jefferson Peace Medal to the Chief." Colby paused, eyes wide open staring at the threadbare fabric overhead. "It would be incredible to find one. Even better would be to find one with both halves still bound together. And even better than that would be to find one of the scar faced medals." His heart began to beat faster as he spoke with a quickened tempo. "Like Paul Harvey said, the die was breaking down at the end of the stamping process so a few of the medals have a crease, or some call it a scar, through Jefferson's face. Only two of those have been found and only the Jefferson half of the medal.

No one has ever found both halves joined, and Jefferson's face creased. I've found lots of priceless artifacts buried with the dead but never one of those. It's the Holy Grail of artifact collecting. Can you imagine? Wouldn't that be something?"

Jimmy grunted in agreement. "Got it."

A moment of tranquility spread through the tent.

"Okay, well, we can talk in the morning," Colby said to the wind as he rolled over on his side pulling the sleeping bag up over his head.

The moon approached the midpoint of its arch when Colby shut his eyes and fell asleep.

5

July 1969

Colby stands in a claw foot bathtub, sensing water above his ankles and rising. Feeling an increased alertness, hands quivering from an adrenaline rush as the water begins over-taking him, he reaches down to unplug the drain. Withdrawing his hand, he realizes that he has the Thomas Jefferson Peace Medal in his hand. Colby looks to his right and sees his parents shaking their heads as they turn their backs and walk away. Pushing against the resistance of neck high water, he slowly turns to his left and Rebecca is standing before him. She has a look of contempt on her face as she uncrosses her arms, turns, and vaporizes out of his sight. She is replaced by an Indian chief. He appears with two black stripes on his right cheek, loin cloth, and a buffalo horn headdress, prepared for battle. The warrior chief fades in and rapidly fades out. Colby is now aware of a tugging on his feet. A whirlpool has him in its unbreakable circular grip, slowly sucking him down the drain.

The green Coleman three burner stove was perched on its stand with the coffee pot on it. Next to it sat Colby, legs crossed, clutching his coffee mug in one hand and reading a book held in the other. Sunrise was transitioning from a yellow orange to a pale blue. Aromatic morning air smelling faintly of grass originating from abundant wheat grasses tickled his sinuses. A gentle breeze carried up from the river a slight nip, which raised goose bumps on his skin. *What a peaceful morning!* He was dressed for a day of digging: khaki pants held up by a narrow black belt, white t-shirt, work boots, and topped with his trademark cowboy hat. An empty lawn chair was next to him. Colby heard the flaps of the tent unzip and raised his head to see Jimmy's hand reach through, separating them in one motion. The opening of the tent faced east, and the sun had just crept high enough to shoot beams of golden light through the gap in the tent flaps. With his head poking out of the tent, he squinted to take notice. Jimmy retreated into the tent to get dressed. Shirt, pants, socks, boots, cowboy hat. The serene morning washed over him as he made his way outside to the empty chair.

"What time is it anyway?" Jimmy said.

Colby looked up from his book. "Huh?" Colby grunted. "What time is it? It's quarter of seven. Want some coffee?"

"Sure. Why are we up so early?"

Colby got up and poured Jimmy a cup of coffee in a metal camp mug. "Ted and his rig are expected here between eight and nine. I don't know how much you heard me talk before you fell asleep, but I want to read you something."

Colby balanced his cup of coffee on the edge of the stove. "This is right from Captain Lewis's diary. It's fascinating and you're going to want to hear this." He looked up to meet Jimmy's eyes. "In all honesty, this is why this trip means more to me than the others. We have a chance to make history." He turned and looked toward the burial field, lost in contemplating what that would mean. Colby had begun to realize that recognition, approval, and appreciation were critical to him. Colby had always been looking for an artifact or treasure that would define his life's work and would separate him from the other archeologists of his day, raising his already lofty status to legendary. He called it a "legacy artifact." Maybe that find would prove to his doubters—perhaps most of all his parents—that his vocation had been a successful endeavor. He still hadn't come to terms with whether he needed to prove it to himself or to others. Over the years, he had struggled from time to time with which entity's opinion he valued more.

Jimmy looked both relaxed and confused to Colby, as he sat with legs extended, ankles crossed, brow wrinkled. His young mind seemed to be racing in a thousand different directions. Colby studied Jimmy's face as he took a sip of the hot coffee. Then the young man focused all his attention on Colby and what he was going to say next.

Colby reoriented his thoughts and began to read from the diary.

'We came around a bend in the river and saw a large village we supposed was Arikara or Mandan. The village was the largest we had seen as it spanned two deep draws and laid out from the ridge to the flat. We counted 80 neet earthen lodges covered in earth.'

"Do you remember our talk about this village the night before we left? How many lodges did I say this village we are at had, Jimmy?"

"80."

"Exactly." Colby continued.

'The village was fortified with ditches and palisades of thick willow or stout cottonwood poles. We dropped anchor for the keel boat and took the smaller boat to shore. Immediately after we passed the squash fields, we were met by warriors hiding in the corn. Behind them we saw women with bone hoes tilling the soil between the rows. We met the hostiles and inquired as to who was the chief among them. They called themselves Star-rah-he in a tongue that was similar to the Platte River Pawnees. Pointing to the one known as Kakawita, we offered beads, sheet metal, rings, handkerchiefs, and a Jefferson Peace Medal.'

"Oh, wow. That's what we heard about on the radio and what you were talking about last night," Jimmy interjected.

"Now you're getting the picture," Colby replied. "I'm tellin' ya, Jimmy, it's here. Knowing what I know after a lifetime of digging and investigation, this is it. We didn't find it last year with the KU group, but we are going to find it this year. If not this year, next. I'm not quitting until every burial on the west side of the Missouri River is excavated!"

"Ok Grandpa, no need to go crazy," Jimmy scoffed.

"Let me continue," Colby replied with eagerness in his voice. *'Some began to recoil at the shiny ornament and began to talk amongst themselves calling it bad medicine. Kakawita proudly and without hesitation, took the ornament and placed the medal around his neck. Kakawita for his part offered tobacco, which was very fine to smoke, and squash seeds in an earthen clay pot. The natives around him seemed exceedingly superstitious and somewhat afraid. We spoke to them of less militant concepts to use, agriculture, and safe passage.'*

"That could be any number of villages along the Missouri," Jimmy countered taking another sip of coffee. "Right?"

"True, but we are right in between the Moreau and Grand

Rivers as described in other documents attesting to where Lewis and Clark stopped. Furthermore, I've read that on their way back from the Pacific, Lewis and Clark crossed paths with a French fur trapper named Tabeau. This guy, Tabeau, lived with the Arikara. He said Kakawita wore the medal all the time until he was ambushed in his earthen lodge by a band of renegades from the Sioux tribe. Knowing the Arikara like I do, he would have been buried with it. The village would have had a very lavish ceremony to honor him as a great warrior chief. Not only would they have buried the medal with him, but they would have buried him with other valued trinkets. The real kicker, and what makes this Jefferson Peace Medal more valuable than all the rest, is it's the first one Lewis and Clark gave out on their historic journey."

Jimmy's lawn chair squeaked as he shifted his weight. "I haven't seen you this fired up about something since, well, since forever..." His voice held a note of admiration and—what was it?—a touch of fear?

Maybe Colby had come on a little too strong. He took a long slow breath and closed the book. With a solemn gaze, he scanned the river, the spaciousness, the rolling grasslands. Colby's prideful confidence was in full bloom. His obsession clear. There could be nothing stopping his lust for the medal and, ultimately, approval.

They sipped their coffee in silence for a time as the sun began its climb. Curls of cirrus clouds drifted overhead to the song of the meadowlark. Generations apart, tied by blood, separated by thought. Colby knowing. Knowing something about the medal he couldn't articulate properly to his seemingly skeptical grandson but felt in his core.

"Time to get to work, Jimmy," Colby said as he tossed what remained of his lukewarm coffee on the hard-dry ground. "The rising river isn't going to wait for us." He opened the back of the Scout to pull out a tape measure, two mallets, and a dozen orange stakes. The plotting stakes were each four feet long with a small 6-inch flag on one end, used to accurately mark a grid for excavation. After last year's dig, there was only an acre of burials left to finish. Hands full, buoyed with enthusiasm, Colby and Jimmy set out for the burial ground accompanied by the sound of their boots slicing and scuffing through the parched but sweet-smelling grasses and flowers. Their swift pace along the way caused wary grasshoppers to launch themselves in every direction. Upon arrival, they meticulously began to lay out the boundaries for the grader. Accuracy was paramount for documentation. Soon thereafter, Grandfather and Grandson went about hammering the stakes into the ground.

Their work within the prairie calm was interrupted by the rumble of the approaching diesel Mack truck pulling a flatbed trailer with an earth mover and retention box. It swung away from their camp and headed toward the rise of the last remaining burials. The plan was to have it cut parallel swaths approximately twelve inches deep and seven feet across to expose any changes in the soil, traces of burial plots, or human remains.

The smell of the diesel engine filled the air as the big rig came to a halt. Colby approached the cab just as the door flew open. A lean driver hopped out and immediately began to loosen the safety chains that held the earth mover.

"Morning, Ted," shouted Colby.

"Fine morning it is, Doctor Phillips." Tall and lanky, he was dressed in blue jean overalls, wearing a local feed company red hat. His white t-shirt showed perspiration stains in his arm pits. The stubble on his face indicated he hadn't shaved in a couple of days. Ted handled the chains without gloves, his gnarly hands larger than normal. Wasting no motion, he moved around the monster unleashing its heavy yoke. A typical hard-working Dakotan doing his job. Colby reviewed his measurements and specifications twice to make sure Ted was clear on how it needed to be done. There was no detail too small for Colby.

Once freed, Ted climbed up into the driver's seat of the giant earth mover to fire it up. With a great roar and a puff of black smoke, the brute came to life and lumbered off the trailer. As Ted moved the big yellow Caterpillar into position, it seemed to bob and shudder across the uneven terrain. The scraper blade, coupled to the back, peeled back the sod as if it were putting up a shade on a window; in both cases, exposing its operator to the unknown on the other side. The rhythmic clatter of the metal slats of the dozer's track offset the occasional belching from its belly. Slowly, tons of sod and topsoil were scooped into the trailing retention box to be set aside to fill in the trenches when Colby's work had been completed. Colby and Jimmy stood with their arms crossed in the shade of the cab, as the trenches were made in perfect symmetry. A swarm of flies kept them company as the thermometer rose. Occasionally, Grandfather and Grandson paced back and forth making small talk to pass the time. Nothing else for them to do but wait.

Two hours later, Ted was finished. Strips of sod were broken up by bands of exposed soil. From where they were standing, it looked like an earthly version of a pleated piece of fabric. The dusty old Caterpillar, with the scraper and empty retention box in tow, crawled its way back onto the trailer. With strict precision, Ted reattached the chains and cables. He grabbed his invoice from the dash and handed it to Colby. In a manner old friends do; they exchanged smiles and shook hands. "Didn't take nearly as long as I thought it would. Good to see ya, Colby. Best of luck with your dig. Take care now." Ted climbed back into the cab of the truck. The diesel engine groaned with the turn of the key. He let it idle for a minute as Colby and Jimmy stepped back. The cab bucked as Ted turned his rig around and left for home, dust swirling in his wake.

Colby and Jimmy wasted no time in returning to the Scout to get their digging sifters, shovels, and hand tools required for their work. The sun was approaching its apex, its strength felt searing on exposed skin. Jimmy opened the tail gate of the Scout and pulled out the tools of the trade. The clatter of activity multiplied the energy Colby felt. They worked together to finish putting together the well-used sifters, which were constructed of oak: two feet by three feet with four-inch sides, bolted to the three and a half foot legs. Jimmy loaded the hand tools and brushes into the screens of the sifters. Colby reached for his knapsack in the back seat to retrieve his university issued notebooks required for recording his findings.

Colby faced Jimmy. "I'm thinking we best get a bite to eat before we start."

"Yeah, let me grab the sandwich meat, onions, and bread." He called over his shoulder, "What kind of pop do you want?"

"Gimme a Ginger Ale. I need something cold and with fizz to quench my thirst. There are some apples in the cooler, too. Grab those."

Jimmy returned with his arms full of lunch fixings, barely getting back to Colby before the mayonnaise slipped from his grip. Colby caught the jar and laid out the food. He slapped together two sandwiches, left one for Jimmy, and sat in his lawn chair to eat. He placed the pop between his legs while two-handing his sandwich so the onions wouldn't fall out. Colby stared toward the burial rise while he chewed his food. Jimmy joined him and devoured his sandwich in half the time it took Colby. Lifting the Clorox jug filled with good Kansas water, Jimmy took long, deep gulps and handed it back to his grandpa. He made another sandwich and consumed that one, too.

Colby took the last bite of his apple when he felt an odd, indescribable sensation hit his consciousness like a lightning bolt. The feeling of someone watching him—watching them. He looked up to the horizon; maybe a mile to the northwest he saw a gleaming light emitting from a grove of trees along the river. He squinted for better clarity but that didn't help. His brain was still trying to process what it was he was looking at. Wasn't bouncing like a head light. Too inconsistent and varied in intensity to be a spotlight. And then it dawned on him.

"Jimmy, we've got onlookers from afar."

"What are you talking about? There's nobody within ten miles of this place."

"Oh, yes there is. Look over there." Colby nodded in the direction from which the flickering light source was emanating.

"What am I looking at?"

"It's the reflection off the glass of binoculars."

"Who and why is someone wanting to look at us?"

"I call 'em 'pot-hunters'. Scavengers or worse. They're amateurs that don't give a damn about history or culture. They just want to dig, sift, and take what they can for their own gain." The tone of Colby's voice was filled with loathing because he'd been burned by these types before at other sites along the Missouri.

The curious look on Jimmy's face turned to confusion. Colby continued, "Back in the summer of '66 I dug at three different village sites south of here and at each one we were watched during the day. At night while we slept at the motel, they'd come in with head lamps to dig in areas we hadn't gotten to but were exposed by the grader. A grader like the earth mover we had here this morning, you know. Or sometimes they would disturb partially excavated burials, so we couldn't examine position, orientation, or if there were any pupae, seeds, or artifacts present with the burial." Colby tossed his apple core in disgust. "Our research would end up less than complete because they would take the various ceremonial pieces that were buried with the remains. These guys are parasites we have no protection from. Even with our camp as close as we are now,"

Colby stopped short of telling Jimmy about the other "parasites" that had interfered with his work three years earlier. Just the thought of Gritzmacher and Calhoun stealing his artifacts—harassing the women and holding Earl Chavey and the other students at gunpoint no less, then giving Earl a black eye when he tried to stop them—turned his guts into a knot. He shook off the memory and waved his arm in the direction of the burials. "We'd have to stand guard all night and then we'd be useless to do our work the next day." He leaned back in his chair to stretch his legs. "When we had more people, we tried to be vigilant by placing sentries to guard the excavations, but these pot hunters, who turned out to be a couple of local trouble makers… they jumped a couple of my students a few years back. Place was south of Pierre. Tall Grass site. Never forget that. Those boys got roughed up pretty good. That was the end of trying to confront them. It's not worth it."

Jimmy leaned forward to rest his elbows on his knees. "So, what are we going to do?" He sounded exasperated.

Colby stood up in plain view and took the last gulp of his pop. With a steely gaze he turned to look down at Jimmy. "Ignore 'em. We're going to just do what we were hired to do…finish the task at hand and find some treasures. One in particular."

Colby slung the knapsack over his shoulder, instructing Jimmy to gather the sifter with the assorted tools inside it as he headed off to start excavating. As they passed the Scout, Jimmy abruptly stopped and dabbed his finger in the pool of green ooze on the ground under the chassis. He rubbed it between his thumb and index finger and stood up with a baffled look on his face, raised his fingers to his nose.

"It smells sweet and is kinda slimy," reported Jimmy.

"Damnit, that's radiator fluid. The same thing happened last year." Colby set the knapsack down, leaned his arm against the right front quarter panel and rubbed his head. He pivoted awkwardly to reach through the grill to unlatch the hood. Up the hood popped with a clunk as the springs released. Colby leaned in to look. He spun the cap of the coolant overflow tank, but seeing nothing out of the ordinary, spun it back on. Next, he slid toward the driver's side and slithered under the front end away from the ooze. Lying on his back he looked up and saw the problem.

"I can't tell if someone was messing with the hose or if it got loose on the bumpy ride in or what happened. Hose clamp on lower radiator hose is gone. Either way we have a problem. Bottom line is we have two options," he began to explain as he wormed his way from under the front fender. "Option one is we bag it for today and tape this up tight and get to town and hopefully Gus can fix it and we get back before dark. Option two is we start digging and sifting today and go in tomorrow morning. I don't like either one, but I really don't like having a questionable vehicle in the event we need to bug outta here quickly. Gonna cost us a half a day no matter which option we choose. Damnit." Colby kicked the ground. A wave of nauseousness passed through him from the stress. "What do you think, Jimmy?"

"I think we should go to town now and start fresh tomorrow. No sense in giving the pot hunters a head start, if that's who is actually watching us."

"Oh, that's who's watching us alright, you can bet on it."

"Could be some tribal folks or government people," Jimmy offered. "You know, like the Bureau of Indian Affairs or the Corps of Engineers. Who knows?" Jimmy shrugged. "I guess it doesn't matter. Let's just put all this back in the truck, patch the hose together, and go back to town."

So that is what they did. Under the relentless afternoon sun, it took about 15 minutes to throw the gear back in the truck, button up the tent, and secure the lower radiator hose well enough to get them back to town.

Back they went, retracing their route in. Through the swales, across the railroad tracks, on the gravel, back to the pavement, and over the bridge to Painted Rock.

"Lost a radiator hose clamp just like last year, Gus," Colby said. The harmony of wrenches clinking and clanking on nuts halted.

"Gimme a few minutes while I finish up here, and then I'll take a look-see," Gus answered.

"Okay, thanks. We'd be mighty obliged."

"Pull 'er in to bay 2 over there. All the way in and don't block the door or hit the tires." Colby turned to head back to the car and Gus yelled, "And leave me enough room in front so I can get to my tool chest!"

"Will do." Colby parked as he was told and left the key in the ignition. Jimmy had already made his way back to the candy rack with his eye on the Salted Nut Rolls. Colby walked back to find a chair but not before checking the coin return of the pay phone located on the wall above the cigarette machine. "Found a dime!" He laughed. Having grown up in the Depression years, Colby knew the value of nickels, dimes, and quarters.

He settled into the tattered vinyl chairs surrounded by walls painted sea mist green and large plate glass windows, passing the time by counting the number of black tiles then the number of white tiles. Free road maps, along with candy, oil, and chips for a price were neatly displayed behind the counter. None of that interested him. Colby's leg jittered as he became impatient and anxious to hear how soon Gus could fix their vehicle.

After a long fifteen minutes, Gus waddled in. "Take me about an hour to finish the job I'm on. Then another thirty minutes to locate the correct clamp and put you back together. Call it two hours."

"Oh, really. That'd be terrific." said Colby. "We'll head over to The Caboose Tavern. I've always wanted to check that place out. See ya in a couple, Gus. We're outta here, Jimmy."

6

They drove back to the Sinclair station and pulled in front of the open bay. Colby felt relieved that they had made it back without incident. A breakdown by the side of the road would have cost them more valuable time. A light breeze blew the suffocating heat into their faces as they stepped out of the dusty Scout. The cinder block garage was filled with, "Sympathy for the Devil" blaring from the transistor radio strategically positioned on the red tool chest.

"Anybody home?" shouted Colby. He marched with purpose toward the bay adjacent to where Gus was working. It was noticeably cooler out of the sun.

Gus was under a station wagon on a creeper and wasn't paying any attention to them. Aside from the strong smell of lubricants, oil, and gasoline, the garage was an atypical service station garage. Tires were stacked neatly in between the bays. The floors were clean, the walls freshly painted light gray. Tools hung in an orderly array that reminded Colby of his old man's admiration for, "A place for everything and everything in its place."

"I'm here," came the irritated response from under the car.

They got up from their chairs and headed back out into the warmth toward The Caboose. There they could escape the unbearable heat of the day and the penetrating smells of the service station. Their walk consisted of one long block to the southwest, toward the rail yard. Together, they crossed the main drag at the corner proceeding up a slight incline past the bank and an abandoned store with boarded up windows. They continued at a good pace past a store front for an insurance agency. The vertical siding showed water damage from the previous winter's snow melt. The painted sign in the window had chipped and faded. Set back in the shadows next to the insurance agency was a door--half glass above two horizontal panels. It had a mail slot in it marked 4201 for the apartment above. Music by the 5th Dimension filtered out through the large dreamcatchers hanging in the open windows onto the street.

"You hungry yet, Jimmy?" questioned Colby.

"I can always eat. A burger sounds good," he replied.

Further down the block, a turn of the century brownstone hotel looked inviting as they passed. Jimmy chose to walk in the sun, rather than the shadow from the overhang. Colby walked half in the shadow and half in the light. "This is a classic," commented Colby looking up at the granite cornice. "I wonder if this was built by the railroad. Would have been convenient to the railyards to house the linesmen, engineers, and yard keepers. Boy, if the walls could talk in that place, the stories they could tell." It had a grand entrance featuring an ornate portico that looked out of place in current day Painted Rock. The leaded glass windows were opaque with dust. A neon sign in the window flashed 'Vacancy'.

Next to the hotel was The Caboose. It was a low building with a flat roof. The outside was fake brick with two small rectangular windows at shoulder height. One window had a neon Hamm's sign in it and the other had a plastic Schlitz sign. The timber door was on the corner facing the abandoned brownstone train depot. Colby stepped up the two cement steps to open the weathered oak door. Once inside, his eyes took a second to adjust to the darkness. The coolness welcomed him along with the faint smell of beer and grease. Standing shoulder to shoulder with Jimmy, he looked around. The tavern itself felt small, with only one high top table in the corner opposite the doors and one Zenith black and white TV centered over the bar. The TV played a rerun of Gilligan's Island that no one was paying attention to because the sound was off. Walls were covered with pictures of trains from long ago interspersed among the beer signs. Bottles of liquor were artfully arranged on the back bar in front of aged mirrors encased by beautiful hand carved oak. The stools tucked under the bar were chrome with faded red vinyl tops that were cracked and tired looking. Colby met Jimmy's eyes nodding at a shoulder mount of a decaying 12-point mule deer hung above the juke box.

A young man with a jet-black ponytail, to Colby's left, bumped, gyrated, and leaned into a pinball machine. The active game pinged and chimed as a round faced young man with a 'Tribal Olympics Boxing Champion' t-shirt on, watched. Opposite them, Colby could see all but two of the bar stools were empty. At the end of the bar, a man in his fifties with a bright red nose sat next to a woman smoking a cigarette. He didn't look up, but her head spun in their direction. She sized them up and down through her horned rimmed glasses. The way regulars look at strangers. Colby could almost hear her thoughts: *You're not from around here are ya?* She gently swayed with Andy Williams', "Moon River" played softly on the juke box. Her companion held on to his bottle of beer as if he were afraid of it getting stolen.

They both seemed lost in reminiscing, but not about each other.

As Colby approached the bar, his boots made a hollow sound on the worn linoleum floor. A woman, with big brown eyes, stood behind the heavily lacquered bar drying glasses. Her salt and pepper hair was up in a bun. She had a weathered face, and her attire seemed to be chosen out of necessity rather than fashion. High cheekbones suggested some Indian ancestry. Colby thought she could have been a looker back in the day. A genial smile broke the ice as they pulled out the stools to sit down. She possessed a light of kindness in her eyes that complimented her cordial demeanor. The bags under her eyes, however, told of long hours trying to make a buck.

"What'll you gentlemen have?"

"Two Hamm's and two cheeseburgers, please," Colby replied. "My name is Colby, and this is my grandson, Jimmy. May I ask your name?"

"Nice to meet you both," she said with a welcoming voice. "My name is Katherine." She slapped her order book on the bar and withdrew a pencil from behind her ear. "You want fries with your burgers?"

Colby looked at Jimmy who nodded.

"Yes ma'am," Colby confirmed.

Katherine poured the two beers from the tapper for Jimmy and Colby and put them on the bar. She called to the young men playing pinball, "Jay, could you and Robert stock my coolers? The Grain Belt, Schlitz, Hamm's and High Life all need to be restocked." She turned pushing through the swinging saloon style doors into the kitchen. There was the buzz of a muffled conversation, then the sizzle of burgers on the grill. She returned in a couple of minutes to place a tray with ketchup, mustard, and napkins on the bar in between them.

"Where you folks from?" Katherine asked in a raspy voice acquired from years of secondhand smoke, no doubt. She was shuffling the glasses under the bar without making eye contact.

"Kansas." Colby took a sip of his beer.

"Oh, a lot of nice folks from down Kansas country."

"I guess that's true." Small talk was not one of the things Colby enjoyed.

Katherine raised her head. "What brings ya through these parts?"

"Just passing through. Had a problem with my truck, so I've got Gus over at the Sinclair looking at it now." Colby thought it best to maintain a low profile because he was not sure how the locals took to anyone excavating Indian burials.

"I know Gus. He'll take care of you. He's a good man." Colby thought she probably knew everyone's business in town because she ran the bar. That ended the small talk as Katherine slid down to the other end of the bar to check on the regulars. A subdued conversation with a couple of head nods and some hushed laughter ensued.

Soon after, through the swinging saloon doors came two plates of cheeseburgers with fries carried by the most beautiful girl Jimmy had ever seen. She had jet black hair, parted down the middle, which hung just over her shoulders. Her skin was a light coffee color, flawless except for a barely noticeable mole above her upper lip. Her eyes were deep brown, her features delicate. She looked to be about 5'5" and curves in all the right places. Her bell-bottomed blue jeans had flowers embroidered on the front pockets. A comfortable cotton light brown t-shirt hung just over her midriff. Despite her bow-legged gait, she carried herself in a poised manner that suggested she was older than she looked.

"These must be for you two gentlemen," she said with a smile that highlighted her dimples. Her voice was soft, her ebullient energy intoxicating, the scent of her perfume appealing. She placed the warm plates in front of Colby and Jimmy. Colby immediately reached for the ketchup, but Jimmy could not stop looking at her. Her eyes met his. Telepathic chemistry exchanged over an invisible, but palpable, wavelength.

Grandson and Grandfather ate their cheeseburgers and fries without conversation. When they were done, she returned to take their plates.

"Hi. What's your name?" Jimmy blurted out.

Jimmy's cheeks flushed and he avoided eye contact with his grandpa in the mirror behind the bar. Out of the corner of his eye, he could see the old man's jaw drop. They both took a pull from their beers. A soft elbow nudged him in the side.

"Sarah." She looked him in the eye reaching under the counter to put the plates and silverware in a tub to be washed. "What's yours?" She looked way more confident than Jimmy felt.

"Jimmy. This is my grandpa, Colby." Jimmy deadpanned, playing it cool with his response.

"Well, nice to meet you, Jimmy and Colby," Sarah said. She extended her hand across the bar to shake hands with each of them.

There was starting to be a level of ease with the exchange when sunlight burst through the door. Two men entered with a swagger and an attitude. Colby and Jimmy looked past Sarah to see the scruffy looking men reflected in the mirror behind the bar. One was whippet thin, the other had a long scar on his face and carried himself with an athletic gait. For a fleeting second, Colby thought he recognized one of them. The thought left him, and he finished his beer. Both Katherine and Sarah met the gaze of the men as they entered. The pair gave a nod of acknowledgement as they strolled down to the high top in the corner. This time the regulars didn't turn around.

"Sorry no table service. If you tell me what you want, I'll get it for you, but you have to come up here and get it," Katherine said in a direct voice.

"We'll have two shots of rail whiskey, ma'am," the athletic one said. Their presence had a threatening vibe. Katherine poured their whiskey in two shot glasses and set them on the bar. They got off their stools and went to the bar. Heads back, they slammed their shots and put the glasses back on the bar. With eyes straight ahead and shoulders back, they threw two dollars on the bar, and walked out. No thank yous, no see ya next time. Nothing.

Colby asked Sarah for another beer. She filled his glass then retreated to leaning against the back bar with her arms crossed scanning the whole scene. To Colby she seemed to be enjoying her newfound connection with Jimmy.

"You get a lot of that?" asked Colby nodding in the direction of the vacated area left by the two men.

"A lot of what?" replied Sarah.

"I don't know. They just looked like trouble." He took a strong pull on his beer.

Sarah scoffed. "Are you kidding me? No, not in this town. Nobody freaks out. Everyone knows everybody and even the people passing through tend to be pretty cool. For the most part it's a pretty laid-back scene."

"Just seemed kinda weird. One of those guys looked familiar but can't for the life of me place them..." Colby's voice trailed off. He paused, staring back at himself, taking a journey through the catalogue of places and faces stored in his memory. Nothing registered. "I guess I'll take our bill, Sarah."

Sarah turned to the other end of the bar. With her voice trailing off she said, "Grandma…"

Katherine set their check on the bar in front of Colby. "$2.50 and we'll call it good," she said. She put both hands on the bar and tilted her head forward. "None of my business, but those two characters came in here earlier asking a lot of questions about a guy that might be in these parts from Kansas. Said they thought this Kansas fella might be headed to the other side of the river." She paused. Neither Colby nor Jimmy spoke. Nobody flinched. Colby looked at Katherine with a blank stare, his chest tightening as she talked. He didn't like what she had to say. At all. Now he knew they were being watched. "I learned a long time ago to keep my mouth shut and will continue to do so. I don't know what they're up to, but I can assure you it's no good. You folks have a friend here if you need one." Folks in Painted Rock, and South Dakotans in general, were known for their gracious warmth and friendliness.

At the word, "friend," Jimmy's eyes darted to Sarah. He looked down at his beer. Colby could feel the boy's attraction to her, something he'd never seen the few times he'd seen Jimmy with his high school girlfriend.

Colby cleared his throat. "Have no idea why you would think it would be me, or us, going across the river. Lots of people from Kansas probably travel this way." He was doing his best to deflect any resemblance of what Katherine implied.

He could tell his attempt had been futile. Katherine was a bartender, and bartenders had a sixth sense about people. She leaned forward and lowered her voice. "Well, my advice to you, sir, is you best watch your back." She uprighted her posture and her bar voice returned. "Come back and see us again next time you're in town."

"We will for sure." Jimmy's voice was louder than necessary, his grin wider than Colby had seen it in a long time. Sarah giggled. Jimmy nodded to Sarah and she gave him the peace sign.

Colby paid the bill and thanked no one in particular and both women at the same time.

7

Once outside, Colby paused on the sidewalk to consider their next move. The diesel smell from the rail yards drifted over them and the temperature felt more tolerable. Long shadows were beginning to cover the street and creep up the buildings across from them. Not much movement of people or vehicles. A quiet afternoon in a quiet town. Colby looked at his watch; there was still some time to kill before Gus would have the Scout fixed.

They walked across the street to head back to the service station to wait. There was nothing better to do. As they walked side by side, Colby processed the danger he'd felt from the two strangers. *I know I've seen those two somewhere…*

Back inside The Caboose, Sarah cleaned up the bar top. She deftly put the glasses in the tub, returned the condiments tray to under the counter and wiped off the bar.

"What was that all about?" asked Katherine.

"What was what all about?" replied Sarah. She feigned ignorance while attempting to polish the lacquer off the bar.

Katherine, hands on hips, laughed out loud, "C'mon, child. It was so obvious you two were infatuated with each other. My gosh, the way you two were looking at each other. I could see it from the other end of the bar!"

Sarah blushed and broke into a big grin as she turned to face Katherine. "He's so cute! I don't know what or why, it just hit me. It just felt…" her voice trailed off as she fell into deep contemplation. "It just felt outta sight."

"Well, don't get any crazy ideas about runnin' off with a boy. They're like a shiny new toy when you first meet 'em." Katherine wagged a cautioning finger at Sarah. "Then pretty soon they want to control your life or they just up and move on. Either way, I don't need the drama of your heart being broken. I need you around here to help me run this place."

Meanwhile, Jimmy took note that his walk was a little lighter and his mood a little brighter. He could feel his obsession growing. *What the hell just happened in there with Sarah?* Cognitively, he couldn't comprehend what had just happened. Emotionally, he liked the euphoria he felt. Sarah had stirred something deep within him. *What is it?* He thought it best to just enjoy the moment and not over analyze it.

The men paused at an open area between two structures. Rectangular in shape, it looked like it might have been a small parking lot at one time. On one side was a boarded-up V-store that contained only empty shelving units. On the other side, were the remnants of a burned-out brick apartment building. Within the space were two wrought iron benches on cracked concrete surrounded by sparse grass mixed with dandelions. The centerpiece was a concrete obelisk about eight feet tall. A lone garbage can overflowed with litter. The spot appeared to be forgotten by the town's folk.

"Huh, look at this, Jimmy." Colby pointed to a monument. The obelisk had a small plaque on it commemorating Sakagawea, the female bilingual Shoshone scout that Lewis and Clark used to guide them up the Missouri River through the Rocky Mountains toward the Pacific and back. "You know the story?" Colby asked.

"Never heard of her."

Colby pointed at the words as he read them out loud.

"The story of Sakagawea...Sakagawea was kidnapped when she was twelve while living in Idaho near the Salmon River region. The Hidatsa tribe from near Bismarck, North Dakota took her during a buffalo hunt to that region. They brought her back to the Hidatsa-Mandan area. Through gambling payoff, purchase, or trade--no one knows for sure--she became one of two wives of French-Canadian fur trader, Toussaint Charbonneau." Colby spoke in an authoritarian voice as if lecturing his freshman Cultural Anthropology 101 class. Jimmy read to himself faster than Colby spoke. "When the explorers Lewis and Clark reached the Hidatsa-Mandan settlement on the Missouri, they recognized her potential value as interpreter."

Jimmy interrupted, "There's Lewis and Clark again."

"I know." Colby said shaking his head up and down. "They left their mark in the area, didn't they? Where was I? Oh yeah... her potential value as interpreter...," Colby continued, "She proved to be an invaluable asset. Her knowledge of the terrain and the Shoshone language as they moved west eased tensions, both for the crew of Lewis and Clark and the hostiles they encountered." Colby took a step back while staring at the worn memorial. "Amazing woman." He paused. "She is certainly worthy of the monument to honor her."

"Huh. Can't imagine how she survived. Really, how any of them survived," Jimmy responded.

Colby sat down on one of the park benches with his back to the sun. Jimmy slid in beside him. A gust of wind swirled discarded wrappers skyward as the smell of the burned building hovered around them. Sparrows darted to and from the top of the monument. A blue jay squawked somewhere nearby.

"We should talk, Jimmy."

"'Bout what?" Jimmy shifted his backside on the bench, trying to get comfortable.

Colby leaned forward, rested his elbows on his knees, and clasped his hands. His eyes were directed at the pebbled walkway surrounding the obelisk. "When your Mom was dying, I made her a promise. I told her I would look out for you, both in what I could give you of my time, and whenever possible, help you out financially. You know, things like college tuition, a little fun money for you, gas money…that type of thing. I didn't want to step on your Dad's toes, but knew money was tight on the farm. Your mom was your grandmother's and my only child. Her death broke both our hearts and…in all honesty…probably contributed to our divorce."

Jimmy leaned back on the bench and folded his arms. He was surprised to hear his grandpa talk in such frank terms about a subject they had never discussed. He got a lump in his throat as memories of his Mom came rushing back to him. The hole in his heart was still patent.

"I wasn't always the best husband and father but always tried to do right by you with my time. I have other financial responsibilities from choices I made in the past." He paused to gather his thoughts. "Let me put it to you this way. Trying to live on a professor's salary with those obligations has left truly little extra. I mean I have an adequate salary and a modest pension, but…one of the reasons we are here," he paused to gather himself. "Okay,

I just gotta say it. Besides me wanting to find the medal as a triumph of my work and wanting to prove something, one of the other reasons we are here is for me to make things right on the financial side of things."

"Okay, now I'm confused. What are you talking about?"

Colby took a deep breath and sighed. He took his white handkerchief from his back pocket and blew his nose. Colby lifted his head and their eyes met. "There were 89 Jefferson Peace Medals that Lewis and Clark took with them on their journey. Only seven have ever been recovered. Of those three were complete, 4 were one or the other halves, including the two of the scar face variety I told you about the other night. They have been sold to politicians, Hollywood types, and collectors for anywhere from twenty-five thousand to a hundred thousand dollars, you know, depending on what condition they were in." Colby lowered his forehead as his eyes widened. "You don't have to be a finance major to understand the positive impact that those kinds of dollars would have on my financial picture if we found one." He readjusted his posture on the bench. "To tell you the truth, I think I could get that if I put it on loan with a yearly stipend to a museum or university. That's how valuable it is."

"Really? I had no idea."

"I have spent countless hours studying this area and know it like the back of my hand. As you know I've excavated many villages up and down the river. I have no doubt in my mind that Lewis and Clark were at this village. It fits the description and location exactly as they described in their journal. Every single one of the medals that has been found was with a burial. I have a strong gut feeling that we can find the medal. Unfortunately, in our case, time is of the essence because of the rising river. In less than a week and a half, the entire burial field will probably be under water and any chance...all my work in identifying this village as a strong potential to have the medal... will be lost."

Colby looked at Jimmy to gauge his reaction.

Jimmy rubbed his palms on his thighs before resting them on the bench. "You know Grandpa, I'm with ya in finding the medal, but our time out here is what is important to me," he said. "When Mom died, I wanted to die, too, but you were there to take me fishing and hang out with me and stuff. You got me through some tough times." He pivoted on the bench, eyes welling up, threw an arm around his startled Grandpa's shoulder, and held him tight for a brief embrace.

Colby rose from the bench, ill at ease with outward signs of affection. "Alright then," Colby stammered, "Just needed to get that off my chest. Let's get back to Gus's place and get a move on."

They left the obelisk and the litter without speaking. Cards were on the table now. Jimmy felt he was beginning to understand his Grandpa's internal struggles, motivations, and drive a little better. On the other hand, he was still working through his sentiments for Sarah. She sparked something in him that he hadn't ever felt before. Between the heartfelt impacts of his Grandpa and Sarah in the last 90 minutes or so, he thought his head was going to explode. Jimmy's limbic system fired into overdrive with so many feelings going in so many different directions.

Colby could see in the distance that the Scout was parked outside next to the service station. He thought that could be a good sign that it was done or a bad sign that it couldn't be fixed. They walked into the bay where Gus continued to labor under the same car as when they left.

"Hey, Gus! Have you fixed our radiator hose?" Colby remarked in a raised voice, so Gus was sure to hear him.

Gus slid out from under the car. Grease was streaked across

his forehead and his hands. "Got ya fixed up and left an extra clamp on your front seat in case it happens again. Strange that the clamp in the same location would give you fits two years in a row." He continued from his prone position, "Left the bill next to the register."

"You take a check?"

"That's fine. Just leave it on the counter. I'll get to it when I'm done here," and he slid back under the car.

Colby turned and exited to the counter, leaving the check as instructed. Out the door, he circled around the corner of the station to the Scout and Jimmy. Both doors were opened simultaneously, and Colby fired up the old beast.

"Purrs like a kitten!" Colby exclaimed with an excited tone as he turned with a smile toward Jimmy. They rumbled back onto Grand Street heading west. As they made the bend in the road, they both put their visors down to block the glare from the late day sun. Colby's foot pushed the accelerator deeper toward the floorboard as they approached the bridge across the mighty Mo. He could feel a freight train full of anxiety travel up the back of his neck. With absolute conviction, he knew that they were in a race against daylight, the river, and pot hunters. Treacherous pot hunters with motives which were not entirely clear to him.

They would be soon enough.

8

The smoke rose in the form of a helix pushed to the north by a relentless breeze as the night chill began to settle in. An irregularly shaped circle of varying sized rocks held a pile of dry cottonwood bark that Charles Ray was using to try to start a fire. Billy watched him struggle as he knelt with his face at ground level and, with a huff and a puff, began to blow into the cinders formed from the burnt sticks and grasses. His cousin looked lightheaded and about to give up, but the coals ignited the bark. The campfire was born.

Billy cautiously stoked the fire as Charles Ray crawled over to his blanket to lie down, took a long drag from a joint he had rolled earlier in the day, and stared at the nighttime sky. His cousin had discovered pot back in high school and became captivated by it in Vietnam because it made the war less intolerable. Apparently it grew everywhere "in country" and he'd come home with a full-blown habit.

The moon had risen a couple of hours earlier and, as darkness fell, it began to reveal its crescent shape against the obsidian backdrop of the nighttime sky. Stars began to spring out of the void above. A strong breeze from the south pushed waves against the bank below gobbling up the soft shale bank with unrelenting fury. The flicker of the fire snapped and popped, sending sparks with the wind.

Billy was comfortable with his back up against a cottonwood tree, out of the wind, field stripping and cleaning Charles Ray's army-issued pistol. He was meticulous because he wanted a gun that would shoot reliably and consistently. With a Camel cigarette hanging from his lip, he had carefully disassembled the .45 laying its parts on his blanket. Slide, barrel, recoil spring, recoil spring plug, magazine, and grip of the gun all placed in an orderly fashion. He alternated the cleaning rod and patches with the bore brush to thoroughly clean the barrel. Next, he put a cotton ball on the cleaning rod and dripped some lubricant on to it. The barrel had to be thoroughly lubricated. After he reassembled it, he slid the magazine in and clicked on the safety. Finally, he rubbed a soft cloth over the entire piece until it had a soft luster. *Job well done.* He guzzled the last of his beer, dropped his cigarette in the can, and threw it on the pile they had started earlier in the day.

That afternoon, while Billy was napping, Charles Ray had been on watch but, after a few beers, had fallen asleep himself. When they woke up to see no activity and no one at the dig site, there had been a rush of panic. There was a lot of cash at stake. They scrambled to their truck and sped to town. *Where else would they go?* After locating the professor and the kid with him, having a shot of whiskey at The Caboose, and grabbing a few supplies, they had returned to their campsite. All in a day's work of recon.

"Is your fire ready for my rabbit?" quizzed Billy.

"I suppose," replied a very mellow-sounding Charles Ray. His eyelids partially covered his bloodshot eyes. Billy had shot the rabbit when they'd returned from town. It had been around since they'd set up camp. Billy thought eating it would remind him of the good times he and Charles Ray had had when they went hunting together.

Billy took his switchblade out of his pocket and sawed off a sufficiently sized branch from an ash tree for use as a skewer. He found a couple of similarly sized branches to use as supports and cut them off as well. He squatted down by the fire. Wedging the vertical supports between rocks on either side of the fire, he ran the skewer through the skinned rabbit and placed it carefully over the fire.

"So, what is the plan for tomorrow?" Charles Ray spoke with a thick tongue. "I mean how soon can we get the hell outta here? Seriously man..." Billy felt Charles Ray was half zoned out, half indifferent to the world at this point. Based on his own experiences with pot, Billy could tell Charles Ray was exhausted, but in a good way. He would be feeling no pain while feeling his body rising above his physical self. Scalp, fingers, toes-all tingling. Mentally, Charles Ray would feel smarter than he had in a while. At least since his last joint.

To Billy, Charles Ray looked like a corpse: his eyes completely closed, lying on his back, hands clasped on his belly. "I told you the plan. Weren't you listening?" Billy's voice contained frustration. "We get paid to bring my man the medal we gonna get from the old man we been watchin'. Until then we gotta just watch and wait. Patience, man." The fire crackled as the fat from the rabbit dripped onto the hot coals. Billy flipped over the rabbit. He chuckled to himself at how much bigger the rabbits always looked before he skinned them.

"What do we do if the old man won't give it to us or he doesn't have it?" mumbled Charles Ray.

"If he has it, we'll just take it. One way or another. Simple enough. My guy, Earl Chavey, knows this Dr. Phillips will find it because of the work him and Earl done in researching this village, the Indian tribe, and Lewis and Clark."

"Yeah, okay, man. Yeah and who is this Earl Chavey guy?" Charles Ray spoke in a slower, deeper, much groggier tone. Eerie shadows flickered on the trees behind him.

"Just a guy that was in my block at Brushy. Has it in for Phillips after Phillips ratted on him over some money issues when they worked together at the University of Kansas. You'll meet him when we get back. Smart guy. Researched the makin' of the medal, told me my ancestor shoulda been the guy to design it… he said prolly coulda been famous or rich or both by now," Billy stared at the fire, contemplating what that would have meant before continuing.

"He's good for the money, too, trust me." Squatting, Billy turned his attention to the fire focused on cooking the rabbit properly.

"How the 'ell did he end up in Tennessee all the way from Kansas?"

"I guess his attorney requested Brushy so he could be near his wife and family 'cause they moved there after he got convicted. Couldn't afford their house no more so she moved back in with her family."

Charles Ray rolled to his side to lean up on one elbow, opening glassy eyes. Billy stared at the different colors of his face being illuminated by the fire. "Okay. The way I figger it, we swoop in and grab that damn coin or whatever y'all call it, take it back to your guy, get paid, then I'm splittin' to go south. Get me a lady friend, some good whiskey, and have some fun. Goin' to the beach…that's what I'm doin'." Charles Ray had expended a lot of energy coming up with that plan, so with a big sigh he lay back down. Charles Ray questioned, "Why didn't he just come out and get it himself?"

"'Cause he's still in jail, ya dumbass." Billy laughed at that as he turned the rabbit again. He knew Charles Ray was down for the count. Charles Ray had a way of rambling when he had crossed the threshold into cannabis land. He had seen it many times. "I told you that on the way out."

"Yeah, you probably did. I was stoned most of the way, 'member?" Charles Ray laughed at that. Now they both started laughing. They settled into the silence of the prairie. An owl from the next ravine over called out. A pop from the fire sent an ember in an arc. The sizzle of rabbit fat, again. Ten minutes passed. Billy took the rabbit off the fire. With his switchblade, he cut off a morsel of thigh with his knife.

"You want some of this," he said looking at Charles Ray, chewing a mouthful of rabbit. He was on his knees now in savage eating mode. "It's pretty good."

"No man. You go ahead. I'm tired. I'm going to sleep right here. I'll take first shift at daybreak." Charles Ray reached over and grabbed the blanket pulling it over his shoulder as he turned on his side. Swatches of light and dark enveloped his body. He fell into a deep sleep under the crescent moon surrounded by the stars.

"Have it your way. I gotta eat." Billy proceeded to cut off several more strips of delicious rabbit meat until he could eat no more. *This sure beats the hell outta prison food.* He tossed what was left of the rabbit on the skewer over the embankment next to the river. Billy pulled the tab of another beer to wash the last of the rabbit meat down. He sat with his legs crossed staring into the fire, his tongue searching for rabbit remnants between his teeth. Tired but content, he let out a loud burp. He snickered then impulsively grabbed Charles Ray's blanket and crawled to the other side of the fire. The embers were dying down as the smoke curled to the heavens. Billy turned to the darkness, away from the light of the fire. He thought he might have trouble falling asleep, but it came upon him easier than expected.

Meanwhile, Colby and Jimmy had returned to their campsite. They unpacked the truck and set up the Coleman stove. Jimmy crawled into the tent. Colby opened a can of Chef-Boy-Ardee spaghetti dumping it into the iron skillet which he set on the stove. He pumped the plunger on the red container of white gas for the stove and lit the burner. While stirring the spaghetti, Colby's eyes surveyed their site. Tent was in good shape, machete used to clear the prairie for the tent still stuck in the ground next to it, water jugs right where they had left them. Nothing had been disturbed. *All good.*

"Everything is right where we left it," Jimmy said exiting the tent.

"Okay, and everything looks good outside the tent, too," replied Colby.

After five minutes of stirring with occasional taste testing Colby announced, "It's ready. Let's eat. Busy day tomorrow. We start the excavating."

Jimmy pulled four paper plates and a couple plastic forks out of the kitchen box by the tent. Colby scooped the warm spaghetti onto Jimmy's doubled-up plate along with a piece of bread. Then he filled his own. They sat hunched over in the darkness on their lawn chairs, worn out from a long day. Canned spaghetti never tasted so good. At this point in their day, it wasn't about cuisine so much as it was about fuel. They ate with only the sounds of lips smacking and teeth masticating, gazing toward the river soaking in all that was around them. The blustery south wind ruffled the tent with an irregular beat as the tin flaps on the sides of the Coleman stove rattled and the vegetation beyond them oscillated. Above them, a ceiling of stars was intermittently obscured by passing cumulus clouds.

Jimmy finished first, got up, and put his paper plate in the garbage bag. He returned to his chair, collapsed it, and laid it next to the tent. He continued past the tent about ten paces, and Colby heard the zip of the zipper and the whiz of Jimmy relieving himself.

"Goin' to bed Grandpa."

"Night, Jimmy. Sleep well."

Colby threw his plate and fork in the garbage. He folded the warm sides of the Coleman and closed the lid. He put his chair on top of Jimmy's, securing it from the wind by putting a water jug on top. Colby shuffled away from camp past the Scout to relieve himself, too. He stood there, in the quiet darkness of the night staring at the cuts over the burial grounds. *So many miles traveled doing something I love. So many villages. A hundred? Maybe more. So much dirt had been moved. Tons! Has it been worth it? Yes, I believe it has. Made a lot of friends, helped a lot of people understand a culture and way of life. Maybe taught my students a thing or two. I know I did. A few even went on to be teachers, professors, or pot hunters in their own right. Perpetuating the craft. I wonder if we will be watched tomorrow. Why are they watching us, anyway? What are they up to? Worry about that tomorrow.* With that, he concluded the conversation with himself and zipped up. It was time for bed.

He turned and headed back to camp but paused by the driver's side door of the Scout. *Should I or shouldn't I?* He thought it best. Colby opened the door slowly pushing the button below the handle so as not to make a noise that would wake Jimmy. Colby leaned forward and reached under the front seat. His left hand searched blindly until he felt the butt of the gun. He wrapped his hand around the grip and pulled it out. The .38 felt good. Just the right weight and size. He like the way it looked. Compact yet capable. Colby made sure it was loaded, double checked the safety, then stuffed it in his belt using his shirt to cover it. No sense in alarming Jimmy. With quiet care, he closed the door and went to the tent. Jimmy was on his side facing the outside of the tent, snoring. Colby snuck the .38 under his pillow. He removed his dusty boots, took off his pants, and slid into his sleeping bag.

The hard ground and smell of the tent reminded Colby of tent camping with his older brother Tim. He hadn't spoken to Tim, his only sibling, in over a year, their relationship eroded over time. Colby's pulse increased as he retreated down the hallway of his memory recalling a couple of scarring experiences from his youth. His exploring days had started in the dense backwater woods of the Missouri River in eastern Nebraska. A hint of a smile formed on his face reliving the sound of the cattails cracking, the heavy smell of the rich organic soil, and the brown river contained within its banks beyond them. Tim and Colby spent hours playing cowboys and Indians, climbing trees, and exploring the flat bottoms. It had been a joyful childhood while in their own private playground. The brothers came home dirty, Tim never as dirty Colby, but never late for dinner. Many supper conversations centered around how Tim had won the west, climbed higher than Colby did, or caught the biggest snake. The look of radiating pride on their parents' faces as Tim pontificated his triumphs in detail, crushed Colby. *I had things I wanted to tell them too, but never could get a word in edgewise.*

Looking back now, that might be where my struggle for attention and love started.

Colby felt wide awake now. He rolled onto his back, arm bent at the elbow with hand propping up his head, staring at the green hood over him. His mind flashed to the day he'd come home from the last day of high school excited to announce that he had been named Valedictorian of his class-despite receiving a 'B' in calculus his last quarter to go along with all A's. Colby remembered dashing up the back steps, throwing open the screen door, ego full of pride. Finally, he thought he had become his brother's equal and worthy of his parents' praise.

His mom and dad had looked up at him with a pained expression. "Well, Colby, Tim was Valedictorian and got straight A's," his dad said. "You should have tried harder. No one outworked Tim, did they, Mother?" Crestfallen, Colby had tossed his report card and Valedictorian notice on the kitchen table, spun around, and walked out the door, red-faced with anger. Once outside, he raced through the backyard, around the buck thorn, and up the grade to the railroad tracks. Outside of his body with rage, Colby threw the coarse granite railroad stones at birds, signs, and trees as he walked toward town. It was dark when he returned. His mom and dad were in the living room. She busy with her needlepoint and dad reading the paper, the radio tuned to "Amos and Andy." Briefly, he stood and waited for them to say something--an apology, a sorry, maybe congratulations? They never looked up, so he marched right past them up to bed.

Tossing and turning, remembering, seething. *How could they be so cruel? Ha, I really thought I could impress them.*

Colby had always thought Tim was their mom's favorite: taller, athletic, better looking. She said on more than one occasion, right in front of Colby, that Tim reminded her of her father. Tim went on to graduate Cum Laude from Johns Hopkins University and became a noted heart surgeon in Baltimore. Colby stayed true to his roots and found exploring people and cultures in the Midwest his passion. Ironically, his mom and dad were the ones that had sparked his interest in Cultural Anthropology and Cultural Archeology when they were on a trip to see the Roche-a-Cri petroglyphs in Wisconsin. They wanted him to go to medical school like Tim, but that never stoked a fire of interest in Colby. Perhaps because that is what they wanted, Colby went in a different direction.

Tim and all his accomplishments and awards were the center of their universe. Even after Colby was named Chairman of his department at the University of Kansas, he thought they would give him some respect. Just the opposite occurred. When Colby called, thrilled to give them the news, his dad had said, "Son, you dig in dirt. Tim saves lives. Now you tell me which is more important."

To this day feel like I never measured up to Tim in my mom and dad's eyes. Maybe this will finally move their needle of affection. I'll get the last laugh on Tim and everyone else when I find that medal. No doubt, I'll receive national, probably even international recognition. Let's see him top that!

The door of self-doubt opened. *Oh God, what if I don't find it...what if all my research indicated we were supposed to be at another village that's already under water....we're too late...I'd be destined to remain just another average anthropologist.* "He was good but not great," they'll say. Ugh! Worse than that, I'll always be 'the other brother' in my parents' eyes.

The irregular puffs of wind on the canvas tent began to mount, serenading Colby to sleep.

9

The bright orange sun peeked over the horizon with flares of blue and purple lancing between the slivers of clouds in the east when Jimmy and Colby woke up. The air smelled clean and crisp with morning freshness. In the distance a coterie of prairie dogs emerged from their underground burrows with a morning squeak. Cabbage White butterflies flitted here and there, busy drinking nectar and pollinating. The day had dawned. Colby made scrambled eggs and bacon, to be washed down with hot coffee. They packed up their gear--shovels, buckets, the probe, sifters, brushes, trowels, and notebooks--and headed to the trenches that Ted had cut so perfectly.

While walking to the burial site, Colby gave directions to Jimmy. "First, we'll do a visual exam to look for changes in the soil color and composition. The soil around and over the burials will be lighter in color. It can be softer by nature, too. We'll probably find some exposed bone. Second, once we suspect a potential burial site, I'll use the probe to verify bone presence under the surface."

The 'probe' functioned as a divining rod made of an old car

antenna with a gear shifter knob on one end as a grip with a welded point on the other to pierce the earth in hopes of striking bone or artifacts in a burial. Colby seemed to have a supernatural ability with the probe. Colleagues had termed him, "The Grave Whisperer" when he used the probe because it always seemed to lead to a burial. "Part savant and part lucky," they said. Because of this sixth sense, he had proven he was the best in his field time and time again.

"What am I supposed to be doing?" quizzed Jimmy. A gentle breeze was at their backs, and the sun had begun to warm the day. The smell of earth moist with dew filled the air. The clouds had drifted off and an azure sky completed the postcard day.

"I'm getting to that. Once we diagnose a burial find with the probe, I'll take a depth measurement to the most superior bone." His hands were active for added emphasis as he neared the burial grounds. "You'll need to record that in the journal. After that I'll start shoveling the dirt into the buckets or the sifter directly. Shake the sifter and we'll both look at what's in the screen." Colby looked at Jimmy as he continued to walk with determination. "Make sense so far?"

Jimmy turned his head to meet Colby's eyes in affirmation. "Yep. Perfect sense." They were moving in concert full of fervor.

"Once we get down close to the actual burial, we can outline it. Then take a length and width measurement which you must also record. At that point, I'll have to excavate using the various sized trowels and brushes. Once we clean up the burial and the body is fully exposed, I will determine head position, body position which'll tell us burial type, any artifacts found within the burial dimensions, sex, and approximate age. I'll dictate all that information to you, and you must record it accurately. That is key."

They stopped at the near end of the first cut and surveyed the area. Jimmy stood silent, waiting for their next move. Colby set down the knapsack, withdrawing the probe from the bundle of tools. Spellbound with expectation, deep in thought, he felt pushed by a cyclone of cosmic energy. He began to walk at a furious pace with his head down, eyes shifting back and forth, searching for a clue, a story written by a disturbance in the soil or by exposed bone. He pressed the probe into the ground, piercing the soft dirt. Half a foot in, he hit a solid mass. Colby withdrew the probe and moved it a foot past his initial penetration. Again, half a foot down he hit pay dirt as the probe flexed between the object and the force of his thrust.

"Here." Colby waved Jimmy over. "Bring me a shovel."

Jimmy closed the ten-yard gap with the sifter and shovel in his outstretched arm. Colby took the shovel and gently inserted it between the two probed spots. He lifted the dirt into the nearby sifter until he had an oblong depression exposing rocks and wood. While Jimmy shook the sifter, Colby got down on his hands and knees and, using the garden trowel, extended the depression to the edge of wood and rocks. The wood was cedar, and the rocks were nondescript, field remnants left by the glacier. He set the wood and rocks neatly aside.

"Anything in the sifter?" Colby asked full of hope.

"Just dirt. No artifacts."

"Shoot. Okay. Now get out the journal and start recording what I tell you. This is super important because it's what I refer to in my writeup for the university, donors, and publication." Jimmy grabbed the journal and a pen out of a pocket in Colby's well-traveled satchel. Colby took the hand trowel to delicately remove the soil exposing only the skull and long bones. He used a horsehair brush to fully reveal all the bones. The entire process took about a half an hour as he removed earth with exacting precision. There was no emotion in his work, just science.

"Burial overlay of wood and rocks. Grave type is pit, 1.3 feet from surface. Maximum length is 4 feet, maximum width is 2 feet. Preservation is good. Body is laid northwest to southeast in a flexed position with the skull at the northwest. Specimen is an adult, no additional artifacts."

"Got it. Can you tell the sex?"

"Put down indeterminate. Let's leave this for now and go on to the next one. I left my camera back at camp, so we'll have to photograph it after lunch. Then we can box it up to take back to the lab at the University for my grad students to study. Catalogue this as burial 001."

They moved a little farther ahead, and Colby saw the crown of a skull cresting the dirt. With caution, he took the trowel again to begin excavating. He exposed the top of the skull to help determine which way the body was lying. He found the humerus, ulna, and radial bone of the right arm resting on the rib cage. Uncovering each bone felt like the euphoria of finding another piece of a jigsaw puzzle. Each bone revealed clues that aided in creating a succinct description of the burial. He continued towards the ilium, femur, tibia, and fibula. He put all the dirt from around the body into two five-gallon buckets which Jimmy put in the sifter. Jimmy began sifting.

"Grandpa, look!" He held up a shell pendant roughly triangular, about two inches on each side, and a hole at the top.

"Beauty," said Colby. Jimmy tossed the fragile and unique piece to Colby.

Colby caught it with two hands. "What the hell are you doing? Don't throw me artifacts, I'll look at them at lunch. Just put it in the smaller artifact box that goes in the bigger specimen box." Colby, annoyed, returned to exposing the mandible as he began to expose the depth of the burial. He continued to remove dirt until the entire skeleton had been unveiled. "Okay, take this down. No wood or rock overlay. Grave type is pit and burial depth one foot to top of skull. Maximum length is 3.3 feet and maximum width is 2.8 feet. Preservation is good. Body position is north to south, with head to the north, and is flexed. Adult female. Shell pendant found with body. Catalogue as 002."

Colby got up off his knees to stretch. With hands on hips, he surveyed his work, disappointed that they hadn't found more with the first two burials. He removed his cowboy hat and wiped his brow with a handkerchief he took from his back pocket.

"Grandpa I gotta ask...where do you get your energy?"

"Huh. In all these years, Jimmy, I don't recall any one ever asking me that." He let the question sink in while he considered how to best answer it. "I'm afraid I'll nev...Oh, I don't know." Colby didn't think it right to get into the whole chip-on-the-shoulder discussion. He preferred to let Jimmy think of him in terms of a lifetime of adoration and admiration. "Let's just say things in my past drive me. Leave it at that." He extended his hand. "Let me take a look at your journal." Jimmy handed over the journal, and Colby reviewed Jimmy's notes.

"Well done. It's not what I had hoped so far, in terms of artifacts, but it's a start." Out of the corner of his eye he caught the reflection of the binoculars again. He felt irritated but chose not to mention it to Jimmy. Jimmy seemed to be engrossed in reviewing his notes, certainly unaware that they were being watched. The South Dakota sun began to beat down on them with clouds in the shape of mares' tails wisped across the top of the blue sky. The breeze was enough to keep the heat manageable. At least for now. Colby grabbed the jug of water to gulp down much needed refreshment. He motioned the jug to Jimmy who took him up on his offer. Colby skipped over to the next trench and began walking with his probe. Off and on, he would see a change in soil and use the probe in hope of finding his next excavation spot. It took him fifteen minutes until he found a promising area.

"Bring the sifter and shovel over here." He started at the perimeter of the area that looked good and took off the top layer of dirt exposing another burial. In a relatively short time with experienced methodology, he had exposed a skeleton. From a squatted position he began to recite the important particulars after Jimmy had finished sifting the removed dirt.

"Pit grave type, again. Wood covering. Depth is 1.7 feet to femur. Maximum length 2.3 feet and maximum width is 1.8 feet. Preservation is good. Fly pupae present. Upper torso intact and lower limbs scattered possibly due to rodent activity. Body position is south east to northwest with skull at southeast. Flexed position. Classify the age as young adult. Sex is indeterminate. A buffalo scapula, not worked, is lying next to the skull. No other artifacts. Catalogue number 003. Let's find one more before we break for lunch."

"What's the relevance of the fly pupae?" Jimmy asked.

"Insects use the deceased as a food source for their larvae or pupae. We think fly pupae are an indicator of the time between death and burial. Their presence would indicate delayed discovery or delayed burial. That's the theory anyway."

"Interesting," Jimmy said. "I have another question."

"Yeah?" Colby responded.

"Why did they bury them so shallow?"

"Fair question. For a few reasons. In the summer, the ground gets baked by the sun. Keep in mind Sound Dakota's annual rainfall is about thirteen or fourteen inches a year. So, the combination of minimal rainfall and sun makes it as hard as concrete. You know that from sleeping on it." Colby chuckled. "Second, they used a buffalo's scapula bone hafted to a stick or just used the scapula with their hands to dig a hole. Once they got through the grasses and gnarled roots, they might have just used their hands. It was tough manual labor. Third, too much further down they were likely to hit glacial till. Bottom line is they only dug as deep as they had to, given the conditions."

"Huh." Jimmy thought about it for a moment. "Okay. Just wondering."

"Yeah enough with the questions," Colby muttered under his breath.

They moved in the direction of the village and found some hand bones. Colby carefully shoveled the bones into the bucket and used the probe to verify there were more. He grabbed the shovel and began the process. The bones were in a random pattern with the skull and long bones missing. The burial had clearly been excavated before.

"What the heck happened here? There seems to be no rhyme or reason to this one," Jimmy wondered out loud.

"By the looks of it, I'd say the pot hunters got this one. Unfortunately, this village and these burials have been dug since 1923. I get why they would dig in the village for arrowheads, bone tools, or other artifacts, but…," Colby's voice trailed off.

"But what?"

"Well, I've just never understood why amateurs would dig in the burials. They certainly can't interpret them. Just makes me angry to no end," Colby threw his hands up. "Maybe for a ceremonial piece or unique artifact. Or maybe just out of curiosity. I can't believe they would have been looking for the same prize we are hoping to find with a burial." Colby gestured with his hand in a dismissive fashion, irked. "This one doesn't count as a specimen. Just document it as disturbed, burial 004. Let's get a couple more complete specimens."

They picked up their gear and headed to the next trench. Jimmy stood by as Colby walked slowly, probe still active, in his own little world, enamored with all the potential that lay beneath him.

Colby found another burial, fully intact, and undisturbed. He guessed from the flatness of the dentition that it was an old individual. The burial was covered in cedar with no fly pupae evident and a few shells buried with it. There appeared to be a handful of seeds in a cluster around the decaying leg bones suggesting rodent activity. The sex was indeterminate, and it had been laid on its back. Catalogued as number 005.

"I need a break. I'm tired," Jimmy said.

Colby could feel the accumulated frustration welling up deep within him. No medal, few artifacts, disturbed burials, trouble with the Scout, and now Jimmy was getting tired? He let out a quiet chuckle that turned into an explosion.

"Jesus, Jimmy. Tired? It's only 10:30! In case you haven't noticed, I've been bustin' my ass," Colby quickly pivoted to point. "The river has gotten fifteen feet closer than when we started, we have no medal, and you're tired? Give me a break." His voice was rising. "Do you understand we are running out of time by the minute? Look Jimmy," Colby pointed at his grandson, "I really wanted to do this trip with you, but so far it's pretty much been a failure and that disappoints me on several levels. The way I see it, you think you have all the time in the world. I did, too, when I was your age. But I don't have all the time in the world," he screamed. He took off his cowboy hat and swatted it on his thigh in anger.

Regaining a portion of his composure he continued, "I know the medal is here. I'm doing this with or without you. My hope was that we would do it together. But, at this point, either way I'm fine." He shrugged his shoulders and extended his arms palms open. "Are you in or do you want to go take a break? Which is it?" Colby stood facing Jimmy with his hands on his hips, his body full of anger.

Jimmy's eyes were wide. "Seems like you care more about this medal than me!"

"Don't you dare make it about a choice," Colby said as he waved his finger at Jimmy. "You signed up for this duty. Now are you in or out?" Spit flew out of his mouth as he spoke.

"Fine," Jimmy huffed. "I'm in." He stomped over to the next trench with the shovel and sifter.

They powered through burials 006 and 007 then headed back down the grade toward their camp. The merciless sun was near its peak as the temperature approached 100 degrees. Colby soaked a bandana with water and rubbed it across the back of his neck. Lunches were made in the only shade they could find, alongside of the Scout, in between chasing flies away from their onion sandwiches. They guzzled water and enjoyed a Snickers bar for dessert. Jimmy leaned his head back on the Scout and closed his eyes. "Damn flies," he barked swishing his hand through the air.

Colby looked at the burial site with a sweeping gaze, planning his next move.

Shortly after finishing lunch they trudged back toward the trenches. They excavated and catalogued another four burials before they called it quits for the day. Colby photographed all eleven exposed burials, and together they collected the skeletons and put them into separate cardboard boxes for further study. The sun's rays along with the pall of intense heat had finally beaten them, sapping all their energy. Dusty and sore, they returned to camp, gathered their towels, clean clothes, and Ivory soap. Off they went to bathe in the coolness of the river which had risen to within twenty-five yards of the trenches. The strip of shore present between the washed-out embankment and the river's edge was soft and muddy. They found a cottonwood tree at river's edge carried up from the original channel with the rising water. The bark and leaves were gone; a smooth remnant of a 30-foot tree uprooted by the Missouri's current. The Corps of Engineers and the Oahe Dam had made sure of that.

Colby and Jimmy sat on the washed-up bald tree and stripped down. The water had a chilling effect on their bodies as they waded in as far as their waists, a welcome relief from the heat. Despite the mud and silt, when they had finished soaping and rinsing, they felt clean and refreshed. With towels over their shoulders and dirty clothes balled up under their arms, they hiked back up the dry wash through the green ash trees to their camp.

The Dinty Moore beef stew and saltine crackers they had for dinner filled them up. The shade had increased, and the temperature had begun to retreat as the sun began its departure. The prairie breathed a calmness into their souls as they transitioned to post dinner relaxation.

"So, what are you taking this fall?" asked Colby, legs crossed, flexing his tired hands.

"Probably a Lit class, Calc 301, and the rest I'm not sure. What are you teaching?" said Jimmy, slouching in his lawn chair, staring straight ahead.

"Probably a 600 level Independent Study on the Arikara," answered Colby. He took a long pull from the jug of water then paused to look over at Jimmy. "Just want you to know that I thought we had a good day today. Moved a lot of dirt. Found some good artifacts, although not the one I'm here for. Hey, sorry about earlier today. It's not you, just a bit frustrated."

"Okay. Yeah, I'm sorry, too. I'll do better tomorrow."

On balance, Colby knew Jimmy had enjoyed the hard, tedious, and sometimes monotonous work that went into burial excavation. Work plus heat plus expectations not met had led to mutual frustration boiling over, simple as that. Colby accepted it for what it was and took Jimmy for his word. Grandpa and Grandson had always made peace after previous tiffs.

The small talk, along with getting organized for morning, happened to be just enough to fill the evening as darkness approached and they got ready for bed. They turned on the transistor radio to KOLW for the weather report. The weatherman, who was also the newsman and head advertising voice, said it would be cooler tomorrow with more wind. No rain in the forecast.

"That's good news. I'm planning to start early and finish late," said Colby turning off the radio. "My intention is to locate and excavate at least twelve more burials tomorrow." He stared in the direction of the adversarial river focused entirely on overcoming its persistence and finding the burial that had the medal.

"I think that's doable," nodded Jimmy with enthusiasm. The dip in the river and a full stomach had obviously rejuvenated him.

Billy and Charles Ray watched and waited.

10

Colby, unable to move, buried up to his neck. Eight warriors on war ponies appeared unannounced from deep within his self-conscious. Arrows whizzed by his head. Why? Why? Are you shooting at me? The warrior whose face was painted white approached him, with stone tomahawk raised, as the arrows continued to fly around Colby's head. "Why must you torment our ancestors by disturbing their graves?" No! No! White face faded out. Colby struggled to free himself from the weight of the earth's grasp.

"Grandpa. Grandpa!" Jimmy said shaking Colby. "Wake up! You're dreaming."

"What? Huh?" Colby sat up in a cold sweat, his sleeping bag disheveled. "I musta been having a bad dream."

"Yeah, you were."

It was only a dream. But it was so real. Ok, just a lucid dream. Nothing to it. Today is the day we find the medal.

Still groggy, Colby mumbled, "Alright Jimmy, time to start the day."

Days two and three were remarkably similar to day one -- stillness and harmony on the prairie interrupted by Colby zig zagging the burial field searching, probing, digging. Jimmy sifted a lot of sterile dirt and took copious notes of each burial. They had success in excavating their targeted number of burials because the weather had turned milder resulting in a revival of adrenalin-driven energy. Occasionally they found sites that had been disturbed by pot hunters. However, by and large, they were pleased with what they had found. Rolled copper pieces, bone tools, shell beads, and an occasional stone point had piqued their curiosity and quenched their thirst to continue looking for more burials.

Sadly, they had continued to uncover more infants than anticipated. Colby gave Jimmy a history lesson over coffee while they were seated in the front seat of the Scout, riding out the passing shower the morning of day four. "The Arikara tribes were some of the last to come in contact with the Europeans and, as such, the last to come in contact with the diseases the Europeans brought. Particularly smallpox. In the period from the 1780's to when Lewis and Clark arrived, the mighty Arikara people went from 30,000 to less than 6,000."

"Holy cow."

"The number of infants we have found this trip and those that were unearthed last summer are in direct correlation with the mortality patterns one would expect when disease is rampant. The youngest were the most vulnerable."

Jimmy sat slumped in his seat hypnotized by the raindrops racing down the windshield from a solitary dark gray cloud that had forced them back to the Scout. "That's horrible. Makes sense though. You wonder if the Europeans introduced disease to the Indians as a way of getting rid them. Kind of like a poisoning all of the Indians with a germ," Jimmy said. Suddenly, the rain stopped, and the sky cleared. The sun resumed its place in the southern sky, prepared to dry things out and warm things up.

"You certainly can find reason to believe that school of thought. Well, looks like it's that time. Let's get to work," Colby offered, and they exited the Scout. The prairie flowers appeared more vibrant and smelled a bit more fragrant, the direct result of the passing shower. As they set off toward the burial field, Colby suggested a more refined strategy than their current approach. "I'm thinking that any royalty within this village must have been buried on the crest of the hill. I should have thought of it earlier." *What the hell was I thinking?* "I must admit Jimmy, guess I was overly eager just to get a shovel in the ground. In my haste, I neglected to take a step back to see the big picture."

"But we have dug near the crest of the hill. Why didn't we just start there?" countered Jimmy. "Plus, by the looks of things, you excavated some from the top of the hill last year, too."

"True, but now we're only going to concentrate on what I'd call the spot on the spot. You have to systematically work through an area," Colby stopped to point out the semi-circular pattern of excavation that had formed. "But every village is unique. I believe that if Kakawita is buried at this site, they would have buried him on the top. With that damn river getting closer every day, I think it's best to play the percentages. I found more ceremonial artifacts with adult burials at the height of a burial field farther south of here at some of those villages I dug along the Missouri. Now that I think of it, the Burns Site and the George Site were good examples of that."

Colby began to probe the top of the hill on the trench closest to the river. The combination of swirling wind with the oppressive sun made Colby feel like he'd entered a blast furnace.

Morning melded into midafternoon as they unearthed scattered burials on the crest. At various times during the day, Colby had scanned the buttes and scoured landscape in the direction of the suspected pot hunters checking for the glint of the glass. As he worked, he put more thought into who could be watching. *I think if they were pot hunters they would have come here by now. Huh. Holy crap! I wonder if it's Gritzmacher and Calhoun, those two State dopes that messed with me and my dig three years ago. That's all we need. Badges shutting down our work. Maybe they're here to rip me off again. That would not be good.* He shivered at the threat of his mission being thwarted. Colby felt the frustration inside him return with a vengeance. His descriptions became shorter and increasingly terse. Colby delivered a continual venomous tone and verbiage in Jimmy's direction, despite his grandson's best attempts to placate him. *He better not ask another question or want a break.* It was starting to look to Colby like this trip would end without finding the medal. The river was now within twenty yards of the trenches, gobbling large chunks of prairie with its rise.

The next spot they chose was to be their last of the day. It was on the downside of the top of the rise facing the river. The probe found the wood and rocks again. Colby began to shovel the dirt into the buckets, fully exposing the periphery of the burial. With his hand shovel, he slowly cleared off the wood. Softball-sized granite rocks lined the edge of the wood clearly delineating the uncommon looking grave. "Jimmy, do you see how all these rocks are nearly identical?" Jimmy shrunk into a baseball catcher's position. Colby rubbed one of the rocks on his pant leg to remove the dirt revealing a smooth polish. "Never seen such uniformity like that before." Colby held the wood up to his nose, and it revealed the aroma of cedar, similar to, but stronger than the other burials that were covered in wood. He neatly piled the wood with the two dozen rocks up on the ridge between trenches.

"Look through the sifter very carefully," encouraged Colby. Jimmy repositioned the sifter and loaded the dirt filled buckets into it. Colby diligently continued to remove dirt with his hand shovel. His focus became laser sharp scraping away the dirt exposing the sternum. As he uncovered the rib cage it became apparent that this body had been positioned on its back.

"Nothing here." Jimmy called from the sifter. He rejoined Colby, bent over with his hands on his knees looking over Colby's shoulder from the uncut rib of prairie above.

Colby continued to load the buckets with dirt from around the lower extremities. Now the hips, long bones of the legs, and feet were exposed. He took the #6 brush and swept the remaining dust, while carefully examining the preservation of the bone. Colby shifted his attention to the skull and began to clear the dirt. After fully uncovering the intact skull, he muttered that the entire dentition had been ground flat. Next, he slowly uncovered the left arm and noticed that both the ulna and radial bones had been broken. Not all the way through, but clearly new bone had been grown for repair. Colby looked up at Jimmy from his knees with a sly smile. He straightened up while still on his knees and pointed at the left arm.

"Jimmy, do you see what I see? This is interesting."

"Yeah. It looks like this one broke his or her arm in two places and it, like, mended back together."

"That's it exactly," Colby said as he returned to dusting the left arm. "Can you imagine the pain this old guy went through? No doubt he was a warrior."

"You think it was a man?"

"So far, judging from the size and orientation of the right and left hip bones, I'd say yes." Colby stopped, took his hat off, and wiped his brow. He put his hat back on and returned to removing dirt with the trowel just below the mandible. One scoop with a copper bead in it. Then another scoop with a copper and shell bead in it. Colby scooped all the dirt from an over exaggerated area around the neck and upper chest area.

"Jimmy, here now, take this bucket and carefully sift it." Colby lifted the bucket onto the sod above the trench. "It appears as if there might be a number of beads in it." Colby stood over the assumed warrior with hands on hips in tune with his surroundings, his face full of contemplation. Something wasn't right. He stepped up from the trench onto virgin prairie. The master digger looked right and left and right and left again. Then Colby turned ninety degrees and looked right and left. He gave an expressionless stare at Jimmy. Colby took a few steps toward the river abruptly turning back around to face the burial ground. Visually, he took note of the excavated area from last summer along with the smaller area they had worked the last few days with his arms folded across his chest. He took off his cowboy hat and scratched his head, pacing. He squatted down and put a piece of prairie grass in his mouth to pacify himself while he tried to figure out what he saw before him. Colby stood up with his hands clasped behind his back, continuing to ponder.

Then it dawned on him. Colby shook his head from side to side. *Why hadn't I thought of this before?* "I got it! Jimmy, the burial ground doesn't go north to south in the direction of the trenches. That was the typical way, more or less parallel to the river. This burial place is more of a semicircle with the straight side along the river and the half circle side fanning out away from the shore. Look at where we have dug! Do you see the pattern? This isn't the traditional rectangle on a hillside burial. It's the Arikara's ceremonial design!" He began to talk faster, effusing excitement. "Let me explain. The burial we are currently working on is actually at the midpoint of the half moon, approximately equidistant from the north and south edges." He saw the puzzled look on Jimmy's face. Colby, facing away from the river, motioned with his arms and hands, "Jimmy, picture a pie with half of it gone with me standing in the middle of the pan. This burial placement is the zenith of all the burials!"

A wave of exhilaration coursed through Colby's body. Colby quickly hopped down to the three quarters exposed skeleton, pawing the dirt with his bare hands like a man possessed, his brain arcing with thoughts of grandeur. He knew this was no ordinary burial.

11

"You think it's the Chief?" asked Jimmy.

"If it's not, it was someone of great importance to the tribe. What did you find in the sifter?"

"Seven copper beads, three elk tooth pendants, and 11 shell beads. Also found this." He held up a circular piece of bone, about the size of a half dollar with serrations around the edges and a hole in the middle. Remarkably, the patina was highly polished.

"I rest my case."

Colby returned to uncovering the right humerus, ulna, and radial bones. As he brushed aside the remaining dirt from the wrist area, he noticed the hand bones went in a deeper direction instead of in a line with the rest of the arm. He continued to scratch at the dirt and began to uncover a reddish object. First the stem, then the bowl.

"He's holding a whole pipe!" Colby turned to Jimmy, pointing. "My God, this guy was special," Colby exclaimed with a smile broader than his ears. There was an unfettered thrill in his voice. He bared the complete pipe cradled by the soil above the palm bones of the hand. "This might be the rarest find in my career. One of the rarest, for sure."

"That is really cool. This has got to be the Chief," said Jimmy, hopping down for a closer look.

Colby sat back on his haunches. For the moment, it seemed like time stood still. He appreciated the royalty before him. He tipped his hat back and with wide eyes said to Jimmy, "This is something. Take a good look 'cause you may never see another burial like it." He pulled his hat back down over his forehead and dusted the pipe where it lay.

Jimmy leaned in closer. "What is the pipe made of?"

"The pipes were made of pipestone; some call it catlinite, probably quarried from southwestern Minnesota. Gets the name catlinite because in the 1830's an explorer and artist named George Catlin visited that quarry. Ever since that time it has carried his name. It was used by the Indians to make their ceremonial pipes. Pipes played an important part in spiritual rituals of many tribes." Colby began to stand. "I left the camera at camp to keep it out of the dust. I'm gonna go get it. The light at this time of day is perfect."

Jimmy extended his hand to Colby and helped his grandpa up. "I gotta say I had my doubts we were going to find the Chief. Not anymore, huh?"

Colby grinned. "I guess not. Just wait here. Play it cool. Don't touch anything. Remember we are probably still being watched." He took off to camp to get his camera, his gait light, his head held high.

Jimmy examined the entire skeleton. He saw the worn teeth, touched the mended arm wondering what this noble Indian's life story had been. *What was his life like? How did he die? How old was he, exactly? Did he have a wife? Wives? Any children?* Colby had scored the entire area around it, and the red stone stuck out in sharp contrast to the brown dirt and pale-yellow bones. He leaned over to look down the blackened inside of the bowl from which Colby had carefully removed the dirt. Jimmy remained on all fours but poked his head up to sneak a quick peek toward camp to see if Colby had found the camera. His grandpa stood by the tent with his hand cupped around his mouth shouting something. Jimmy rose up on his knees and shrugged his shoulders, with his arms outstretched as if to say, 'What? I can't hear you.' Colby waved him off before entering the tent.

Jimmy stared at the pipe paralyzed with curiosity. He hadn't ever seen a whole pipe before. The workmanship was beyond reproach. Smooth surfaces, gently rounded contours, the stem scribed with flame lines. He put his hand over it to gauge its size in two dimensions, length and height. *I wonder how wide it is.* He thought about carefully retrieving the pipe just to cure his interest, but then thought better. He looked toward camp again. Colby had moved to the back of the Scout. Jimmy's impulse connected with his impatience to overpower any sense of reason. He reached for the pipe to see if he could pull it straight up without disturbing the soil around it. Slowly, he lifted it straight up without disturbing any soil. The remaining outline of the pipe was clear. The clay and dirt mix had held. The pipe felt heavier than it looked. *How in the world could the Indians craft such a beautiful piece of art? How did it last centuries without being broken or chipped?* Awestruck by its beauty, he wanted to examine this magnificent artifact further, but knew not to push his luck. He leaned over from his knees and with a slight tremor in his hands, began to place the pipe in the exact spot from which he had taken it.

Then he saw it. *What the...* He grabbed the #10 brush to delicately dust just a portion of the circular object. *How the hell could I have missed it?* His brain had become so focused, so locked in on the pipe so as to not get caught moving it, that he hadn't bothered to look underneath it. My God, he thought, as excitement welled up inside of him taking his breath away.

There in the dirty and windswept plains of the South Dakota prairie overlooking the rising waters of the Missouri River lay a tarnished Thomas Jefferson Peace Medal. He sat back screaming out loud to no one, but to everyone. He couldn't contain himself. He scrambled to his feet waving to Colby. He began to jump up and down yelling. Colby poked his head out of the Scout and waved back. Jimmy stopped. He gathered his wits thinking it best to put the pipe back and let his grandpa be the one to find the medal. With surgical precision he placed the pipe back in its original resting place. He looked up only to see Colby yards away walking rapidly toward him with a concerned look on his face. He had the camera slung over his shoulder.

"What the hell was all the commotion about? I thought I told you to play it cool. That looked like anything but." Colby glared at Jimmy. *You have no idea what's at stake here.*

"Oh, yeah, I forgot. I couldn't help it. I'm sorry but I was just so excited," Jimmy said. Colby tried to catch his eye, but he looked away.

"Don't ever let that happen again," Colby pleaded. "Seriously, those are the type of antics that could attract attention from our voyeurs."

"Yeah, got it. It won't happen again. What took you so long, anyway?" Jimmy asked.

"I found it the last place I looked," said Colby forcing a smile. "I had left the camera on the front seat of the vehicle when we were sitting out the rain."

"Yeah, I figured you forgot where you put it again. Let's get this catalogued and get some pictures." Jimmy stepped aside, making room for Colby to see the chief and resume his work.

"Good plan." Colby set his camera down and got down on his knees. He rummaged in his front pants pocket, withdrawing the tape measure. "OK, grave type is pit, 2.9 feet from surface, maximum length of pit is 5.9 feet, maximum width is 3.1 feet. Preservation is remarkable, no put down extraordinary," he chuckled. "Body is in prone position with head to the east and body extending to the west. Sex is male and I would guess in his late 30's by the wear of his dentition." He paused to instruct Jimmy in a very businesslike manner. "You should list the copper, shell, and elk teeth by number and description. And don't forget to list the bone disc. Obviously, the pipe, too."

"There may be more, Grandpa."

"No, I think that's it. Did I miss something?"

"Well, I was thinking that after you get your pictures and you remove the pipe, you have to excavate the hand and …"

"Yeah, okay. Good point." Jimmy was being more thorough than usual. Nice. "I guess there could always be more."

Colby retrieved his camera and began taking photos from all angles to properly document his amazing find of the whole pipe. Thankfully, the light remained ideal, so the shadows were at a minimum. "This is the kind of stuff journals and banquet circuits love."

He took the last photo then picked up a research box he would use to store the bones and artifacts. "Okay, set the box over here where I can reach it." With Jimmy standing by his side, he plucked the first of the two hundred and six human bones from the pit and placed it in the box. He continued up the legs, through the torso, rib cage, right arm, and skull. Clavicle, scapula, left arm bones. Colby paused, admired the exquisite pipe, then bowed his head in a holy moment of respect for this apex member of the tribe, to match the reverence with which he had been buried. With appropriate caution, he removed the pipe before grabbing the handkerchief from his back pocket to wrap it up with for safe keeping. Colby felt like he had just gone to the funeral of an old friend.

"I'll put the pipe away; you dig out the rest of the hand," Jimmy said as he exchanged with Colby the pipe for the mini trowel.

Colby reeled in his emotions and happened to look back down at where the pipe had been. He saw the medal. Opened his mouth but nothing came out. His chest tightened. He tried to catch his breath. Stunned silence. *Are my eyes playing tricks on me? What the hell?* Trembling, he put his fingernails under an edge. With the touch of a surgeon, he picked up the medal-both halves still joined. Tarnished to black by a combination of moisture, oxygen, and trace metals in the soil over time, but intact. He knew the medal would be well preserved, if he ever found one, in large part due to the dry conditions and the loess soil type. *Yes!* Examination revealed a slight crease on Jefferson's face. Tears began to puddle in his eyes. At long last, Colby had found the much sought-after Thomas Jefferson Peace Medal. It felt beautiful and familiar.

This was it: the holiest of holy grails. He had found Kakawita. Lewis and Clark had indeed visited this village. Vindication for the master at last. Relief and repose filled Colby's soul as he inspected the medal. Deeper he traveled introspectively, recalling the journey he had been on to get to this point in his career. Doubters, both inside and outside his family, always feeling like he had to prove himself, an unbridled obsession to find this medal. Finally, the dam broke and a dribble of tears rolled down his face streaking the dust earned over the course of the day. *If only my parents and Rebecca could see me now. This would show them.*

I know it. Finally, I would have won their approval and love. He looked up at Jimmy, kissing the medal. A triumphant culmination after decades of searching.

"We did it! We did it!" said Jimmy, as he stepped down into the trench, his hands slapping Colby's back.

Colby rose to his feet drained of energy. The façade of the tough old digger and taskmaster had melted away. He righted himself then gave Jimmy the strongest bear hug he had ever given him. They held the embrace for longer than normal relishing all that was good in that moment.

"Yes, we did Jimmy," Colby sniffled. "Yes, we did."

12

Charles Ray and Billy had spent the last few days taking shifts staring through their binoculars. They were looking for any clue that might lead them to believe that the two men they were watching had found the medal. Hour after hour, it proved to be tedious, boring work, but they kept at it. When they weren't watching, they played 'chicken' with their switchblades just for giggles, smoked some pot, and reminisced about their childhood. Billy whittled to pass the time but even that became monotonous. Charles Ray played the harmonica, poorly. By now their food supply was running low and their patience was growing thin. Both were dirty, sunburned, and tired.

Finally, Billy saw a marked expression of excitement through his binoculars. "The younger one is jumping up and down. Somethin's goin' on."

"What do ya see Billy? What do ya see?"

"Get over here quick and look for yourself."

Charles Ray quickly crawled up the short ridge and grabbed the binoculars. He peered across the grassy expanse. "Shoot, he's lost it. Looks like he got stung by a bee or got bit by a rattler. Maybe the sun got to him."

"Nah. It's more than that. Somethin's happening." Billy's impatience boiled over. "That's it, I've had enough. I think it's time we pay those boys a visit." He grabbed the binoculars back from Charles Ray before the two slithered back down the ridge. "Let's just go over real nice and all and just ask them what they're up to," Billy said. "We just say we're out here huntin' and were wondering what they're doin'. Poke around a little bit and see what turns up," Billy pointed in the direction of the burials. "They're takin' more pictures than normal. Gotta be a special burial. At this point we got nothing to lose and maybe we get something worth a buck or two."

"I'm with ya," Charles Ray nodded. "This God forsaken prairie has done me in. I'm itchin' for some action. Time to roust 'em up a bit, and then head to town."

"Right on, cousin, right on. Give me the keys, I'll drive."

Billy grabbed the pistol off of the blanket and tucked it in his pants behind his back. Charles Ray put on his dirty t-shirt before tossing him the keys as they marched to the truck. They barreled out of the draw, bounding over the irregular surface of the grassland and onto the plateau that would take them to the dig site.

By this time, Colby had taken his shirt off. He ripped a piece of it, wrapped the medal in the scrap, and placed the rare prize in a small cigar box. The bones of this once proud and powerful warrior chief had been respectfully placed in a standard issue museum box for transport. He placed the cigar box on top of the bone box. Chest swollen with pride, full of respect for its contents, he began to carry the box toward the camp. Jimmy had already made one trip with some of the other burials of the day and returned. He gathered the remaining boxes and tools, joining Colby on the walk back.

All at once, a pickup truck charged out of the distance, coming from the direction where they had seen the sparkle of the binocular reflection. It seemed to be moving much faster than it should, given the terrain.

Their heads turned in synchrony. "Well, well. Looks like we're going to have visitors. Let me do the talking, Jimmy," Colby said with urgency, his mind full of worry and concern. "I was wondering when they were going to show their faces."

Once back at camp, they neatly stacked the boxes next to the truck. Jimmy began to organize the tools in the back of the Scout. Colby bolted for the tent. His thoughts teetered between cautiousness to paranoia. He wasn't ready to share with the world the most prized find of his life. He took his gun from under his pillow, flipped open the cylinder to make sure it was loaded, then shoved it in his boot. Unexplained and unwelcome visitors demanded prudence. He wasn't looking for trouble but no telling what could happen. Better to be protected than unprotected. He crawled back out of the tent and met Jimmy at the back of the Scout. Colby glanced up while he started putting the specimen boxes in.

The light blue pickup truck with the Tennessee plates pulled up close to the Scout. The pit in Colby's stomach made him feel sick. He wished Jimmy had brought his twelve gauge. Strength in numbers. As the truck doors slammed, Colby came out from behind the Scout to greet them.

"Howdy!" The man looked familiar, but Colby couldn't place him. "I'm Billy," he nodded his head to the side, "and this here's my cousin, Charles Ray." Billy stopped with his hands on his hips and Charles Ray crossed his arms across his chest retreating to lean his bony frame against the warm hood of their pickup truck.

Neither Billy nor Colby extended their arms to shake hands. "We just been bird huntin' these parts. Saw you folks out here so we thought we'd be neighborly and stop by." Billy looked in the direction of the burial field and pointed up the slope. "By the looks of things, you been doin' a lot of diggin'. Whatcha been up to?"

Colby thought it important to credential himself. "My name is Dr. Colby Phillips and I'm a Professor and Chair of the Cultural Anthropology and Archeology Department from the University of Kansas." Colby glanced over his shoulder to see Jimmy approaching. "We are excavating Indian burials for study before the river overtakes the burial ground there on the rise."

"Did you find any?"

"We found a few. How's your hunting been?" Colby said deflecting the conversation.

"Haven't shot anything but heard this was good country."

Colby decided to put them on the spot. "You're the ones who've been watching us, aren't you? I've seen the reflection from your binoculars."

"Nah, we ain't been watchin' you," Billy said with a nice tone. "We seen you here, but we've been glassin' birds, that's all. Hey, mind if we see what you found? Curious, ya know."

"Yeah, as a matter of fact, I guess I do mind." Colby locked eyes with Billy. Billy's expression didn't match the cordial voice he was putting on.

Jimmy joined Colby in the face-off standing a half step behind him. "This is my grandson, Jimmy." Jimmy stepped forward starting to extend his hand for a handshake. Billy glared at the hand. Jimmy pulled it back. Grandson stayed silent, but Grandfather knew his mind was actively taking inventory of the situation. Colby could feel Jimmy's presence behind him, pictured him crossing his arms like a sentry at his post.

"Anything and everything that we have found is University property. You understand why we can't show you, right?" Colby smiled as if they were colleagues.

"I see. Huh." Billy paused, anger brewing. His head shot back up in a vertical direction. "No, I don't understand, mister." He took a step forward, an arm's length away now. "No sir, no, I don't." Billy tilted his head to the side as he spoke. "The way I figure is we come over here neighborly like to just say hi, and you're being kinda rude and unfriendly." Billy's blue eyes remained locked on Colby's. "Do you think they're being unfriendly, Charles Ray?"

Charles Ray slowly nodded his head and said, "Yeah, I do."

Billy lifted his chin, "So, why don't you show us some of that Kansas hospitality y'all preach about and let us see what you found? Or are you tryin' to hide something?"

"I know you've been watching us. No reason to lie to me. Why is that?" Despite Colby speaking with a calm voice, the jousting had become more intense. Out of the corner of his eye he saw Jimmy take a step forward while taking his hands out of his pockets.

"I already told ya," Billy scoffed. He kicked the ground, nodding his head from side to side. "No, that must be someone else, mister." Flashing a broad, smile, Billy said, "You accusin' us of something?"

Amid an uncomfortable interaction in the middle of the Great Plains, Colby experienced a moment of crystal clarity. He realized that these were the two men he had seen drive by when they left the grocery store upon their arrival in Painted Rock, the same men that did a whiskey shot at The Caboose. Probably the guys that Katherine said were looking for them.

The escalating tension between the two men became palpable. "Not accusing you of anything. Just wondering why you'd be watching us. And, like I said, I can't show you anything." Colby's brow became taut. "Now, if you'll excuse us and be on your way, we are actually just packing up to leave."

Billy's eyes narrowed shifting his glare between Colby and Jimmy. Billy had stared down lots of folks much tougher than Colby. He sensed he had the upper hand in the verbal dance they were engaged in. He scuffed at the ground with his boots pivoting toward Charles Ray. His cousin snickered, shook his head, and readjusted his position by crossing his legs.

Billy said, "Really got nowhere for us to go. What's your hurry anyway? There are two, maybe three, more hours of daylight. We can hang out. Hey, I've got an idea!" He got a predatory look in his eye and flashed a sardonic smile at Colby. "So as not to trouble you while you break camp, I think I'll just help myself to see what you found."

He began to pass by Colby. Colby reached out and grabbed his upper arm, "Look, buddy, I told you twice. I can't show you what we found."

Charles Ray straightened up and took two steps forward, ready to pounce like an alley cat. Billy pulled his arm away from Colby and raised his hands above his head as if to surrender. He motioned to Charles Ray to stay put.

"Ok. Ok. How about this--" Billy took a step back, his facial muscles relaxing. He had a lifetime of very successful experience reading weaknesses in people, then exploiting it, to get what he wanted. With a relaxed posture, he took a deep breath, then exhaled through his nostrils. With great effort, he spoke in a reasoning tone of voice. "Let's agree none of us want any trouble. Right?" He held his arms out vulnerable, pleading. Then, his glare hardened, so that his face became contorted with anger.

"Let's also agree that if you don't show us what you found real nice and friendly like I'm gonna to have Charles Ray beat both your faces to a bloody pulp. Maybe rearrange a few things, shall we say."

The old man stood still as a stone.

Billy kept one eye on Colby and Jimmy and the other eye toward Charles Ray as he spoke, "Charles Ray, why don't you tell them about your time in 'Nam. Maybe help them make the right choice."

Charles Ray's hand shook as he took a long pull of his cigarette held between his thumb and forefinger. He dropped it, rubbing it into the hard ground using the toe of his boot for emphasis. He stared at the duo from Kansas. His head twitched. That damn tic again. He looked away, simultaneously rubbing his neck. "I can't, Billy. They don't want my version no way anyhow," Charles Ray said.

Billy volunteered, "No problem, Charles Ray. I'd be happy to do it for ya." He focused on Colby and began. "My cousin was in country in the early days of the war with a crew of five in an AC-47 gunship named, 'Puff the Magic Dragon,' flyin' out of Laos for close air support. Funny name, huh?" Billy's upper lip raised up on one side as he acted like he was at a lectern on a podium, "Anyway, it was pretty dangerous 'cause they flew so low and at night, but the gun he had could put a bullet on every square inch of a damn football field from a pivot point above the enemy." Billy talked using his hands to demonstrate. "He actually liked to bring the hell down on them Vietnamese Cong or whatever ya call 'em. The resulting carnage was impressive. I mean women, children, oxen. The way he told me, didn't make no difference to him," Billy snickered. "I ain't gunna lie to ya. He likes to inflict pain."

Standing rigid and unfazed, Colby's face showed no emotion. "What's your point?"

Billy's eyes got big and round as he laughed, "My point?" He looked at Colby but tilted his head toward Charles Ray, "You want somma that?"

Colby looked back at Jimmy longing to protect his only grandson from the seemingly unavoidable conflict racing toward them. He felt cornered. *God have mercy.*

Only one way out. He bent over to reach for his gun, but before he could pull it out, *Thud!* Boot on bone. Colby spun around and landed face first sprawled on the ground. His cowboy hat went flying.

"Grandpa!" Jimmy exclaimed rushing to his grandpa. Colby turned his head and looked up at Jimmy, blood streaming from his lip and nose.

Jimmy knelt down next to Colby. He turned to Billy, "What the hell did you do that for?"

Billy pointed his finger at Jimmy. "You shut up. I gave him every chance to make the right decision, but he made a bad decision instead." Billy stood over Colby. "Sorry old man but you had it comin.'" Billy pushed Jimmy onto his backside before rolling Colby over onto his back. Colby felt Billy wrenching the gun from his boot, heard him open the cylinder and empty the bullets onto the ground. And then, over his shoulder, Billy tossed away Colby's best chance at defending himself. The gun was gone.

Charles Ray doubled over in laughter. "He just folded over like he was hit by a two by four. Hot damn that's good stuff."

Colby laboriously rolled onto his stomach and got up on all fours. In one motion, he turned his head to look at Billy spitting blood in his direction. Billy took a step forward to kick Colby again, this time in the rib cage. *Uff!* Boot on torso. Colby let out a loud groan as he crumpled to the ground.

Jimmy got to his feet and charged Billy in an attempt to tackle him, but Billy caught him with a right uppercut to his jaw. *Whack!* Bone on bone. Jimmy looked uncoordinated trying to regain his balance, shook his head trying to clear it. He swung wildly hitting nothing but air. A straight left jab from Billy staggered Jimmy back against the truck. He slumped down with his back against the tire. Out cold. Blood trickled out of the side of his mouth. His chin fell to his chest. Like a marionette, Billy imitated Jimmy wobbling and falling. Like hyenas over a kill, Charles Ray and Billy filled the air with laughter.

"Now, may we have a look at what you found?" Billy asked as he leaned over with his hands on his knees to look at Colby. His voice dripped with sarcasm. "Pretty please?" Billy kicked dust on him.

"The ol' man pissed me off and they both paid for it." Billy said turning to Charles Ray. "Seriously, we could have just looked, taken something, and left. But no, they had to try to be the tough guys. Not my fault," he chuckled. "Guess you just can't fix stupid." Billy hadn't even broken a sweat. He pointed to the light blue pickup truck. "Get the rope out of the back."

Charles Ray went to the back of the truck and grabbed a section of three strand Manila rope about eight feet long.

"They need to chill out while we do some lookin'. Let's put them back-to-back with their arms locked at the elbow and tie them together behind their truck." Billy grabbed Colby under the armpits to haul his semi-conscious body behind the truck where he sat him up. Jimmy was starting to come to, but barely resisted Charles Ray dragging him over to where Colby was.

"You'll never get away with this," the old man grumbled. Flies buzzed around his head.

"Oh yeah? Who's gonna to know? There's no one within miles of us. I guess you can tell that to the coyotes when they come to visit you tonight." Billy fetched Colby's hat and dusted it off. He pushed it onto his head over his eyes. "Best ya keep your mouth shut. Now go ahead and lock your arms at the elbow. Let's not make this any more difficult than it has to be."

He complied. Charles Ray looped the twisted rope around their torsos, double knotting the ends.

Charles Ray took a seat on the rear bumper. Billy had begun to open boxes.

"Yikes. Look at this, Charles Ray! Must be Halloween!" Charles Ray came around the truck and gasped. Together they peered into the box and saw a skull and bones. They closed the lid and went to the next box, opened it, and started laughing. "Y'all are crazy. The Indians know you're diggin' up their relatives?"

Colby blinked deliberately, croaked his answer. "They don't care. We are on a Sioux reservation, and this is an Arikara village. Historically, the Sioux and Arikara hated each other. Some say they still don't get along."

"And what do we have here?" Billy opened the small cigar box and unwrapped its contents from the ripped t-shirt. "Hey, Charles Ray, it looks to me like we found the mother lode," Billy exclaimed. He held up the medal with a big smile.

"Whoa, is that it?" Charles Ray's eyes got big and his mouth froze open. "Is that what you were talking about?"

"Yes, sir. This here is a Thomas Jefferson Peace Medal." Billy let out a big yeehaw. "I'll be damned. We're about to get paid!"

"You don't know what you're talking about. That's nothing," Colby muttered.

"Oh, really? Well let me tell you something, Doctor Colby

Phillips from the University of Kansas. We know all about you and your digs. You see, I met a former colleague of yours, Earl Chavey. That name ring a bell?" Billy squatted down to look Colby square in the eye. "Me and him got to be real tight at Brushy Mountain. Know what Brushy Mountain is?"

The old man showed no reaction as his head wobbled from side to side.

"It's a prison in Tennessee. He got sent there because of what you done to him. He told me you stole university money by fixin' the books but because you're some big important fella they couldn't charge you. He told me," Billy cocked his head as his volume increased, "he got railroaded and sent to jail by YOU!" He jabbed his finger into Colby's chest for emphasis. "He also told me all about how you were obsessed with finding this medal. We spent hours in the library researching and looking up the history of this medal."

Colby looked away as if ignoring Billy's words.

"Hey," Billy tilted his head to the side and slapped Colby's face to redirect his attention, "you need to hear this. I promised Earl I'd make sure you understood in no uncertain terms how bad you hurt him. My buddy, Earl, said his goal in life was to get even with you, and the best way he knew how was to get this medal from you. His wife told him you were here last summer and heard you were coming back this summer."

Billy paused and softened his tone to a whisper. "Did you know he had a wife and two small kids? They're livin' on government assistance now because of you." He stood looking down on Colby. "Earl figgered if you were coming back you still hadn't found it. I was fixin' to bust out anyway, so we made an agreement. I needed work and he needed to get even. It was a deal made in heaven. He gets the medal and his revenge, and I get a nice paycheck." Billy bent over to go nose to nose. "How am I doing so far? You with me Dr. Phillips?" Billy put his hand on the top of Colby's cowboy hat to make him nod in agreement. Blood dripped from Colby's nose. "Good. I figgered a smart guy like you would connect the dots and agree with me."

At the mention of Earl Chavey, Colby's body stiffened. He hoped Jimmy was too out of it to understand the incriminating story Billy was weaving. Colby needed to defend his honor before his grandson by telling his side of the story. In a hushed voice he began, "I didn't steal any money from the University. I was entitled to that money, but they didn't see it that way. It was supposed to be a loan, damnit." Colby licked the taste of blood from his lips. "I showed the University all my reimbursement slips and ledgers from my trips. Earl accompanied me on most of those digs. I'll tell you one thing for certain," Colby looked at Billy, "they aughta be thanking their lucky stars I work for that University. I bring them a lot of grants and endowment money!" Colby's lip had already started to swell, and his ribs ached with every breath. "Earl Chavey didn't keep his records as well as I did." He spoke with no remorse. "That's his fault. There was tremendous pressure from the higher ups to bury this and get it out of the headlines. Somebody had to be held accountable. I'm sorry for Earl. I liked him." Colby stopped to catch his breath. "If he wants to be mad at someone, he should be mad at the Trustees. I never wanted Earl to get hurt. You gotta believe me." On the inside, Colby felt pangs of guilt because the truth was, he had misappropriated funds to pay for his daughter's medical expenses. Despite the fact that he'd eventually paid the funds back, the guilt lingered. He had fudged the numbers and testified against Earl. She was dying. What was he supposed to do?

"Shut up." Billy began pacing like a caged animal. "Your

bullshit story doesn't mean a damn thing to me. He got screwed by you and that's final. I know it and you know it. Now, the other thing about Earl that I liked is that he holds grudges. Just like me. I do hold grudges, don't I, Charles Ray?"

"That's a fact."

"The one weird thing that Earl found researching during our free time – there's lots of time to research in prison," Billy stopped in front of Colby, raising his right index finger, "is that this medal actually should be in my family." Billy shook his head in the affirmative. "That's right. Your buddy Earl told me so. He said he did a lot of research into my family genealogy. How about that for a coincidence? See, I kinda started to study it when I was lookin' up the medal, but Earl said he already done it, so I didn't have to. How's that for a friend? Earl told me 'by now you shoulda been rich or famous or both'." Billy drew quotation marks with his index fingers. "Instead, I'm a nobody from Morgan County Tennessee. I guess my great-great-great," Billy began counting on his fingers to recall how many generations back he should go but lost count. "Okay, well anyways, if them records Earl told me about is right," Billy stopped, "and I ain't got no reason to believe they ain't accurate, my distant Grand Pappy was Robert Scot. He was the guy supposed to design this medal for Thomas Jefferson, but he got screwed, too, because they gave the work to some immigrant, Johann somebody or other. Sooo here we are." Billy's arms were outstretched with his palms facing upward looking down at Colby. "I figure my distant relation Robert Scot got screwed; therefore, I got screwed, you screwed Earl, now we're gonna screw you!" He and Charles Ray started laughing that same evil laugh. Only this time it was longer and with deeper conviction.

"You're sick," Colby countered in agony. "I don't believe a word of what you just said. Stupid hillbilly. You're not smart enough to follow the branches of a family tree. Ha. Earl sold you on a fairytale. That cheap whiskey you drink…"

"Whoa, partner. In case you haven't noticed you're in a bit of a predicament. No sense in getting' all personal and whatnot. See, we're fixin' to take this medal," Billy said as he bent at the waist while dangling the dusty medal in front of Colby's face, "and make our fortune. You get to sit here with your grandson and rot. So, I don't care what you say. You can save your sob story for the pearly gates. C'mon, Charles Ray, let's go to town and slam some of that cheap whiskey the professor says we drink and celebrate." Billy straightened up and began to walk with confidence toward their pickup truck.

"Hey," Charles Ray shouted after Billy, "Let's see what else is in 'dem other boxes. We only looked in a few. Shouldn't we check the others? Maybe your buddy wants other stuff besides just the medal."

Billy turned and gave a dismissive wave, "Nah, this medal is all Earl wanted. C'mon now, let's hit it."

Charles Ray turned back a step and stood over Colby and Jimmy, smiling. "Sounds like a splendid idea to me. I might even find me a woman for the night. That young one at the bar would do me just fine." Colby felt Jimmy's body stiffen. He squirmed, but the rope held Grandfather and Grandson tightly. "Well, lookie here! Billy, I think I might have touched a nerve." Charles Ray got in Jimmy's face. "I'll give her your regards when we're together." That got them both laughing again. Deep and sadistic.

"You're both worthless pieces of shit. I hope you both go straight to hell!" Colby shouted.

Billy abruptly stopped and spun around all-in-one motion, quickly back traced his steps, pulled out his .45 from behind his back, and shoved it under Colby's chin. "You think you're all high and mighty and important. Earl told me that's how you was. Now look at ya. You're just a tired and broken old man. You deserve to die here on the prairie where you made your name on the backs of all those that came with ya. You're a disgrace." He got down on his knees putting his face about two inches from Colby's. Colby could smell his sour, hot breath. Billy pointed the gun at Colby's forehead and cocked the hammer. Colby strained not to flinch. "Let me be clear, I would just as soon blow your brains out as look at ya. Earl would probably want that, but that would be too nice. I'd rather just let the coyotes or rattle snakes get ya." Billy released the hammer, spun the gun skyward, and returned the gun behind his back. He turned to Jimmy, "Sorry kid. Can't pick your relatives."

"So long, suckers!" Charles Ray said in a mocking tone as they both made their way to the pickup. They hopped into the cab grinning from ear to ear. Out their windows they waved a taunting goodbye headed to town, treasured medal in hand. Jimmy and Colby watched helplessly as the red taillights got smaller and smaller. The peace and quiet of the prairie returned. No sound except the occasional cackle of a ring-necked pheasant in the distance. High above, three turkey vultures circled on warm thermals in the clear blue sky of early evening.

13

Jimmy turned his head to the side. "You okay, Grandpa?" Anxiety knotted Jimmy's stomach.

"Sore, but I'll heal. How are you feeling?"

"Same. I think my jaw might be broken. I can barely open my mouth." Jimmy could taste the blood in his mouth. He ran his tongue along the broken edges of his two front teeth. "My top front teeth are chipped!" The rising anger inside Jimmy had reached a crescendo. "Grandpa, I want that medal back!"

"Sorry to hear that about your teeth," Colby whispered. It hurt to breathe in. "Forget the damn medal. Right now, we have to think of a way to get outta here. Any suggestions?"

Jimmy thought for a second as he looked around. The new rope had been tied too tight to wriggle out of. Then he saw a bright reflection from the blade. "Can you bend your knees? I have an idea."

"Yes, I can, but what's that got to do with anything?" Colby said.

"I was thinking that, by pressing our backs against each other, the resulting force will help us get our legs under us and we can hobble over to the machete. We'll use the blade to cut the rope."

"I knew I brought you for a reason. But you make it sound so easy."

"Best idea I got." He paused. "The only idea I got."

"Where's the machete?"

"I used it to clear the area for the tent and then stuck it in the ground right over there." Jimmy motioned with his head in the direction of the machete. "Luckily, I left the blade pointed away from the tent. Once the ropes are cut, we can go to town and find those guys."

"Then what? Absolutely not. Are you crazy? They'll be long gone. They're not sticking around. We just need to concentrate on getting free. First things first." Colby let out a sigh.

"Alright, so I will count to three, and then we push against each other," Jimmy said. "Bend your knees and push with your legs back and up. Ready? One, two, three…" Attempting to get a foothold, they both dug their heels in and with every muscle in their legs began to push in a direction up and back. Groaning, straining, they slowly began to lift themselves up.

Colby was struggling. His frail legs began to shake and quiver. "I can't. Cramps," he hollered. In an instant, they tumbled onto their sides, unable to stand. Colby let out a guttural cry as he landed on his ribs.

"Let's take a break. Let you get your strength back," Jimmy said. His chest tightened from the stress of hearing Colby's suffering. "You're going to be okay, right, Grandpa?"

"I hope so." Colby sighed.

For a few minutes, they lay in the dust and flattened grasses, drained of their energy, sore bodies, dried blood, cracked bones, and no medal.

Colby knew this couldn't end well. Doubt announced its presence as he began to contemplate whether this whole manic search for the medal had been worth it. "I'm sorry Jimmy. Damnit, I shoulda never got you into this mess." The tone of his voice spoke the pain in his heart. "I got my priorities messed up and put you in danger. My blind ambition and cavalier attitude have gotten me in trouble more than once in my life. My marriage, the University, and now this. Damnit. I shoulda never brought you on this trip." His voice was gravelly, his eyes moist. "I wanted this to be special for you and me because I knew I was close to finding it. Oh, God, I'm so sorry." The three turkey vultures had landed about twenty yards away and were just staring at the two hapless diggers.

"It's okay, Grandpa. It's not your fault we got ambushed. We were having the best trip ever until those jokers showed up. Probably didn't help that I lost my mind jumping around trying to get your attention when you were looking for your camera. But hey, like you always say, it's always an adventure when we're together, right?" Colby could hear a smile in Jimmy's voice. "We'll get out of this and we'll get your medal back. We just gotta take our time."

"Hope you're right." Colby had been in control of pretty much every facet in life up until this point. He liked getting his way, being the Alpha. Over the course of his professional life, he had done what he wanted when he wanted. This had earned him notoriety and tenure, among other perks. And maybe a little bit of trouble to go with. With Jimmy in charge at the moment, Colby's position shifted from being *in* charge of his circumstances to being *a* charge of someone else. It was not a position that felt comfortable to him. He also knew there was no choice. Funny, he'd had an unsettling feeling about this trip from the time they left.

On the drive up, confident in his purpose, he just couldn't draw from his subconscious exactly what was giving him that uneasiness. Possibly thinking that too many things could go wrong and hinder his quest for the medal. That definitely made him feel vulnerable. Maybe it was something else? He'd just known this trip would be different. He just didn't know how different. He had thought to himself that perhaps it might be his last. Outwardly broken, internally conflicted. Both gnawed at him, weakened his soul.

"Ready to try again to sit up?" Jimmy seemed to be doing his best to be encouraging as the sun began to kiss the horizon. Nightfall would be coming soon.

"I'll do my best." Colby's pain approached unbearable.

"Let's do it, Grandpa. Nice and easy. One more time, slowly. You ready?"

Barely audible, Colby whispered, "Okay."

"One, two, three…" Colby could feel Jimmy lightening up on his pushing to counter their weight difference. Soon, their force reached an equilibrium and up they went as if in slow motion, pushing to get their legs under themselves. "C'mon, Grandpa! Keep pushing! We're gaining on it!"

Through the hurt and misery he was feeling, Colby pushed as hard as his busted body would allow. His right foot slipped, but he caught it just in time to avoid another tipping disaster. Once their knees were at a forty-five degree angle the rest would be easy. Searing pain rocked his entire body again. They paused for a second. Jimmy held steady and continued to rise feeling the weight of the push becoming lighter. As they approached the magical 45-degree knee bend, Jimmy hollered, "We got it. C'mon only a couple more inches!" Like that, they stood up straight and erect. "Ha! We did it," Jimmy hollered.

"So now...we shuffle over...to the machete?" Colby, head down, limp body emptied of strength, felt as if he couldn't go on. *Lord, take me now.*

"Yep. We'll take it slow." They only had to go about five yards, but one misstep would put them right back on the ground having to start the process all over again. "Just take small steps."

"I can't move...Jimmy. I can barely staaan. That took about everythi...I...had left. I don't know if...can make it." The strain of inhaling and exhaling made Colby's words garbled.

"C'mon you can do it. I didn't quit when I said I was tired a few days ago, and you're not going to quit now," Jimmy said emphatically. "Okay, we go to Plan B. This is going to hurt, but just bear with me. I'm going to use my butt as a pivot point and put you on my back. I can carry you over to the machete. Once there, we will sit back down and cut ourselves free." Before Colby had time to respond, Jimmy bent his knees and with a determined lift hoisted him onto his back. Colby let out a cry that pierced the quiet. With measured steps, Grandson and Grandpa lumbered toward the machete.

"I'm going to set you down now." Gently, he straightened up, lowering Colby back to his standing position. "Now, Grandpa, we are going to slowly sit down. Do not knock over the machete. If that gets tipped over, we ARE going to be in even bigger trouble."

"Okay...Okay." Colby's breathing had become even more labored as he tried to get his wind. They pressed backs, squatted, and sat down.

Four feet to freedom. "Now I'll slide my right leg toward the tent, and you slide your left leg. Then we slide our butts in unison. This is going to work. Go." Colby was feeling the finish line nearing. "Don't stop now. Two more. Go." They rested. "One more. Go. Perfect. Holy crap, Grandpa, this is going to work." They were right next to the sharp blade of the machete.

The twilight hour brought coolness and shadows that stretched and distorted. Daylight would soon begin to run out at an exponential rate. Two more turkey vultures landed near the other three. Ten eyes on dinner. Darkness meant danger.

14

The good news was that Charles Ray had bound them so tightly together that the rope was taut. Therefore, they didn't need to cut through all of the loops around them. Cutting through just one would loosen the rope enough for them to escape. They both had a surge of energy that powered them as they rubbed the rope up and down on the blade. Their shoulders, elbows, and clenched fists raised and lowered in chorus. Faster and faster. Up down. Up down. The machete held firm with the increasing pressure against it and the quickened pace. They were making progress one twisted strand at a time. Jimmy's farm strength carried most of the burden of cutting at this point. Colby was literally along for the ride, barely able to move. Without warning the rope went slack. They were soon to be free.

"We are going to raise our elbows away from our bodies and that will give us more slack. Do it now," shouted Jimmy, despite the accompanying pain. As they lifted their elbows, the rope began to unravel from around them. Jimmy could feel the blood rush back into his biceps. He quickly shook off the rope and tossed it aside. Colby leaned back and lay flat on his back. Jimmy lifted Colby's head, cradling it in his lap.

"I need water," Colby whispered, his face ashen. Jimmy grabbed the water jug from next to the tent.

"Just a little to start," Jimmy instructed. He lifted Colby's head enough to pour a little water in his mouth. "How are you doing?"

"Not so good, Jimmy." Colby's eyes squinted with pain. "But better than when I was tied up."

"You think I should get you to a hospital?" He waited for Colby's response. "Or should we contact the town cops?"

"I don't think that will be necessary. I'll be alright. Plus, I don't want people to know we're out here or what we are doing. I've got a better idea. I think we should go visit our friends."

"Who are you talking about?" Friends? No hospital, no cops? Maybe his grandpa had lost his mind. "We don't have any friends out here. We know no one."

"Well, we did meet two people at The Caboose who said they were our friends." Colby struggled a wry smile then winced.

Jimmy raised his brow while rubbing his aching jaw. "I like the way you're thinking, Grandpa. Let's get you up and into the truck and take a drive into town. If nothing else, we'll get some ice for our bumps and bruises. Maybe a little sympathy, too." Jimmy poured a little more water into Colby's mouth.

Colby's color began to return as he sat up to get his bearings. Jimmy stood behind him sliding his arms under Colby's armpits. As sore as Jimmy was, he still managed to lift Colby's dead weight off the prairie with a backwards bear hug. They both let out a grunt as their broken bodies completed one more task.

Jimmy took Colby's right arm and wrapped it over his shoulder to help him walk to the truck. For further assistance, Jimmy put his left index finger into one of Colby's belt loops. Colby said,

"Kinda ironic isn't it? I used to take care of you, now you're having to take care of me. Humph, didn't figure on that for this trip."

"No worries, Grandpa." Together, they slowly hobbled toward the Scout gaining energy, but no relief from the pain. Grandfather and Grandson suffering together, leaning on each other for strength, and looking like they were going to survive this predicament.

"I think you're gonna to have to drive," Colby said.

"What do we do with the tent, tools, all our specimen boxes and all the rest of our stuff?" wondered Jimmy out loud.

"Leave all of it. We will come back later tonight or tomorrow and pack up," Colby replied with a hint of rejuvenated determination.

Jimmy used his left arm to open the passenger side door of the Scout for Colby to get in. Despite the obvious pain in his ribs, Colby was able to elevate himself into the front seat. Jimmy hustled around the front of the truck and flung open the driver's side door. Before he could get in, Colby said, "Get my .38, the bullets, too." Jimmy found them behind the truck, hurried back to settle into the driver's seat, and passed Colby the gun and bullets. Colby wiped the dust off the bullets then systematically returned them to the cylinder. He placed the gun in the glove compartment under a road map of South Dakota.

Jimmy turned the ignition and pushed the accelerator to the floor. The Scout fishtailed forward as Colby maintained a steeled demeanor. "So, what's our next move once we get to town?"

"Jimmy, if we do find them, I'm not sure what we'll do. They're professional criminals. We can't fight them with our fists. I can't just shoot 'em. If they see us first, we might both get shot, anyway." Colby's face revealed feelings of exasperation and hopelessness. "Talking isn't going to get us anywhere. I'm not sure why we are going to town. I think we have to sneak up on them somehow or maybe Katherine and Sarah can help us." Colby paused. "I guess some of this we just might have to figure out on the fly." Another pause, then a head nod. "Let's just get to town first and see if we can find their truck. We can adapt and adjust from there."

Given their beat-up condition, Jimmy knew this would be a bad time to confront Billy and Charles Ray. However, the thought of getting the medal back for his grandpa and the resulting joy that they both would experience far outweighed the risk. At least that's what he was trying to convince himself as logic wrestled with emotion.

Over the prairie, through the gates, back to the pavement, and over the bridge they traveled. They passed a few westbound cars coming into town. By the time they arrived in town, it was completely dark save for the hollow glow of the streetlights and occasional neon business sign. As they neared the Sinclair station, it was plain to see Gus had gone home for the night. Shadows drawn from solitary light poles intermittently darkened the street as they took the long way toward their destination. Jimmy drove at a moderate speed. He could feel his grandpa's eyes scanning back and forth. Litter whipped by the wind danced across the street as they continued their way east. A group of high school age youth walked along the main drag in a tight cluster. Nowhere to go, nothing else to do. It was a placid night in Painted Rock. As they reached the eastern edge of town, Jimmy took a right on Railroad Street toward the river which eventually turned them back to the northwest, ending up parallel with the railroad tracks. Red and green lights dotted the railyard as abandoned train cars lined the spurs.

"The Caboose is up a couple of blocks on the corner," Colby said pointing ahead.

"I see the sign. Let's drive past and circle around the block, see if they're there," Jimmy suggested.

"Sounds like a plan." Colby sat slumped down. His head was on a swivel constantly surveying the parked cars and sidewalks. "I don't see any sign of them or their truck."

Jimmy took a right turn away from the railyards to pass in front of The Caboose where the only vehicles on the street were parked. Jimmy rolled ahead slowly. Car, truck, truck, car - diagonally parked, dusty, and all with South Dakota plates. The next vehicle was a light blue pickup truck with Tennessee license plates.

Jimmy abruptly stopped the Scout. Colby's voice cracked, "Oh my God, they're here."

15

Katherine eyed the haggard looking strangers drinking celebratory shots of whiskey. Each shot made them more contentious. The shorter one with the long scar on his face seemed to be the "brains" of the two if you could even use that word to describe him. The other was sinewy with a wild look in his eye. From appearances alone, they didn't fit in with the normal evening crowd. Their clothes were perspiration soaked and dirty, clear evidence they hadn't bathed in a couple of days. The odor emanating from their corner of the bar confirmed it. She remembered them from the last time they were here and didn't like them anymore this time around. She served their drinks with a cool politeness but kept a wary eye out for trouble. Behind them, Johnny Rivers crooned from the speakers of the old Seeburg M100C jukebox next to the busted cigarette machine.

The shorter one with the scar on his face got off his barstool and reached into his pocket. "Hey lady," he barked in the direction of Katherine and Sarah. "Hey, come 'ere."

Katherine sighed. It was going to be one of *those* nights. She nodded to Sarah to head for the kitchen and meandered down the bar. She stopped in front of the man.

"What's your name, anyway," the short one mumbled.

"Katherine. What's yours?" Katherine couldn't have cared less.

"Billy." He swallowed hard. "Billy Dalton. And this here is my cousin Charles Ray."

"What can I get ya, Billy?" She felt on edge as frazzled nerves fired within her. She had seen the bulge of the guy's gun when the two men had walked by on their way to take a seat at the end of the bar.

"You ever hear of the Peace Medal?" Billy slurred. His eyes looked like they were having trouble focusing. His movements were soft and rounded. He pulled out what looked like a tarnished silver dollar and set it on the bar. "That there is a one and only Lewis and Clark Peace Medal."

Katherine pulled out her bifocals from her dress pocket and leaned forward to get a better look. "I've heard of the Thomas Jefferson Peace Medal that Lewis and Clark traded with the Indians. Is that what this is?" She looked over her bifocals feigning interest. She eyeballed the other guy who sat with his head down looking at the bar, both hands clasped around his glass. At least he probably wouldn't give her any trouble tonight. Looked like he was about to put his head down and fall asleep. Or pass out.

"Yeah, yeah, that's what I said," Billy snarled. "It's worth a fortune and we aim to cash in."

"Is that right? Well, good for you." Katherine said in a tone meant to appease them. Beginning to sense trouble, the last thing she wanted to do was upset either one of them. She knew of the medal and a little of its story, but not its value. "That's pretty cool. Where'd you get it?"

"Took it off a dead guy!" He let out a loud laugh and elbowed his barely coherent cousin so hard the imbecile nearly fell off his stool.

Katherine wasn't laughing.

Billy's demeanor switched from jovial to serious. He leveled his drunken gaze as he shifted his weight. "I mean we found it." He hesitated then tipped forward. "Wha', you don't believe me?"

"I believe you found it. I was just wondering how and where you found it. Just asking a question." Katherine had one hand on the bar and the other on her hip. She was calm on the outside but was losing her patience with the guy's act. She'd dealt with this type of situation one too many times.

"Well, none of your damn business, lady." Billy stared at her. "I'll have another whiskey," he demanded. "Give it to me neat!"

Katherine huffed, "You haven't paid me for the last one, sweetheart."

He set the medal on the bar. Fumbling in his pocket, he pulled out a bunch of singles with a ten-dollar bill mixed in. The copious consumption of alcohol seemed to have flipped Billy's anger switch. His brow tightened and his nostrils flared. "There's for the last one and the next one that you'll get me right now." He leaned in with both hands clutching the bar rail.

"Coming right up." Katherine took payment for both drinks from the handful of bills and went to get the rail whiskey and a new glass. She returned to set the tumbler of whiskey in front of Billy. She grabbed his empty, left without saying a word, and made a beeline for the kitchen.

"I'm calling Jay and Robert," Katherine mumbled to herself in a panicked voice. "We gotta get those guys out before there's trouble. I hope they're home."

Jay and Robert were friends and classmates of Sarah's. Their given names were Jay Red Feather and Robert Yellow Knife. They were proud, full-blooded Sioux. Jay's father had been made the Tribal Chairman years earlier. His mom taught third grade at the school in Painted Rock. Good kids with steady jobs now working for the power company as linemen. The three of them had been friends since kindergarten and both always looked out for Sarah. They had been over to Katherine's house more than a few times over the years to hang out with Sarah while they were growing up. Katherine had been like a second mom to them. In return, they would occasionally pitch in at the bar cleaning, serving, or doing whatever Katherine needed done. She was grateful for their help and happy to throw a few bucks their way in return. The young men had grown up on the reservation and had been raised to serve others through a sense of community fostered by their tribe. Their commitment hadn't ended when they'd moved into town.

Jay picked up the phone on the second ring, "This is Jay."

"It's Katherine. Thank God you're home. I've got trouble. The one guy, I guess his name is Charles Ray, is stone drunk, and the other guy, his name is Billy, has a gun to go with his bad attitude. Trust me, you'll know 'em when you see 'em. They need to leave."

"We're on our way."

People took care of each other in Painted Rock.

16

As Jimmy put the Scout in park behind the diagonally arranged cars, Colby sat up to see out the driver's side window. "Yep, that's their truck alright." He pointed to the intersection. "Keep going. Go up to the corner and take a left."

"Where are we going? They're here. Shouldn't we park and go in?" Jimmy's voice held nervous excitement.

Colby turned his attention to the two young Indian men running up the street and entering The Caboose. *They look familiar. Was it pinball?* "No way. I want to go around back, so we can get in the kitchen to try to draw Sarah or Katherine's attention," he explained. "I want to talk to them and see what the scene is inside the bar. I'm not convinced this is the time or place to confront them."

As instructed, Jimmy rolled on toward the intersection, taking a left at the corner.

"Make another left here," said Colby pointing. 'Here' was a gravel alley flanked by telephone poles and aging single car garages. On one side, gnarly buckthorn grew around the garages, bookends to the vacant lots along the alley. On the other side, the backs of the store fronts had parking stalls, garbage cans, and an occasional fence that delineated property lines. A gust of wind off the river pushed a wave of leaves at a diagonal down the alley. The pop of the tires on the gravel was interrupted by a high-pitched screech. A grey and white cat darted across the illuminating beam from the headlights. They bumped along until they saw the rectangle of light passing through the back door of the tavern. "Park in front of the dumpster," Colby ordered.

Jimmy pulled into the gravel area big enough for three cars. A lone amber light from above the open screen door in concert with the wind cast ghostly shadows in all directions. Two of the stalls were occupied, with only the stall in front of the dumpster open. Next to the electric meter above the dumpster a sign read, "No Parking in Front of Dumpster." Jimmy looked at Colby for direction. "Just park here, anyway," Colby said pointing to the open space. Jimmy pulled in and turned off the engine.

The moment of truth descended upon Colby. He had a choice to make. Go back to the village and head back to Kansas in the morning or enter through the back door into an uncertain world fraught with peril. He sat in silence, crossed his arms, and contemplated his options.

Concurrent to Jimmy and Colby's arrival behind The Caboose, Katherine returned from the kitchen to the sound of Glen Campbell flowing out of the jukebox just as Jay and Robert entered the dimly lit bar. Heads turned as they stood inside the door. Katherine acknowledged their presence with a nod. "What can I get you boys?" she asked.

Katherine's shoulders relaxed and she softly exhaled now that the boys were there. A reassuring level of comfort--no, it was relief--came to her.

Jay spoke for them both as they walked forward. "Couple of High Life's." Robert faced the TV, but his eyes scoped out the scene.

Katherine bent to slide open the door on the top of the refrigerator unit and pulled out a couple of beers. She popped the tops off the bottles, handing them to Jay and Robert, who each put a dollar on the bar. She looked them both in the eye then slowly moved her eyes to her left, indicating the direction of the trouble. She mouthed the word "gun." Neither of them immediately looked toward Billy and Charles Ray. They took a swig from their beers and turned to face each other. Jay looked over Robert's shoulder. Charles Ray's head was down. He stared at his glass. Billy looked in the mirror drumming his fingers on the bar to the music. The whiskey train had taken them far from where they were seated. Next stop, Comatose Junction.

Jimmy waited patiently while his grandpa mulled over their situation. When Jimmy couldn't stand it anymore, he volunteered to go in the kitchen door alone using Colby's compromised condition as the excuse. He got out of the Scout, walked to the back of The Caboose, and cautiously tip-toed up the two cement steps. He slowly opened the door. The gleaming stainless steel in the kitchen made the room particularly bright. He proceeded past the walk-in cooler and turned the corner. He stood behind a shelving rack of large containers of condiments, pots, and pans. Sarah was at the fryer putting in a basket of onion rings.

She jumped back. "Oh, my gosh. You scared me."

Jimmy approached her with his index finger over his mouth, "Shhhh." Without hesitation, he gave her a hug.

She hugged him tight but reflexively pulled away as she looked at him. "Your teeth are chipped!" With a gentle touch from caring hands, she stroked his face. "You have dried blood on your chin. What happened?" Her soft voice expressed concern. "Are you alright? Where's your grandpa?"

Jimmy spoke in a quiet voice fearing they could be overheard. "Long story. Grandpa is in our truck parked out back. He's hurt bad. We both got beat up and robbed by these two guys. The same two that were in here the last time we were." Jimmy drew shapes in the air with his hands to describe them. "Very rough looking, unshaven, from Tennessee, ordered whiskey. You know who I'm talking about? Are they here?"

"Yes, but not for long," Sarah said shaking her head. "They're at the bar drunk off their asses. My grandma wants them gone. She called a couple of my friends to come over to get them out of here. They should be here by now."

Jimmy contemplated what to do next. "Can you go out there and see? If I go out there, they will recognize me, you know? Then we'll all have a problem."

"Okay. You stay right here, and I'll go out to see what's going on. I'm not too worried. Jay and Robert can handle themselves." She pulled the basket of onion rings out of the fryer dumping them into a wax paper lined wicker basket. "Wait here."

Jimmy retreated behind the shelving.

Sarah took the basket from the counter and headed through the swinging doors. Patsy Cline's hit song, "Crazy," was just ending.

"Who ordered the rings?" Sarah questioned with authority, scanning the bar.

"We did," said the middle-aged man sitting next to his wife. They were regulars at The Caboose.

"There you go. Watch yourselves. They're hot!" Sarah reached for the ketchup and mustard carrier placing it in front of them. She placed two small plates on either side. She stepped back to put her hands on her hips and flashed a warm smile. "Nice to see you, John. How have you been, Jean?"

"Doing well," Jean responded. "Could we get some napkins, too?"

"You certainly can." Sarah collected a short stack of napkins from under the bar setting them in between John and Jean while making eye contact with both Jay and Robert. Their beers were almost gone.

Sarah pivoted to look at Katherine with wide eyes. "How's it going?" Turning her back to the bar Sarah tilted her head down and lowered her voice, "Those folks from Kansas are in the kitchen. Well, just Jimmy. I'll take over tending so you can go back to talk with him. The grandpa stayed in the truck. I think those two idiots at the end of the bar robbed them and beat them up."

"You're kidding," Katherine said rolling her eyes. Acting like she didn't have a care in the world, she walked back through the swinging doors to the kitchen.

Katherine looked around and didn't see anyone. She stood there for a second rechecking. *He's gotta be here somewhere.*

"Over here," Jimmy whispered. He poked his head out from behind the rack.

"Oh, boy, they did do a number on you," Katherine said pointing out the obvious. "How much money did they steal from you?"

"They didn't steal money; they stole a rare artifact my grandpa and I dug up west of the river."

Katherine raised her chin putting two and two together. "Ohhh, so that's where they got that Jefferson Peace Medal. One of them just showed it to me. They're both pretty drunk. The one was spilling his guts about it."

"They left us for dead, all tied up. My grandpa is in the truck waiting for a report on what those two guys are up to. I just want that medal back. My grandpa has been looking for one for his whole life. Maybe we should call the cops?"

Katherine smiled a big smile as she pondered Jimmy's innocence. "I forgot for a second you're not from around here. We have three cops total in our town. Keith is deer hunting over west river. Andy is off tonight, probably home with his family. That leaves little Donny Sully as the only one on patrol. Bottom line is I got this handled. They're leaving, but the medal ain't."

"You weren't joking when you said we had a friend here at The Caboose. What should me and Grandpa do? Where should we go? I feel like I have to do something," Jimmy's voice was getting louder as he grew more agitated.

"Shhh. Keep it down. Keep it down," She gently guided Jimmy toward the back door. "Seriously, don't worry. Go sit in your truck and wait. I know this sounds strange, but you must trust me. You don't know me, but…"

Jimmy interrupted. "Okay. I'll go wait in the truck for fifteen minutes. Then I'll come back and see what's happening."

Katherine watched Jimmy rush out, catching the screen door before it slammed behind him.

17

Returning to the Scout, Jimmy could see Colby slumped in the front seat with his head back and his eyes closed. Colby's eyes opened when Jimmy knocked on the window. *Good, then he wasn't unconscious.*

He climbed into the driver's seat. "Katherine said they were in there and to sit tight. They're showing off the medal. And yes, they're drunk."

"Sit tight? For how long?"

"I told her we'd wait for fifteen minutes. I asked her if we should just call the cops, and that's when she said to sit tight. My impression is that she can handle it."

"Alright. I'm not sure what our next play is going to be, so we might as well see what develops." Colby took another swig of water then pulled his watch out of his pocket. Neither one knew what to do, so they sat in silence eyeballing the back door. A gust of wind kicked up leaves onto the hood of their truck and the repulsive smell from rotten food fermenting in the dumpster blew in their direction.

Back inside, Katherine pushed through the swinging doors

from the kitchen to the bar. June Carter and Johnny Cash were belting out, "Jackson" as she entered. Robert sat at the bar, facing the front door. Jay remained standing watching the schemers in the mirror. The "crowd" had thinned out leaving only the two of them, John and Jean, plus Billy and Charles Ray. Quickly, Katherine took John's tab and scribbled, NO CHARGE, and below that, WE ARE CLOSING EARLY. She slid the bill on the bar to John and smiled.

John looked at the bill. "Well, much obliged, Kitty." She smiled at the name all the regulars had used for her since she'd taken over the bar decades earlier. "I guess that means you're kicking us out?" He looked confused.

"Yeah, sorry, John. Have some things to get caught up with at home, so we'll see you the next time. You folks have a good night and drive safe." Katherine took their basket, napkins, and beer glasses and put them under the bar.

"I've got some field work to get ready for my second cut of alfalfa to do tomorrow, so it's best we head out, anyway."

John and Jean got up from their stools, pushed them in and toddled toward the door. John donned his Stetson giving a tip of the brim to Katherine. "We'll be back Friday. Hope y'all have a very good evening." The wind rushed in through the open door as they left. Katherine nonchalantly went over and locked the door behind them.

The music machine thumped to the beat of Tom Jones. "Sarah, will you help me carry this stuff to the kitchen?" Katherine grabbed the silverware tub. Without saying a word, Sarah picked up the tub of dirty plates right on Katherine's heels. They both set down their tubs next to the sink. Katherine turned, grunting as she pushed the heavy butcher block in front of the swinging doors. For added insurance, Sarah helped her move the rack of pots and pans up against it. "That will keep them out there. If nothing else, it will slow them down enough to give us a chance to run outta here." They backed away and huddled behind the bread rack.

The music had stopped, so Jay walked over and stood looking at the juke box. He saw the outline of a pistol under Billy's t-shirt. Drowning in whiskey, the two looked oblivious to the people leaving or the music stopping. Charles Ray had his eyes closed, head propped up by his fists, glass empty. As he scrolled through the music selections, he could feel Billy staring at him in the mirror. He looked up from the juke box to see Robert headed toward him. Robert looked every bit as tough as when he won the gold medal in the heavyweight division of boxing at the Tribal Olympics in Rapid City two summers ago.

"Play thomthing goood, you draft dodger," Billy hiccupped in a drunken stupor.

Jay turned, flipped his jet-black ponytail over his shoulder, and set his chin, "You talkin' to me?" His considerable biceps tightened. Jay's facial expression and stance said, "Don't mess with me." To no one's surprise, he took the gold in calf roping at the same Olympics.

"Ain't nobody else in here playin' no music. Yeah, Imma talkin' to you." Billy was raising his voice. "Nice ponytail, Chief." The scar on his face shortened as he laughed.

Jay took a step forward and in a subdued voice he said, "I'm no draft dodger. I haven't been called up yet. If my number gets picked, I'll serve. Didn't your momma teach you any manners?" Jay took another step forward.

Billy turned his body around, his head at the level of Jay's puffed out chest. As if sensing an imminent confrontation, Billy made an exaggerated move with his right hand for his gun, but

Jay reacted before he even got close to pulling it out. Jay took a small step to his right and bent his knees to solidify his base then exploded a left hook that smashed into the right side of Billy's face sending him flying off his stool. He ended up face down on the floor, motionless. Rapidly moving to position himself over the limp villain, Jay quickly grabbed the gun from under his t-shirt. Jay raised his right foot and stomped on the back of Billy's head with the heel of his cowboy boot as Billy's nose, along with a few facial bones, broke with an audible crunch. A torrent of blood flowed onto the linoleum.

Charles Ray, mired in an alcohol induced fog, turned to his right, trying to lift himself off the bar. By the time his eyes uncrossed, Robert had grabbed him by the back of his neck and drove his forehead into the bar. Whiskey tumblers flew in every direction, shattering. Charles Ray's head bounced on the lacquered pine surface as blood poured from a three-inch gash on his forehead. Robert took hold of his sinewy shoulders, spun him around, delivering a hard-right fist to his mid-section. A loud grunt filled the room as the air left his lungs. Robert finished him off by pushing his listless body onto the floor. Charles Ray was out cold. The criminals were finished.

An eerie silence came over the bar. For a moment, no one moved, a calm after the storm. The only motion were lights from the juke box painting the inside of the bar with primary colors in a random sequence and the pinball machine blinking white light. Broken glass, tipped over bar stools, and the conjoined smell of sweat with alcohol made it feel like a post-fight scene out of an old western movie. Despite being surrounded by violence, the peace medal remained on the bar.

Billy rolled to his side in an effort to get up, his face covered in blood. Jay straddled him, lifted him by his shoulders, standing him up. He locked down Billy's arms by forcing them behind his back, turning him to face Robert.

"Teach him some manners, Robert," Jay said.

Like pistons on a race car, Robert pounded four heavy fisted punches into Billy's face and gut. Billy went limp and Jay pushed him forward onto his partner. A pile of losers; the victory was complete.

"You can come out now," Jay shouted. "These two won't give you any more problems."

Katherine and Sarah reappeared timidly through the kitchen doors. Sarah put her hand over her mouth to muffle her gasp of surprise.

"Robert, run and get your truck and bring it to the back door," Katherine said. "Jay if they make a move, shoot 'em."

Jay took a seat and kept the gun pointed at the two defeated thugs.

Colby sat up, dumbfounded by the screeched wail of a pickup skidding on the gravel to his right, then rapidly backing up to the back door of The Caboose. Jimmy started to put his hand on the door handle, but Colby put his arm across Jimmy's chest. "No. Let's just wait and see what's going on." He pointed to the driver. "Who is that guy?"

The thick bodied young Indian man got out of the truck, sliding around to the back to open the lift gate. He turned, leaped to the top step, and opened the door to the kitchen. He looked through the screen over his left shoulder at Jimmy and Colby as he went inside, paying them no mind. Inside, neither Billy nor Charles Ray had moved. Jay handed Billy's gun to Robert and took Billy by the armpits dragging him out through the kitchen. Standing by the swinging doors between the kitchen and the bar, Robert kept one eye and the gun pointed at Charles Ray, at the same time his other eye monitored Jay's progress. Jay used his foot to open the screen door before he let Billy thump down the steps. In an awkward attempt, he tried to lift Billy's limp body from the bottom step into the truck. They had expended a lot of energy in taming the bad guys.

Jimmy and Colby were witnessing Jay's ordeal. "That's Billy!' Jimmy exclaimed. Without hesitating, he rushed out of the Scout to Robert's pickup truck. "Here, let me help you."

"Who are you?" Jay questioned; his shirt splattered with blood.

"I'm Jimmy. Friend of Katherine and Sarah's. This guy and another guy beat us up and robbed me and my grandpa."

"I'm Jay. My buddy's name is Robert. I'll get in the back of the truck. You lift him to me, and I'll lay him in back."

That is exactly what they did. Jay quickly tied up the unconscious Billy with baling twine like the animal he was, ankles to wrists.

Wincing, Colby got out of the truck, and slowly ambled toward Jimmy as Jay went back inside. By the time Colby got to Jimmy, Jay and Robert were already carrying Charles Ray out, followed by Katherine and Sarah. He, too, was still unconscious. They got him into the back of the truck as Colby and Jimmy stood idly watching. Jay, with rodeo speed, hog tied Charles Ray next to Billy. From start to finish, the entire ordeal of getting them out of the bar took less than fifteen minutes.

Katherine stood on the top step with Sarah. "You best get goin', you two," Katherine instructed them. "You know what to do from here. When you come back, don't forget to get rid of their truck that's parked out front."

"Yes, ma'am," Jay responded. "Mind if I make a quick phone call?"

"Go ahead but make it a quick one."

Jay scampered back inside, returning within two minutes. Colby watched Robert and Jay as they hopped into the front seat, ululating out their windows with the dignity of their heritage as they sped away, passing the evening train rumbling into town, horn blaring its arrival.

Colby looked up at their friends on the stoop. "Guess that's the last we'll see of those guys. Where are they taking them?"

"Oh, just west of town across the river," Katherine said in a manner of fact.

"To the reservation? Not that I care, but why are they taking them there?" Colby questioned.

Katherine responded with a wink and a smile. "Because the reservation is where things go to disappear."

18

"Let's get you some coffee and some ice on those bruises," offered Katherine. The four of them went back inside. Katherine closed the screen door, shut the weathered hollow core door, and locked it.

"Sarah, get the guys some ice, and I'm going to get a bucket of water and some rags to clean the floor," Katherine said. "Have a seat at the bar, you two."

The languishing smell of stale cigarette smoke mixed with beer and grease repulsed Colby as he passed from the kitchen to the bar. Colby leaned against the bar appraising the mess before him, each breath a needle to his ribs. How surreal the last few hours had been. He shook his head as the silent jukebox continued to splash colorful patterns and the pools of darkened blood before him coalesced. His eyes followed the smeared crimson streaking the linoleum toward the kitchen. *If only those that made, carried, or wore that valued piece of history could see the current wrath of turmoil that surrounded that little medallion.*

"Here's some ice for you two," said Sarah.

"Thanks. I'm not sure just one bag will be enough," countered

Jimmy. He placed the bag of ice on his lip and the sting jolted his head back.

"Do you have any aspirin?" Colby asked as he put a bag of ice on the welt under his left eye.

"I sure don't, Colby," Katherine said as she got down on her hands and knees to wipe up the sea of blood on the floor.

With worry in her voice Sarah said, "So, what's next for you guys? Are you going back to your camp tonight?"

Colby hadn't considered what would come next. He had been so focused on tracking down their nemesis, the pain he was experiencing, and the medal, that the thought of their next step never occurred to him. *Wait…the medal.* "Where is the medal, anyway?"

"Last time I saw the medal it was on the bar by where those two guys were sitting," Katherine said looking up and pointing. She stood up and lugged the bloody bucket of water to the kitchen to dump.

"I'm pretty sure it was there when I was cleaning up the broken glass," Sarah added.

Jimmy got off his stool and walked down to where Billy and Charles Ray had been sitting. He looked on the bar, pulled out the stools to see under them, turned in a circle scanning the floor. He did not see the medal. "Maybe it's back by you, Sarah. It must be there."

Sarah reached for the flashlight behind the cash register. With a sweeping motion, she moved the beam of light back and forth across the floor behind the bar. She turned back, "I don't see it."

His physical and emotional tank empty, Colby felt like he was going to pass out. His body hurt like he'd never experienced, and he couldn't believe he had been so close to owning Kakawita's Jefferson Peace Medal. His eye followed Katherine as she returned from the kitchen. *She wouldn't lie about the medal, would she?* "If it's not here, where is it?"

An awkward silence followed. Nobody present had the answer – or at least no one felt like sharing their thoughts. Katherine spoke up, "Well, look, the medal didn't just disappear into thin air. We can look again in the morning when we're refreshed, and it will be lighter in here. Why don't you both stay with Sarah and me tonight? I have two spare bedrooms, and we'd love the company. You two have had a hell of a day."

"That sounds like a good idea. I think we're all tired, and you two need some medical attention," added Sarah.

"My guess is that I've got some cracked ribs," said Colby with a hint of resignation.

"I'm so tired right now," Jimmy chimed in.

"Yes, thank you. I believe we should take you up on your offer. It's late and I don't want to travel. You're sure it wouldn't be too much of an inconvenience?" Colby was relieved at the offer. The prospect of sleeping on the hard ground made his ribs ache.

"Not at all. Okay then, it's settled. I'll lock up and you can follow us to our house. It's on the north side of town, just five minutes from here," Katherine responded.

The three of them walked out through the kitchen and stopped at the back door.

Colby noticed Katherine was not with them. He turned to Sarah. "Where's Katherine?"

"Grandma won't leave until she makes sure the front door is locked, then she will turn off the jukebox and pinball machine. Next, she will close the blinds and turn off the overhead lights." Sarah pointed toward the bar predicting Katherine's movements. "Then she goes behind the bar to straighten the bottles on the shelf but leaves that light on over them. It's the same mental checklist she goes through every night. I've seen her do it a million times," Sarah shrugged.

Katherine finished her closing tasks and joined them on the back stoop.

"We'll follow you," Jimmy shouted as he walked to their truck. Sarah gave a wave of acknowledgement and stepped into her truck. Katherine locked the back door and hopped into her sedan. One by one the vehicles pulled down the alley and headed for Katherine and Sarah's place.

Soon, they pulled into the gravel driveway next to the two-story farmhouse on the edge of town. Surrounded by acres of untilled fields on three sides, the property looked like an oasis in the middle of a desert. The distinctive burr oak trees that dotted the expansive lawn cast ghostly shadows from the bright full moon suspended above. The light from the streetlight nearby helped reveal that the years of dust and weather had dulled the white clap board siding and white trim around the double hung windows to a light beige. An aging garage with a service door and an overhead door big enough for two cars sat off to the side of the house. Jimmy parked in front of the garage door then offered Colby a hand getting out of their truck. A subtle breeze carried the rank odor of pig manure from the farm down the road. They trudged single file up the back steps through the three-season room with shelves filled with jars of pickles, tomatoes, and jam.

Katherine unlocked the door, leading the posse into the kitchen. She turned on the lone overhead light and set her purse on the brown kitchen table which was surrounded by six chairs upholstered in a brown and yellow vinyl floral pattern. The spacious kitchen featured white appliances nestled between white metal cabinetry. The Formica countertops were a soft grey with flecks of muted colors dispersed throughout. Colby felt at home immediately.

"Jimmy, your bedroom is just to the left of the bathroom here on the first floor. It's all made up. Follow Sarah to the bathroom. She'll get you a warm washcloth to wipe that blood off of your face. Colby, I'll get an Ace bandage for your ribs out of the drawer," directed Katherine. "The aspirin is on the table by the salt and pepper shakers." Colby took a seat at the kitchen table and found the aspirin. Jimmy dutifully followed Sarah.

Katherine found the Ace bandage in the first drawer she opened and got a glass of water from the faucet. She turned around, handed him the water, and he popped two aspirin. "Stand up. I'm going to wrap your ribs. You may be more comfortable sleeping in the easy chair. If you prefer, you can sleep in the southwest bedroom upstairs. Up to you. Now lift your shirt."

Over grunts, Colby uttered, "Easy now. I'm pretty tender."

"I know. I'll be as gentle as I can." She unrolled the Ace bandage as she wrapped it around his mid-chest four times and fastened the end with two metal clips. It felt snug and didn't allow his chest to expand much, which reduced his pain. She led him into the adjoining living room that had a couch, easy chair, coffee table, and Zenith TV.

"With your ribs in tough shape, I would think you ought to try to sleep here," she said removing the multicolored afghan from the easy chair. You can adjust it to lay back or sit up. Whatever is most comfortable for you."

Not one to argue at this point, Colby politely said, "This will be fine. I'll make do. Thanks again for your hospitality." He gingerly sat in the chair as Katherine handed him the afghan. She unlaced his boots, placed them on the floor, and tilted the chair back slightly. She helped Colby spread the blanket over himself.

A faint whiff of her perfume stimulated his senses. He felt grateful for her kind touch. His face softened to allow a slight smile to form. It had been a long time since a woman took the time to care for him.

"I'm going up to bed. The bathroom is back there," she said, turning and gesturing back in the direction they had just come from. She reciprocated a smile and lightly placed her hand on his shoulder. "Do your best to make yourself at home. Get some rest. We'll find your medal in the morning. I'm sure of it. Good night." Her voice trailed off as she turned to head up the wooden stairs.

"Good night. Thanks again," Colby answered, closing his eyes. Soon, his breathing became shallow, his pulse dropped, and he was fast asleep.

Light streamed from under the closed door of the bathroom as Sarah took a warm washcloth and dabbed the dried blood from Jimmy's face. The warmth of the washcloth soothed his aching muscles. Her touch brought comfort. A tear formed then trickled down Jimmy's left cheek.

"Are you crying?" Sarah asked. "Was I being too rough?"

"Nah, must have something in my eye."

"Oh, Jimmy. You can tell me. What's the matter?" Her caring tone matched the concerned expression on her face.

"It's just…," Jimmy's shoulders slumped. He tilted his gaze to the ceiling as tears welled up in his eyes, his voice trailing off. He looked down, rubbing his jaw, contemplating how much he felt comfortable sharing. His throat tightened with vulnerable trepidation not knowing how Sarah would react to baring his deepest emotions. He shuffled his feet, then rubbed his eyes free of tears. He tried to read her, feeling small in her space. *What is she going to think of me?*

Her arms hung relaxed at her side with legs less than shoulder width apart. In Sarah's face, he saw gentleness and understanding through her head tilt, with the upturned corners of her lips communicating happiness in his proximity. He could feel his face becoming warm and flushed, thinking this to be an early crossroads in their relationship. Jimmy's voice became a whisper. "Can I trust you, Sarah? I mean can I tell you something personal?"

"Well, yeah, of course. What is it Jimmy?"

Jimmy looked into her inviting eyes telling himself she was safe.

"I've had my mom on my mind," Jimmy started as he tried to quell his quivering lips. "I just miss her so much. She died a few years ago from cancer. I tried to talk about it with a girl I dated senior year in high school, but she dumped me right after, so I was afraid to bring it up with you. I don't want to scare you away."

"Oh, my gosh, no Jimmy" Sarah said as her voice changed from surprise to condolence. "I'm so sorry."

"Yeah, thanks. I don't know." Jimmy sniffled and put his hands in his pockets while scuffing the tile floor. "I think Grandpa brought me out here to help me get over it, and then I met you and…I just feel like I got a lot of mixed emotions goin' on, you know?"

"Well, at least your mom was around for most of your life. Mine left when I was little, and I don't really see her that much." Sarah told him that Katherine had raised her since she was four. Her dad was AWOL from birth and her mom, Katherine's daughter, had moved to Bismarck with a musician to find work and live the lifestyle. She visited Sarah from time to time and sent money when she could. She loved Sarah but loved her freedom more. Grandma became mother, too, nurturing Sarah with love and wisdom. "Katherine is more my mom than my mom is my mom."

Sarah turned to lean her backside against the sink with arms folded.

Jimmy took a Kleenex from the box on the shelf and wiped his eyes, letting out a nervous laugh, "Well it sure seems like Katherine is the best combination mom and Grandmom you could ask for. Anyway, thanks for listening. I feel better already."

Sarah turned her head to meet Jimmy's eyes. With a confident tone she said, "I like you, Jimmy. I can tell you've got a good heart. I can see in your eyes how much you loved your mom. Thanks for trusting me enough to share that. You know, you're different than the guys around here. None of them would have the courage to be honest with me like you just were."

"Sarah, you are an amaz…" She got off the sink and put her index finger to his mouth to stop him from talking any further. Their closeness fueled the burgeoning mutual lust of passion.

"You don't have to say a thing, Jimmy," Sarah whispered. She stood on her tiptoes, put both her arms around his neck, and gave him a light kiss on the lips. They both pulled back ever so slightly and then without hesitation went back for more. For the moment, his jaw pain dissipated. Tongues twisted as desire soared. Hands traveled over and around. He felt so strong and she so soft.

They paused as Jimmy's hands rested on Sarah's hips and her arms looped around his neck. "This just feels so right," said Jimmy with a hushed voice as her body was pressed against his. Their shared affinity continued to override his pain. "You feel so good."

"I know. Kinda crazy, isn't it," Sarah replied, eyes dreamily focused. Jimmy believed her mind and body were caught up in the amorous moment, too.

"My grandpa is right out there, and your grandma is right

above us," Jimmy said. "We should probably play it cool and call it a night, don't you think?" With great reservation, Jimmy was doing his best to be a gentleman.

"Yeah, I guess we should." Sarah sounded disappointed. She released her arms, and there was an uneasy silence as she draped the washcloth over the tub.

"Honestly, I really need a shower," Jimmy confessed.

"Um, yeah, of course. I'll get you a towel. When you're done, I should take one, too." She went into the hallway and returned with two towels. He leaned in and gave her a kiss on the cheek.

"Thanks. I won't be long." Jimmy showered off the day's exertion and fear. He dried off, wrapped the towel around his waist, and picked up his clothes.

"Good night, Sarah," he whispered through the door of her bedroom.

"'Night."

He went to the guest room closing the door behind him. He dropped his towel, put back on his underwear, pulled back the covers, and crawled into bed. A bed had never felt this good. He lay on his back staring at the ceiling letting his mind fill with thoughts of Sarah. *What is happening? Is it possible to get the crap kicked out of me and be falling in love, all in the same day? Is there such a thing as love at first sight?* Quickly, his mind switched to the medal. He turned over on his side. *That's the other thing. Where is it? Worry about that tomorrow.* His mind went back to how beautiful Sarah is. *Oh man.*

Sarah got off her bed and went to the bathroom. In routine fashion, she took her shoes and socks off, unzipped her Wrangler jeans, and slid out of them. The tiled floor felt cool on her feet. She took off her shirt, unhooked her bra and threw them on the pile of clothes she had started. Sarah took her shower while trying to process her feelings for Jimmy. *I barely know this guy, but I've never felt so strongly towards another man. Is this really happening? Can I fall in love with a total stranger? There can't be love at first sight or can there be? No, that's ridiculous.* She got out, dried off, wrapped up in a towel, and brushed her teeth. Sarah checked herself in the mirror on the wall mounted medicine cabinet as she brushed her hair. A smile looked back in front of her.

Turning off the light she went out the bathroom door. Sarah stood in the short hallway waiting for her eyes to adjust to the darkened house and her mind to decide. She glanced to the left, the safe emotional choice, her bedroom, and sleep. She swung back to the right, the risky emotional choice, the man she hoped had existed. *What should I do? No. Yes. Not tonight my love.* Softly, she tip-toed back to the safety of her own bed.

Soft summer breezes lapped against the curtains in front of the open windows as surrender would have to wait for another day.

19

Colby is standing silent and unmoving as the wind whips around him. The warriors carrying coup sticks adorned with eagle feathers gallop over successive undulations of prairie in full throat with his ex-wife leading the charge. The charging horses, eyes bright red, breathe in rhythm with every step. Colby turns to run but can't move. He's paralyzed as the ground around him shudders upon their approach. A voice... "You don't know what you have in your possession." Colby opens his palm and it's on fire. The warriors laugh as a blindfolded Rebecca draws back her bow.

Colby woke up disoriented by his surroundings, chasing the remnants of his indistinct dream. *Just a dream. Just another dream.* "Ughhh," he moaned. The pain in his ribs brought him back to the real world.

Colby slowly opened his eyes to see dust mites dancing above him in the pale sunlight streaming through the opening of the curtains. His nose picked up the smell of the bacon, and he could hear muffled conversation coming from the kitchen. He carefully pulled himself up from the recliner, neatly folded the afghan, and gingerly made his way to the kitchen. Sarah poured him a cup of coffee. Katherine stood at the stove. "Morning, Colby. How are those ribs today?"

He tried to shrug as if to say, "Not bad," then winced.

Katherine pulled out a chair and guided him into it. "Hey, Jimmy!" She called from where she stood. "Your breakfast is ready. Get it while it's hot!"

"Yes ma'am. I'm on my way," answered Jimmy exiting the bathroom.

Sarah set full plates on the table. Each place setting was completed with a glass of orange juice.

"How did you sleep?" asked Colby as Jimmy pulled out his chair to take a seat opposite Sarah.

"Really good." His grandson stole a glance at Sarah and took a couple of small bite of his eggs. He tried to take a bite of bacon and then seemed to think better of it, setting the bacon down and rubbing his temples. Instead, he grabbed a piece of toast and tore it into little pieces. "My jaw is a little stiff, though. How are you feeling, Grandpa?"

"My ribs are sore, but I actually slept pretty well. I think wrapping them helped. Thanks to Katherine." He nodded toward Katherine.

"I'm glad that helped," Katherine said. "You should probably see our traveling doc, but she won't be back for three days."

"No, I'm fine. I don't want to see a doctor. Better if I don't have to answer a bunch of questions," dismissed Colby with a wave of his hand. "I'll bet she's probably booked anyway."

"Suit yourself," Katherine paused to take another bite of her eggs. "So, here's what I'm thinking. You guys go back to west river and pack your stuff up. Sarah and I will go down to The Caboose and start looking for the medal. We have to get the bar ready to open at 11 for the lunch folks, anyway." Given his condition, Colby appreciated Katherine taking charge. She dabbed the corner of her mouth with her napkin. "Colby, how long will it take you to go out there, get packed up, and come back to town?"

Colby thought about it as he calculated the time to do all Katherine was suggesting. He considered going down to the bar first; then going to pack up. He had no idea where the medal could be. *Who has it? Katherine and Sarah? Was this all a ruse to divert attention from them? Where could it have possibly gone? Not planning on leaving without it. It couldn't just disappear, could it?*

Colby tasted the mild bitterness of his coffee as he set his cup down and raised his eyebrows at Katherine, "Well, I'd say an hour and a half to two hours, tops. But I really think I should go down to the bar first and look."

"I don't think that will be necessary. Sarah and I can look just as well as you can. I'm sure you don't want your things left out there any longer than you have to. I'm sure we'll find it before you get back," Katherine reasoned.

"Okay. Well then...," Colby started.

The ring of the phone interrupted their breakfast. Katherine got up to answer it. "Hello? Oh, hi Jay." Katherine's facial expression turned to stone. "What's so important?"

Colby, Jimmy, and Sarah looked at Katherine looking at them.

"Okay, I'll be there. Come to the back door. The front door will still be locked. You took care of their truck, too?" Katherine cradled the phone on her shoulder while taking her apron off. "Okay, just tell me when I get there. I know, I know," Katherine nodded her head as she looked at her attentive audience. "Thanks, 'bye."

With a loud clang, Katherine hung up the phone. "Jay wants us down at the bar, pronto. He has something to tell us. He wouldn't say what it was. Sounded urgent. Just leave everything where it is, and we'll clean up later." She looked directly at Colby and Jimmy, pointing her finger, "You two best get going and we'll see you at the bar whenever you get there. Drive safe."

Colby found himself captivated by this strong woman, admiring her willingness to put a plan in motion as he struggled to get up from the table.

They all marched out the door into the morning sunshine with the screen door closing behind them with a resounding bang. They were acknowledged by a basset hound barking from across the street. Colby and Jimmy headed out of town to pack up camp. Sarah and Katherine sped into town to meet Jay.

Jay stood perched with his hands in his Dakota Power windbreaker pockets on the back steps as they rolled to a stop. He waved to them as Katherine and Sarah exited their sedan and truck, respectively.

Katherine approached him. "What have you got to tell me that's so important?"

"Let's go inside to talk. I've only got a second, and then I gotta get to work," Jay answered, a staccato rhythm in his voice. He seemed uncharacteristically edgy and in an unusual hurry. He stepped off the steps to let Katherine pass, so she could unlock the door. "'Morning, Sarah."

"'Morning, Jay." Sarah was unsure of what to make of Jay's tense demeanor. "You okay?"

"Yeah, just in a hurry," Jay said on his way inside while Katherine began to turn on the lights. "Not much sleep last night, you know."

Once the three of them were gathered in the kitchen, Jay

spoke. "First of all, we dumped those two guys in an empty box car way out past Boulder Lake. The train had over-nighted on a side rail headed west. One of them had come to, the short guy with the scar on his face. Man, was he cussin' up a storm. The other one, the guy that was passed out, was still out of it." Jay continued, "Second thing is that I saw that blackish metal thing on the bar and took it. Figured it probably was theirs and I had earned it. When I looked at it, I realized it was a Thomas Jefferson Peace Medal. I thought, what the hell! I remembered studying Lewis and Clark senior year in history class. Read about the medal but never thought I'd ever see one. I knew that the medal was a big deal and could be pretty valuable."

Katherine raised her index finger. "You know, I wondered if you had grabbed it last night."

"So, you have the medal?" asked Sarah excitedly.

"Not exactly." Jay evaluated Sarah's skeptical eyes then locked in on Katherine's surprised expression as he continued. "I stopped at my dad's place on the way back to town to ask him what I should do with it. He looked at it and said he'd take care of it. He didn't look happy and barely wanted to touch it. Said he didn't want it in his house. My brother, Barking Coyote, happened to be there so he took it to keep in his safe at his shop. It was all kinda weird, ya know?" Jay shifted his weight, feeling tightness in his chest. "Dad said he would have to talk to the other members of the Tribal Council before he did anything." Jay's eyes widened. "I got this freaked out feeling by his reaction. Something tells me I'm not sure I want to have anything to do with it either."

"Does this medal have some supernatural powers or something? What the hell?" Katherine wondered out loud. "Those two guys from Kansas found it and sure seems like they want to hang on to it. I get that it's rare and valuable but your dad's, I mean Standing Bear's, reaction is certainly odd."

"So, that's all I wanted to tell you," Jay said rubbing his forehead. "Oh, we took the plates off their truck and dumped it in the river south of town."

Katherine spoke, "Good enough. We'll have to let Colby and Jimmy know if they want the medal they should go and see your father."

Jay was headed to the door, "I guess. Robert's waiting for me so I gotta go. Catch ya later." He flew out the back door leaving Katherine and Sarah to make sense out of his story. They looked at each other for a moment, processing.

"The good news is that at least now we know who has the medal," commented Sarah.

Katherine finished, "But the bad news is they might not be able to get it back."

20

The call had gone out from Standing Bear before sunrise. Dawn air hung heavy, soothed by the soft cooing of a mourning dove, as the tribal elders made their way into the Tribal Council tepee. A current of greetings and grumbles passed between the assembled until Standing Bear called for their attention.

"I've called the Tribal Council together this morning to discuss something very important," Chief Standing Bear sat stone-faced at his place of honor, on the west side of the tepee. He gazed around the circle of elders seated on the ground inside the tepee made of canvas and twenty-eight lodgepole pines. Standing Bear preferred council meetings in the manner of his forebearers as a way to keep traditional customs alive with his people. A small fire burned in the center with smoke exiting through the two smoke flaps at the top.

"Sorry I'm late," Standing Bear's older son Barking Coyote panted, bursting into the tepee, handing his father a plastic jewelry box with the medal in it.

"My son, you look like you've been up all night," chastised Standing Bear with a scornful look.

"I worked most of the night finishing a piece for a friend. My apologies, Father." Barking Coyote covered his mouth, his hands blackened by chemical residue. He coughed and took his place as a hush returned to the gathered leaders.

Standing Bear tried to quell his disappointment toward his son as he withdrew the tarnished medal from the small box to hold up for all to see. A few of the chosen recoiled at the sight of the medal, recognizing it, and knowing what it possessed. They were all there- Eagle Elk the tribe's medicine man, White Cow Bull, Fools Crow, Black Deer, Bright Moon, Snow Face, Barking Coyote, along with two others. "My son, Red Feather, brought this to me sometime late last night." The Chief continued. "He came upon it as a result of a dispute among Whites. Red Feather brought it to me asking for advice as to what to do with it. Now I am bringing it to you." Each elder looked at Standing Bear with reverence in their eyes. "It is a Thomas Jefferson Peace Medal. The White archeologists who have been digging on the reservation north of here found it in a burial of our ancestors at Kakawita's village. We know this is his village because we are descendants of those whose true word has been passed down through generations. No doubt then that it had been found with Kakawita, the great Arikara chief. You also know of Kakawita's fate. All of us are aware of the dangerous spirit that lives within this medal. We have a decision to make. First, I must ask Eagle Elk to lead us in prayer."

Eagle Elk, in his seventh decade, sat shirtless. His upper body was painted with multi-colored animals and spiritual symbols. He wore a headdress of four eagle feathers representing the four directions: east, west, north, south. In his youth, he had been taught the sacred lore of his forefathers. Through prayer and fasting he received visions which gave him special powers for the good of his tribe. His current role as medicine man, prophet, and spiritual leader had been called upon over the years whenever the tribe faced adversity.

They all closed their eyes in respect for a deep connection with the Creator. Eagle Elk, seated to the right of Standing Bear, shook a stick with the small, dried gourd fastened to the tip in the direction of each member. Out of the silence, the medicine man's voice began a solemn Lakota chant that floated above the group. Some nodded their approval as they felt the omniscient spirit wash through them. Others chanted in response, carrying them into that spiritual dimension at the core of their soul. He concluded his prayer chant, and the tepee fell silent again.

Eagle Elk rose, taking an eagle feather from his headdress and began to sing in Lakota the Four Directions Song, dancing around the fire pit in a sunwise or clockwise direction, waving the feather above him. He stopped opposite the east-faced opening letting the rising sun bathe him with glorious beams of wisdom. Sworn to live a life of truth, he addressed the council, "I have communicated with the Great Father and Wakan Tanka, the Great Spirit. They have shown me the future. This medal began the white man's appropriation of our culture. It is a symbol of treachery. We must remain autonomous from the white man or lose our identity, our sovereignty."

The assembled exchanged eye contact as heads nodded. Whispers of approval filled the tepee. "To keep this medal and what it represents to our people would further prostitute ourselves to the white man's ways through assimilation. The future that has been shown to me is a patronizing appropriation meant in subjugation. We will not be complicit. If the white man wants it, he can have it." Eagle Elk closed his eyes, tilted his head and torso back, extending both his arms skyward. Softly, he chanted the traditional prayer of thanks for clarity toward the heavens. Remaining seated, the rest of the elders likewise extended their arms, joining in a prayer that had been passed down for generations.

"You have spoken words of wisdom," Standing Bear said turning toward Eagle Elk as he resumed his seat next to the Chief. "All that you say I believe. What say the rest of you?"

Fools Crow spoke up. "I agree with Eagle Elk. His sacred words are pure." He used his hand to vertically slice the space in front of him, signifying the 'straight way.' "With respect, Standing Bear," he continued looking around the circle, "you must tell the white man our position. He must also know the hazard associated with the medal. Perhaps the truth will enlighten him, and he will not want it either."

"I think we should rebury it at the village of our brothers," blurted Black Deer. "Put an end to it. We share its location with no one." Mumbled agreement circulated through the council.

"I do believe he will want it, Fool's Crow. He is known to us from travels this way in the past. The White Digger has been working with the government to excavate burials for many years. Because of his toil, he will not surrender it back to Mother Earth or to anyone," Standing Bear said. The elders shook their heads in disgust.

Snow Face spoke up. "Let's just give it to the government in Pierre. We would gain their respect for the offering."

A hush settled within the group. Standing Bear looked at Snow Face. "They have never shown our society proper respect. We don't owe the government the courtesy of its return."

"We should throw it in the river," opined White Cow Bull, followed by another round of satisfied nods and inaudible murmurs. "Why do we care about it, anyway? It is from the white man's culture." The murmurs became shouts of affirmation for White Cow Bull.

Out of the boisterous din Bright Moon suggested, "Why not just melt it in a fire ceremony. Wouldn't that melt the evil that is within it? Destroy it once and for all!" A roar of approval erupted.

Standing Bear raised his right hand to quell the noise. "You make a good point, White Cow Bull." Standing Bear rotated his head to focus on Bright Moon. "I, too, thought of melting the medal. However, we must remember, it is sacred to the Arikara. At one time we, that is the Arikara and the Sioux, had a mutually beneficial relationship. Their crops for our trade goods. We must show respect to them and our joined history." Standing Bear continued as he used his hands to reinforce his reasoning to the Council members. "If we make the medal to be like a ghost in the wind as has been suggested, the government will be all over us. I know this because, when Red Feather gave it to me, he said he thought his friends in Painted Rock knew he had it. He stated many whites would come looking for it with a vengeance. "It is not wise to invite that kind of trouble on our people." Standing Bear's commanding presence had all eyes centered on him. "Furthermore, my belief is that we can use this medal to tell the White Digger our truths, as Fools Crow has suggested. When I am contacted, I will offer to parlay. It will be as Eagle Elk has told. We must rid ourselves of the medal and the bad medicine it contains."

Standing Bear watched as Eagle Elk took the pipe bowl and the stem out of his pipe bag, an otter pelt-trimmed pouch with buckskin fringe and trade beads. He filled the bowl with a sanctified tobacco herbs mixture and joined it to the stem made from hollowed out green ash. To ignite the mixture, he took a thin stick of dried cedar to the fire in the center of the Council lodge and carried the fire to the top of the bowl. "From this pipe you will become the truth. The pipe cannot lie. No man that has untruth inside him may touch it to his mouth." He drew a deep breath then blew into the stem sending prayers to the Creator. Using his right hand, he circled the smoke over his head as a blessing.

Eagle Elk passed the pipe with a nod of validation to Fools Crow. Similarly, Fools Crow drew deep, puffed the smoke skyward, and passed the pipe. Around the Tribal Council circle, the pipe got passed in a sunwise direction, each member deep in supplication. Snow Face offered it to Barking Coyote, who declined. Snow Face hesitated, looking at him expectantly, pulled the pipe back, then reoffered it with a bob of his head. Barking Coyote took the pipe but passed it to Black Deer without touching it to his lips. With raised eyebrows of surprise Black Deer took the pipe before puffing and passing it on. Standing Bear was the last to use the pipe, then returned it to Eagle Elk who disconnected the stem, placing the pipe in his medicine pouch. Smoke dissipated overhead leaving a sweet aroma inside the tepee, as Standing Bear and the men quietly exited.

"Barking Coyote," Eagle Elk softly motioned making eye contact. Barking Coyote separated himself from the others to sit before the medicine man. "I saw." The medicine man padded his medicine pouch. "I am sensing your confliction." Eagle Elk tilted his head, raising his eyebrows, curious. "Perhaps you will join me in the sweat lodge for Purification."

"Thank you, Eagle Elk. I am honored by your request, but not today," Barking Coyote said, nodding in submission. "I'm meeting with a customer in Timber Butte at noon to finalize some business."

The corners of Eagle Elk's mouth became pinched with disdain, then relaxed. "Go then…with my blessing." With reluctance, Eagle Elk nodded his approval. "Tend to what you must."

21

Heading out of town toward the village, Colby, sedated by the still of the morning, began to reflect about all that had transpired so far on this trip in the context of his career. What had his life been to this point? As he looked through the windshield across the stunted grasses of the prairie toward the river, he remembered his years of study, research, and fieldwork...all those digs. Images of the many miles traveled flashed through his mind, the blistering hot days, the thrill of the find. He thought about all the people that had worked with him, endured his scorn, and were rewarded with his praise. Colby acknowledged to himself that, perhaps, his obsession with approval and recognition had scarred his relationships with family and friends. *But it's been my internal fortitude that has allowed me to make a positive difference in the world of cultural anthropology. Hasn't it?* He scratched his head. *Does the good outweigh the bad? Were all the accolades, financial rewards, and notoriety worth the pain I'm in now?*

Colby looked over at Jimmy thankful for the times they had spent together, whether driving or digging in the dirt. Colby felt a certain euphoric energy when he was around Jimmy, a transference of optimism and youth, really. The grandpa in Colby treasured those days watching Jimmy grow into the young man he had become. He was enormously proud of him, yet he battled with his lack of ability to express it. Had he been a good grandpa to Jimmy?

Colby rested his head against the back of the car seat. His stomach ached as he speculated on what life would be like if Jimmy's mom were still alive. It had broken his heart to see her body ravaged by the cancer, but he had marveled at how she kept a positive outlook until the end. *She was always so proud of her dad.* He would never get over the void she left in his life. Jimmy probably wouldn't either.

They arrived at the village as the day shook off the morning cool and began to warm up. The slate gray colored river rippled ever closer to the burial field. A calmness had filled their camp where violence had been. The trenches, once a dark brown color, were now a light brown, baked dry by the sun. Colby and Jimmy packed up their personal effects and collapsed the tent. They crammed their excavating tools, sifters, and boxes for university study into the Scout without method or organization. They finished in less than an hour and made tracks back to Painted Rock. Time continued to be their master in the search for the medal. Earlier in the trip it had been the rising river, now the clock ticked as the search renewed.

Once on the pavement, they rolled their windows down and listened to Roy Orbison on the radio. Jimmy raised his eyebrows. "Do you think we'll ever see the medal again?"

Colby shrugged. "I have no idea. We found it once; maybe we can find it again. I'm having my doubts though." They were silent the rest of the trip. Colby grappled with notions of the medal and getting home. He'd had just about enough of this trip with little to show for it. Moreover, how could he journal this trip with any degree of plausibility? Who would believe his story? In all the excitement, he had completely forgotten to take a photo of the pipe and the medal where they lay. *I need that medal in my possession. I have to have it.*

They pulled into the back of The Caboose and parked in front of the dumpster again. The back door was unlocked, so they went inside. They found Sarah and Katherine busy cleaning the bar and stocking the coolers. It would be a half an hour before they started serving lunch.

"We found the medal. I mean, we know where it is," Katherine excitedly began, palms up fingers wide. "Jay picked it up off of the bar last night, thinking it belonged to those scoundrels. He realized what it was and, long story short, left it with his dad. Well, actually his brother." Her face went from expressive to a relaxed confidence and explained, "I know this sounds confusing, but for sure it's being held for safe keeping on the reservation. Jay's dad is the Tribal Chairman, so no need to worry."

"Interesting," said Colby. A wave of hope cascaded over him tempered by the reality that the medal remained beyond his reach.

"So, we just go and get it from him then, right? Let's go, Grandpa," Jimmy said eagerly.

"Something tells me it's not going to be that simple," cautioned Colby, cocking his head to the side.

Katherine interjected, "It might not be. According to Jay, his dad had a weird reaction when he saw it. Like he didn't want to touch it. Said he was going to have to talk to the other Council members before he did anything with it."

"I guess we will have to go talk to him. I don't know what else to do at this point." Colby sounded defeated. "What have we got to lose?"

Sarah offered with wide eyes, "I could go with you. I know Jay's dad."

"That would be a good idea," Colby agreed. "With you there, he might listen. He doesn't know us from Adam. Katherine, could you call him and see if he'll meet with us?"

"I'll do it right now. Howard is a reasonable guy. I agree that Sarah should go, too." Katherine went in the kitchen. Colby followed her through the swinging doors to listen to the call. Jimmy and Sarah waited in the bar.

Jimmy shifted his weight on his bar stool to look into Sarah's brown eyes and spoke first, "You okay? I mean with us and everything?" His voice rose an octave.

"Very okay. I don't know what's next for us, but I do know I have feelings for you that I've never had before," admitted Sarah, grinning with happiness. She reached out and took his hand in hers.

Jimmy felt the warmth and smoothness of the back of her hand. "Me, too." Jimmy returned a relieved smile. "Thanks for listening last night."

The doors swung open, and they quickly let go of each other's hands.

"C'mon Jimmy. We have to meet him in 30 minutes. Katherine set it up for us. You too, Sarah," Colby commanded.

Sarah led the way past Katherine through the kitchen. "I'll drive. I know the roads and where he lives." Sarah turned her head as she scurried down the steps. Colby limped along as fast as he could. Sarah continued, "We have about twenty miles to travel and the roads are not great." Jimmy opened the passenger side door of Sarah's truck, boosted Colby into the middle of the cab, and hopped in beside him. Sarah threw the truck into reverse, backed out of the alley, and sped west.

They passed through the crisscross of shadows from the bridge's super structure as they crossed the river and turned southwest. The sun arched toward its apex as white pillowy clouds of varying shapes and sizes loomed in the tall sky. Their route followed the contour of the land which had been carved by glaciers long ago and, more recently, by erosive water. The highway was dangerous with sharp corners, its gravel shoulders overgrown with weeds or nonexistent, and it lacked proper signage. The speed limit was forty-five mph, and Sarah kept her speedometer right between the four and the five. They traveled up and over worn hills, around and through dry narrow valleys, each occupied with their own thoughts.

Jimmy snuck a peek out of the corner of his eye, feeling content to be in Sarah's presence. Still he felt there were some emotions he had to reconcile to himself about her. He smiled, feeling confident in Sarah's ability to empathize with the deeply personal sentiments he had expressed the night before and knowing he could trust her after their talk. Her responses comforted him. He felt a connection. *Is it the uncertainty about our possible future together that has my feelings all twisted? I guess sooner or later it comes down to fate. If it's meant to be, I guess it will work out.* Jimmy leaned forward, scooching in the seat to get comfortable. He turned his head and their eyes met. *Mom would have loved Sarah.* God, he missed his mom.

Colby stared out the window. All he could think about was how they had gone from hunting, to being hunted, to now hunting again. Chasing the elusive medal. That was the one constant between the east and west sides of the river. No one could get a tight grasp of that tarnished piece of silver. He played out different scenarios in his head and the possible outcomes of their meeting with Howard. Only one scenario and one outcome mattered to him.

As they drove on, Colby began to get a feel for the poverty the Indians were experiencing. He had never traveled this deep onto the Reservation. The Scout passed dilapidated single wide mobile homes with abandoned cars sitting next to them. The ground surrounding the homes was worn down to exposed dirt, littered with garbage. Clothesline poles leaned inward as the wind dried the morning's wash. Often, solitary burn barrels sat away from homes with brightly colored bicycles lying nearby. He also saw small, abandoned buildings that at one time might have been homes. On either side of them were spacious fields of grasses, with horses grazing as their tails chased flies. These sights were interrupted by broken wooden fences or intermittent sections of barbed wire fences along the side of the road. Colby felt he had crossed over into a different world.

Sarah broke the silence. "Be sure to address Jay's dad as Standing Bear, not Howard. Respect of the Indian people and their elders is important to them." A gospel tune by Porter Wagoner could be heard above the buzzing of the wind through the rolled down windows. Sarah turned to Colby and Jimmy while using a sweeping motion with her hand from left to right. "You can see life out here is much different than Painted Rock. It was an eye-opener for me when I first visited Jay's house when I was in grade school. Probably different than where you live in Kansas. Please don't judge them by their color or economic status. They're good people, authentic, and a lot of them are friends of mine."

Colby and Jimmy nodded.

In the distance there appeared a water tower with the words Wanbli Ohitika painted on it, which Sarah explained meant, 'Brave Eagle.' Clusters of willows, poplars, and osiers partially concealed their view of the Indian town. They were getting close. The road eased up a slight grade as Sarah reduced her speed. To their left, they passed a rusted Quonset hut on the edge of town with three-foot fire weeds surrounding it. A group of young Indian men were clustered outside it smoking cigarettes. Beyond them sat a gravel lot next to an unpainted grey cinder block garage set back from the road with two overhead doors and a brick chimney painted white.

To their right sat a two-story dark brown post and beam log building that housed the "Last Chance General Store" on the first floor and a jeweler above it. The chinking had large pock marked areas or missing pieces in several areas showing its wear from the years of hot summers and harsh winters. Behind the store, small houses sat atop a ridge next to the water tower and dotted the hillside. A spider web of telephone and electrical wires ran between the houses. Some of the homes had additions mismatched with the original architecture. Many of the homes had peeling paint, broken windows covered with cardboard, or missing shingles. The dwellings were connected by a winding gravel road with scrub buckthorn sparsely scattered throughout.

They turned right after the General Store and headed up the gravel road to their appointed destination. At the top of the hill sat a man gently rocking back and forth in the shade of his front porch. Sarah pulled up next to the house. A telephone pole with a basketball hoop sat at the end of the driveway. The top of the Tribal Council tepee peeked over the roof line from behind the tan colored house.

Standing Bear stood. He was broad shouldered and 6'4" with long arms and long legs. He had on jeans and a white t-shirt covered by an untucked black and gray flannel shirt. His cowboy boots were scuffed and dusty. Standing Bear's jet-black crew cut had been recently trimmed. His large round face, weathered and deeply tanned, partitioned by furrowed creases, spoke of both of his wisdom and his age. He wore a large ceremonial arrowhead within a sterling silver mount surrounded by turquoise pieces around his neck, emblematic of his position as Tribal Chairman and Chief.

Sarah slammed the door of the truck and strolled toward Standing Bear. Jimmy and Colby exited the truck wary and lagged a few paces behind her. She marched up the steps to greet Standing Bear with a smile and an embrace. "Standing Bear, it is so good to see you. It has been too long."

"Please call me Howard, Sarah. You are family to me and always welcome in my home."

"Thank you," said Sarah. "I'd like you to meet my friends, Colby and Jimmy. They are from the University of Kansas."

Standing Bear extended his hand as they came up the stairs and said, "Yes, I know of you both. On behalf of the citizens of the village of Brave Eagle, welcome."

Colby and Jimmy took turns shaking Standing Bear's firm handshake. His hand was the size of a grizzly bear's paw. Colby looked straight into Standing Bear's eyes and began. "Thank you, Standing Bear. It is a great honor to meet you. Thank you for making the time to meet with us on such short notice."

Standing Bear's piercing dark eyes stared hard at Colby. "I did so out of respect for Kitty and Sarah."

"Well, we appreciate it very much," Colby replied with a head nod of thanks. "Jimmy and I share your respect for Katherine and Sarah." Colby felt an awkward pause, not sure what to say next. Standing Bear's eyes narrowed to a squint. Colby recovered. "That is a gorgeous bolo tie worthy of its owner. Where did you have it made?"

"Jay's brother, Edward Barking Coyote, is a jeweler. You

passed his shop above the General Store." Standing Bear's massive hand pointed down the hillside. "If I might say so, he is a talented artisan with silver. He can make anything custom or even duplicate an existing piece of jewelry. Thank you for noticing."

Standing Bear reached for the door to his house. "Please join me at the dining room table. We have much to discuss."

22

The inside of Standing Bear's house proved modest in appearance and spartan in accommodation. Front door and back door connected by a straight hallway the length of the house. To their left, a dining room connected to a kitchen behind it. A pine dining room table big enough for six was centered in it. The walls were covered with wallpaper that had a muted pattern of wildflowers. To the right, a living room. A rose-colored couch, with maple end tables on either side, appeared worn, but serviceable. An avocado green easy chair faced an RCA console tv. The walls were painted a tawny color. In stark contrast to the vanilla flavor of the rest of the house, brightly colored woven Indian rugs filled the hallway, living room, and dining room.

Standing Bear offered his outstretched arm toward the dining room, "Please have a seat." They all stood by the table waiting for Standing Bear to take his seat at the head of the table and when he did, in concert, they pulled out their chairs and sat down. A shell with what appeared to be herbs in it adorned the center of the table.

Standing Bear reached into his pocket and pulled out the

small box containing the prized artifact. He looked directly at Colby, who was seated on his right, and set the medal on the table between them. Colby sat impassively with his hands folded in front of him but could barely contain himself. *I can't believe I'm seeing what I'm seeing.* It appeared to have lost some tarnish since the last time he saw it. The medal still had a black tinge to it but not as black as he remembered it when he'd pulled it out of the ground. *Well, what do you know? Those idiots must have cleaned it up.*

Standing Bear spoke first. "We have been watching your charade from afar since it began. You must know, nothing happens west of the river without my knowledge." He was very calm, and his deep voice communicated control. "We saw you arrive; we saw you dig, and we saw those two men assault you. We saw it all."

Colby, Jimmy, and Sarah listened intently with engaged eyes as Standing Bear continued. "We are not in favor of you digging on our land. That being said, we also understand why you dig. We know the politicians in Pierre and Washington think it's a necessary exercise in documenting our heritage because of the rising river water covering our ancestor's villages. Doesn't mean we have to agree with its offensiveness."

Colby spoke as his brow rose into wrinkles. "With all due respect, Standing Bear, our work offers your people an opportunity – I mean all people – the opportunity to better understand Indian history."

"Is that right," replied Standing Bear incredulously, his fingers interlaced. "Which part? The part where the white man stole our land? Or the part where they brought diseases and wiped-out entire tribes? Maybe the part where the white man chased my ancestors down and murdered innocent women and children?" Standing Bear paused to regain his composure. His face showed no emotion. "Oh, you must mean the part where they slaughtered our sacred buffalo in the name of sport? My people have been living with this 'history' for centuries."

Heads bowed, Jimmy and Sarah remained silent, but tension filled the room. Colby offered, "You're right, those things did happen. I can't deny or erase any of it, but perhaps through my work a better understanding, in fact a mutual respect, might emerge."

"On your way in you saw the conditions we live in. The federal and state governments do little to help us. We have under-educated children, rampant alcoholism, and unemployment runs about 85%." Standing Bear went on with fire in his words from tensed lips, "Their programs and their money haven't freed us, those programs have enslaved us. I have gone to Pierre, and I have gone to Washington, and the oppressive white leaders both say the same thing, 'We're working on it.' They disgust me with their lies and false promises."

"It is good for Jimmy and me to hear these things. I have to admit, I was unaware of the extent and severity of conditions within your community." Colby paused because he was concerned that what he was about to ask could open a can of worms. A can that could not be reclosed. "So, with respect I have to ask, what does all of this have to do with the medal?"

"It has everything to do with this medal, because in many ways the white explorers Lewis and Clark started it all. They were the first organized government expedition to our native lands." Standing Bear pointed to the medal, "Ironically, they were the first to offer that hollow token of peace. It was the start of the white man's incursion. We offered little resistance, believing their purpose was noble. In many cases, we welcomed them to our villages, our lodges, our lives. Truth be told, the medal was the start of the white man appropriating our culture, hijacking our customs, and subordinating my people by attempting to assimilate us into your world." In a calm voice he concluded, "In simplest terms, to us it represents an invalidation of who we are as a people."

"I guess I never thought of it that way," said Colby, with a sideway tilt of his head, rubbing his forehead, eyes cast at the table. He took a deep breath through his nose and let it out.

Standing Bear kept the heat on. "Kakawita was a noble Arikara warrior and Chief. We are Sioux but recognize his bravery as we are bound by the Hoop. A sacred circle of the universe." The Indian leader used his right hand to draw a circle above the table. "An Indian brotherhood, if you will, that binds the Sioux with our friends and our foes. Kakawita's story has been passed down through the generations. It is a story of leadership, trust, and sacrifice. After Lewis and Clark gave Kakawita the medal the village was beset with two years of dry summers, brutal winters, famine, and the small pox. Virtually wiped out the village," Standing Bear's face became full of sadness, the corners of his mouth drooped, and he puffed out his lower lip. "Shortly thereafter, he was murdered in his own lodge by my Sioux ancestors. It has been told that his dying wish was to be buried with the medal to save his people from its spell. The legend of Kakawita tells us that this medal holds bad medicine to anyone who encounters it. You, no doubt, can attest to that," he nodded, eyes locked with Colby's.

Standing Bear steepled his fingers as he stopped to observe those gathered around the table. Sharp eyed, he made eye contact with each one of them. A fog of uneasy silence consumed the room as they waited for Standing Bear to continue from his de facto pulpit. Quick peeks ricocheted around the table.

The wooden ladder-back chair creaked as Standing Bear

leaned back folding his arms across his chest. "When Jay brought the medal to me last night, I immediately knew I needed to go into session with the Tribal Council to discuss what to do with it. We all agreed. Avenging spirits inhabit this medal. Evil intentions come from it. We don't want it." He pushed the medal in front of Colby. "You can have it."

There was an uncomfortable pause as Colby shifted in his chair, rubbed his hands together, and softened his gaze. Colby could hear his heart beat as his shoulders rose from the tension. "Standing Bear, I want you to know that there is significant monetary value to this medal and that could really help your people. Maybe you should keep it," charitably offered Colby.

"I am well aware of its value to those only concerned with money," answered Standing Bear in a caustic tone. He crinkled his nose, showing his upper teeth. "We want nothing to do with the oppression it represents or the pain and suffering that comes with it." He leaned forward, opened his hands on the table, and looked directly at Colby. "Our Indian nation is not imprisoned by your values, your definition of happiness, nor is our self-worth defined by achievement and material things, such as this medal represents to you. Our race is in this world but not of this world. The Great Father of the universe gives us our self-worth: we don't have to earn it." He paused to let his comments sink in. "Take it at your own peril."

No one spoke as a cautious gaze bounced from person to person with Sarah and Jimmy folding their arms across their chest to settle on looking at Colby. "Very well, then. You have spoken and we," Colby gestured to Jimmy and Sarah, "appreciate your kindness and your honesty. I don't want to take any more of your time. We will be on our way."

"So, it shall be," Standing Bear's voice dropped. "But, before you go, you must join me in a smudging ceremony," Standing Bear said. "It is our custom on such occasions." He pointed at the center of the table. "In the shell are four sacred plants-cedar, sage, sweetgrass, and tobacco." He struck a wooden match, lit the sacred mixture, and softly blew them out. He took an eagle feather and wafted the healing smoke over himself. "If you please," he motioned for them to lean forward and use their hands to inhale the smoke. "This will cleanse your soul of negative thoughts." Colby pushed down his doubts and, out of respect, leaned forward and complied.

Ambivalent about the meaning of the smudging ceremony, Colby awkwardly stood at its seeming completion to shake hands with Standing Bear. With the transfer complete, both remained expressionless as Colby put the medal in his pocket.

With a relieved silence, they shuffled to the door. Jimmy extended his hand to Standing Bear. "It was a great honor to meet you, sir. Thank you," Jimmy said tilting his head with a submissive nod of his head.

Standing Bear stared at him with a paternal look in his eye as his hand swallowed up Jimmy's. "I can see you have an attraction to Sarah. You must be good to her."

Colby looked over his shoulder at Sarah and Jimmy to see Jimmy's face turn from pink to red. His grandson stammered for words but nothing audible came out. Standing Bear released his grip.

Sarah's face turned bright red, too. "Oh, Howard," she said, as Standing Bear bent to give her a fatherly hug. His stone-faced expression melted into a slight smile.

"Dr. Phillips, may I have a word?" Standing Bear asked. His tone had transitioned from tutorial to collegial. Jimmy and Sarah exited, closing the door behind them, to wait on the porch as Colby pivoted to stand face to face with Standing Bear.

In an authoritative voice, Standing Bear said, "My people say the eyes are the window to a man's soul." His face was impassive. "When I look into your eyes I see the torment that has bothered you for many years. It is wretched, and it has controlled you for far too long." He gently placed his hand on Colby's shoulder. "This medal you covet is merely a symbol for your discontent. You cannot find true happiness when you are chained to the desires you expect from others when their desires aren't yours. You, and you alone, have the power to cast off the shackles of others not meeting your expectations and recognize your true self-worth. Only then will the ever-present spirit, Wakan Tanka, fill your heart with peace."

Colby stood with hands on hips, staring at Standing Bear, absorbing his wisdom. He averted his guilty eyes to the floor, speechless, wondering how the gentle Indian knew. He lifted his head to see the Chief's fixed glare. Colby bobbed his head once in acknowledgement.

They paraded down the steps, across the worn yard, back to the truck to take their same seats for the trek back to Painted Rock. Standing Bear sedately stood on the porch as Sarah's truck headed back down the hill.

The white clouds present at the time of their arrival had been replaced by an overcast cloak of gray. A sense of unease encircled Colby as they backed out of the driveway. Standing Bear's earnest remarks had left an indelible impression. Just as they left the winding gravel road and hit the pavement by the General Store, Jimmy broke the still within the cab. "So we got the medal back, but you don't seem happy, Grandpa."

"Yeah, I've got some *serious* thinking to do," mused Colby as a shadow of doubt crept over him.

23

Katherine sat down to read the weekly newspaper after the last of the dirty dishes were stacked next to the sink for Sarah to wash and the bar had been wiped clean. It had been a light lunch crowd at The Caboose and now the bar was empty. Around 1:30 two men walked in, both dressed in black suits, narrow black ties, and crisp white shirts. Their wrinkled brow and blank facial expression revealed they meant business. They stood away from the bar, arrow straight with feet shoulder width apart.

"Good afternoon, gentlemen. What can I get ya?" Katherine surmised they might be ex-military.

The taller one stepped forward removing his fedora. "May we speak to the owner? Wonder if we could ask a few questions?" he asked.

Katherine stood behind the bar with her hands on her hips, "Depends what you are asking. Who are you?"

"My name is Special Agent Paul Gritzmacher, and this is Special Agent Roger Calhoun." Both removed their badges from their inside coat pockets and flashed them in Katherine's direction. "We are from the Department of Indian Property out of Pierre."

205

"I'm the owner. What would you like to ask me?"

They both took another step forward. Agent Gritzmacher pulled out his notepad. "An anonymous caller to our office said that you might have knowledge of a Lewis and Clark Peace Medal otherwise more formally known as a Thomas Jefferson Peace Medal being found. Is that true?"

"Yes, I am aware that one was found." Katherine nodded, trying to figure out what they wanted to find out. The chess match had begun.

"And how did you come to know that?" Gritzmacher asked, tilting his head as he wrote.

"Two men were in here last night showing it off. They laid it on the bar right down there," Katherine said pointing to the other end of the bar.

"Any idea where they might have found it?"

"No idea. The one guy just said he got it off a dead guy."

"Dead guy? Who was the dead guy?" The vertical lines between Gritzmacher's eyes deepened.

"Mister, I have no idea. I just work the bar trying to keep my customers happy. Might I ask why you are so interested in that medal?"

"Well, you should know that it has significant cultural, historical, and monetary importance to some. If it was found within the high-water mark of the Oahe Reservoir, or Missouri River as most still refer it, we are duty bound to get it back because it's government property."

"Sorry, I don't think I can help you." Katherine shrugged. Her answers were becoming blunter, fueled by her impatience as she folded her arms across her torso.

Gritzmacher smirked, "Oh, I think you can. Who were the two guys that had it?"

"They said they were from Tennessee. They had a couple of drinks too many and left."

"They take the medal with them?"

Katherine tilted her head back with a laugh. "I guess so. It's not here," she said extending her arms in a 'see for yourself' motion.

"And what time was that?"

Katherine looked at the ceiling, taking a moment to recall the time. "I guess it was around nine or ten. I'm not really sure. Kinda lose track of time when we're busy. You know how it is." Katherine nodded her head presuming agreement while smiling.

Gritzmacher shrugged. "They say where they were going?"

"No, sir, they did not. Now if you'll excuse me, I need to finish cleaning up."

"Sure, no problem. Here's my card. If you hear anything, could you give me a call? We'd be much obliged if you could help us recover that medal," Gritzmacher gave her a friendly smile.

"I will certainly do that," Katherine said, having no intention of calling.

"Thanks for your time."

They turned and headed for the door and Katherine turned to head for the kitchen. She left the card on the bar.

"Oh, ma'am, just one more question," Gritzmacher said with a hand on the door.

"What's that?"

"Have you ever heard the name of a Professor Colby Phillips?"

Katherine paused for effect. "Nope, that name doesn't ring a bell." She pushed through the swinging doors and sat down on a stool by the grill. Head down, her hands shook. She glimpsed over her shoulder toward the bar apprehensive about the two men.

Five minutes after Gritzmacher and Calhoun left the bar, Sarah, Colby, and Jimmy walked through the back door of The Caboose. Katherine was working in the kitchen, busy with her preparation for the evening bunch. She battled frayed nerves while doing her best to maintain her composure. She didn't want to alarm the others.

"Howard gave Colby the medal," Sarah announced, setting her purse on the counter. Shuffling behind, Colby and Jimmy seemed much less excited than she'd expected.

"I had a strong suspicion that Howard would give it to you," Katherine said lifting her head as she peeled potatoes. She appraised Colby and Jimmy's expressions. "You two don't look overly happy about it."

On the ride back from Brave Eagle the dreams had begun to give Colby pause as his psyche absorbed Howard's cautious words. "It's just been a trying last few days. I'm glad to have it back," Colby said.

"I need to tell you of two visitors from Pierre I just had," Katherine began as she wiped her hand on her apron. "They were looking for the medal and let me tell you, they were asking a lot of questions. Paul and Roger somebody. Special Agents from the Department of Indian Property."

Colby's jaw clenched.

"I told them two guys from Tennessee had it and left with it. What I told them was mostly true. Except the part when they asked me if I knew you, Colby, and I said I never heard of you."

"Paul Gritzmacher and Roger Calhoun. I know who they are. They have hassled me before. My guess is that they told you they wanted it back because it's government property," Colby grumbled. "Probably gave you a song and a dance about its cultural and historical value."

"That's exactly what they said," Katherine replied, hands on hips.

"I've got all the necessary paperwork to refute their claim to the medal," Colby explained. "They both know I'm working with the State, the Corps of Engineers, and the University of Kansas. Have for years." Colby leaned on the stove with his arms folded across his chest. "They flash their badges to confiscate valuable Indian artifacts and somehow the artifacts never make it back to Pierre. According to various people I've talked to, their stories… or more accurately their lies go like this…they tell their bosses that the artifact or artifacts were either never in their possession or what they said they took wasn't documented correctly by the intake clerk. In other words, they take a high dollar valued artifact from a pot hunter or authorized legitimate party like me and document that they took an artifact of much lesser value and turn that over to the State. Then they sell the high dollar artifact on the black market and pocket the cash." Colby paused to let his listeners catch up. "Get this, the best story they tell is that they turned an artifact in, and the State lost it. Thus far they've managed to not get caught. Their threats and intimidation keep the victims quiet, and the State is too busy with documenting sites ahead of the rising river to verify the paperwork they turn in. Gritzmacher and Calhoun are as crooked as it gets."

Katherine, Jimmy, and Sarah looked wide-eyed. "Oh my God," exclaimed Katherine.

"Hard to believe, isn't it?" Colby held his hand with index finger extended. "Wait, there's more. They arrested me once on a site west of Harris. They threw me in jail, and I spent over 12 hours behind bars until the South Dakota Attorney General got me released. I had gotten all the approvals, filed all the paperwork, but didn't have copies on me. Wouldn't have mattered anyway." Colby shuffled to stand, extending his hands and arms for emphasis. His eyes met the attentive trio. "They were trying to get me to give them artifacts to sell. Strong arm me, you know. When I said 'No,' they cuffed me. They even threatened to blackmail me. Thankfully, my pal, Earl Chavey, got the right people to bring up the documents. When I went back to the site, all the artifacts we had found with the burials were gone. They stole everything. I had to plead with the National Science Foundation to get a grant after that. I didn't get anything the next year, which really compromised my research." Colby continued with raised eyebrows, chin lowered, and his arms folded across his chest, "The river took a lot of good villages during that time. Thank heavens, two years ago, I returned to the good graces of the NSF and received their funding. But I lost what would have been a very productive year because of them. Gritzmacher and Calhoun screwed me over good."

"Are you kidding me?" Jimmy looked astonished.

"No, I am dead serious. They want the medal for its cash value or the notoriety, even though they never found a single artifact themselves. It's true this little gem is worth some money to me indirectly through speaking engagements, appearances…maybe I'll even write a book." The corners of his mouth raised to a grin. "The difference between us and them is WE found it." Colby extended his arms with his palms open. "Furthermore, I can see the good that could come out of it being in a museum or university setting where people can appreciate it. I can promise you one thing," Colby's face darkened, "if they get their hands on it, that medal would never make it back to Pierre. They'd fence it in a heartbeat. If by some stretch of the imagination it did make it back to Pierre, their bank account would be even fatter than it is already. I can also promise you I will never give it to them," Colby's scathing tone adamant and defiant. "They're opportunistic thieves of the worst kind."

"They left but I have a feeling they will be back. I could tell they didn't like my answers," interjected Katherine.

"The only way they would know we are still in town is if they see us or they see the Scout," Colby said with grave concern in his voice. "The Scout is hard to miss with the KU logo and Kansas license plates. We need to put the Scout somewhere they won't find it."

Jimmy offered, "What about on the reservation?"

"They might have headed that way toward the village site, so that's probably not a good idea," Katherine said.

"What about in your garage? It's so close," Colby countered.

Katherine nodded her head pointing to the back door. "No time to waste. Get going. Follow Sarah and she can let you in the house. Stay there for the time being until we can figure out how to get you outta here without them seeing you or your truck."

Upon Katherine's direction they bolted for the door and hurried to their trucks. Sarah took the most direct route to the old farmhouse with Jimmy right on her heels. Sarah parked in front of the garage, hopped out, and lifted the large garage door. Jimmy slid the Scout into the vacant garage and killed the engine. Sarah reached up and pulled the door shut. Colby opened the glove compartment, collected the .38, and put it in his pants pocket. The two of them exited the service door, hustled up the back steps, and met Sarah in the kitchen.

"You guys make yourselves at home. I've got to get back to The Caboose to help Grandma. We'll call you later," Sarah said as she rushed out the door.

Colby and Jimmy looked at each other as the chimes from the grandfather clock resonated through the empty house. "Make yourself comfortable, Jimmy. We might be here awhile."

24

Once outside the bar after grilling Katherine, Gritzmacher and Calhoun stood on the curb in front of their white Ford Galaxy 500 with a cherry on top, joined by the diesel smell of the railyards. Gritzmacher put on his sunglasses and turned to Calhoun, "What do you make of her story?"

"I think she's lying."

"Yeah me, too. I'm just not sure what she's lying about. What do you think the chances are that there were two guys in the bar from Tennessee?"

"Oh, I'd say slim to none," Calhoun replied without emotion, eyes surveying up and down the street.

"Let's take a drive around and see if we see anything that might be of interest. Let's start at one end of town and take it a block at a time." The two investigators got in their car and began driving southeast along the railroad yard.

Gritzmacher and Calhoun rolled through the entire town at a slow speed, block by block. Their AM radio played no music. Large elms lined the streets neatly laid out at right angles to each other. They passed small houses with well-kept yards bordered by cement sidewalks. Other larger houses had love seats suspended over expansive porches waiting for occupants. Occasionally, they drove by a lawn being mowed. Some had split rail fences, some had white picket fences, and some had no fences at all. Behind the houses, single car garages faced the alleys that bisected the blocks. A lot of the houses had their drapes closed to keep the heat out. Comically, Dakotans referred to it as South Dakota air conditioning. Boys and girls were riding their bikes or walking home from summer school. Without a doubt, some moms were waiting for the children at home with freshly baked chocolate chip cookies. Conversely, darkened homes with no visible activity made it seem like some of the townspeople were not home. Some were probably at work for the highway department, a business in town, or one of the spacious Black Angus cattle ranches surrounding Painted Rock. Perhaps others were gathered at one of the churches for quilting, bridge, or to catch up on town gossip.

"This town seems like it belongs in a Norman Rockwell painting," Calhoun quipped.

"Or a Twilight Zone episode. Did you see the way she looked away when I asked her if she knew Colby?" Gritzmacher asked Calhoun.

"I did see that. I also noticed she was vague about the two guys that she said had the medal. The guys from Tennessee," Calhoun offered with a nod of his head. "A woman like that sees and hears everything."

"We get that medal and I'm retiring. We're talking big bucks to the right buyer," chuckled Gritzmacher. "The first call I make is to JR Stedgeman in Billings. He's been good to us in the past. He'll give us a fair price. Not to mention that he will keep his mouth shut."

"How you gonna play this one?" questioned Calhoun.

Gritzmacher half turned his head toward Calhoun while keeping an eye on the road. Never know when a rabid jackalope might dash in front of them. "Kinda seems like it would be good to say we never recovered it. We came close, but could never get our hands on it," Gritzmacher said with a snicker. "Gee whiz, sir, we're sorry sir, but nobody we talked to had it. Or Maybe we try to pin on Phillips. Not sure…something like that. I remember when my dad was working the extorting and blackmailing racket for the mob in Chicago after prohibition, he'd have me tag along. He'd say, 'Son, we get ourselves pinched by the law, the less we say the better.' First things first, though…we gotta get our hands on the medal."

"True. I do like the idea of pinning it on Phillips," Calhoun said as they shared a laugh.

"We've got some nice money with our other work, but this would be our best job and biggest payout yet," Gritzmacher assured Calhoun. "I'm going to pull in here and fill up." Gritzmacher pulled the Galaxy 500 into the Sinclair station and they got out to stretch their legs.

"Fill 'er up, sir?" the attendant asked as he ambled through the afternoon heat toward their car.

"Yep, and check the oil, too," Gritzmacher instructed as he slammed his car door shut.

Calhoun headed from the car to the men's restroom. Gritzmacher casually walked back to chat with the attendant who seemed preoccupied with resetting the pump and unhooking the nozzle. "Fine day we're having." Gritzmacher read the name on the front of the coveralls. "Gus is it?"

"Yep. We haven't had one of these in a while. Predicting some sort of storm later today. Never know in these parts though."

"No, I guess around here you never know," commented Gritzmacher. He looked around, keeping his eyes peeled for Phillips, the Professor's truck, or Tennessee plates. "Nice looking station you have here. You must be the owner. Only the owner would keep a service station this neat and tidy," gushed Gritzmacher. The back of Gus's coveralls looked sweat stained and Gritzmacher got a whiff of the associated sour body odor.

Gus beamed with pride. "Thank you. Yep, I've had this place for prettinear twenty years. Originally was my Pop's. Been at this location in one form or another for forty."

"That's impressive! Say, gotta ask you…have you seen an old International Harvester Scout with Kansas plates come through here recently? Has University of Kansas written on the side."

Gus topped off the cruiser's tank, hung the nozzle, and brushed by Gritzmacher on his way to check the oil. "Let me think." He stopped and scratched his head. He lifted the hood and removed the dipstick. Wiped it clean with the rag from his back pocket and inserted the dipstick back. Pulled it out and looked at it carefully. "Oil's good." He slammed the hood, took the rag out of his back pocket again, and rubbed his hands with it.

This guy was stalling. He had to know something.

Gus looked right at Gritzmacher, "I see a lot of cars and trucks here, you know, over time and all. Nope, can't say that I recollect a vehicle like that."

So he wanted to play that way? "I understand. I'm sure you do see a lot of vehicles through here. That's just kind of a unique truck, so I thought you might remember. Let me settle up with you and we'll be on our way," Gritzmacher followed Gus into the waiting area. He handed the owner his business card. "Give my office a call if your memory improves or that truck stops here. I need to get him an important message about a member of his family. I guess there's a family emergency. We're trying to find the guy that owns it and help him out."

"Ohhh," Gus answered, glancing at the card. Now he hesitated. Absent-mindedly, he tapped the business card on the counter. "You know," he said with a wide-eyed expression of epiphany, "there might have been one of them pass through." The business card tapped more rapidly. He withdrew his red rag from his back pocket, blotted sweat from his brow, then changed his tune. "But that was months ago, I think. You know, at my age, the memory just isn't what it used to be. I just can't say."

"So, there wasn't, there was, or you're not sure?" Gritzmacher loved to put people in an intellectual vise, loved the inevitable irritability that followed.

"I said, I don't remember!" Gus yelled, nostrils flaring, eyes bugging out, face shaped with anger.

"Okay, Okay. Easy, old timer, I was just asking. Thanks for the service," He grabbed a toothpick from the dispenser on the counter and walked out the door.

Gritzmacher got in the car where Calhoun was already waiting. "What was he yelling about?"

"I pushed him too hard. Well, actually, he and I both knew he was lying about seeing Phillips' Scout," Gritzmacher confidently said with a toothpick in his mouth. He sat erect in his seat and continued. "The good Doctor has definitely been in town. He's definitely been to this gas station and that bar," emphasizing his point with a nod of his head toward each property. "I think it was Phillips and another guy in the bar last night with the medal, not two guys from Tennessee. We need to pay another visit to the bar and have a heart to heart with the owner."

"You think they left town?"

"Something tells me they are still around," Gritzmacher took the toothpick out of his mouth and rolled it between his thumb and forefinger. "People wouldn't have to be lying if they'd up and left. They'd have no reason to cover for him, you know. I'm still trying to figure out who the other guy would be."

"Maybe we should head out to the village. He might still be there."

"It's getting late and I'm not exactly sure how to find it. Lots of prairie between here and there. Let's hit the bar and put the squeeze on."

It was approaching 4PM at The Caboose. Katherine wiped glasses and Sarah filled ketchup and mustard bottles while Jay, Robert, and their co-worker Mark drank their second beers in celebration of Robert's 23rd birthday. The keyboard intro to The Doors, "Light my Fire", danced from the jukebox.

The door opened and Katherine looked up reflexively. The two agents were back. They took a seat right in front of the darkened TV.

Katherine put down her towel and glass and walked down to greet them. "Back so soon? What can I get ya?" She put a couple of cardboard coasters on the bar in front of them. She struggled to hide her anxious disdain behind her forced smile.

"Nice to be back," Gritzmacher said with a reciprocating smile. "A couple of Hamm's would be just fine."

Katherine put the ice-cold beers in front of them. "Would you like menus?"

The agents spoke in unison, "Yeah."

She reached under the bar and put the one-page lunch menu in front of each of them. She walked away to give them a couple of minutes to look, then returned. She pulled a pencil out from behind her ear and an order ticket from her apron pocket. "What'll it be?"

"I'll have a hamburger and fries," said Calhoun matter-of-factly.

"Gimme a ham and cheese sandwich and fries," Gritzmacher stated.

"Coming right up," answered Katherine while gathering up the menus and putting them back under the counter. She walked down to where Sarah was talking to the boys and handed her the order. As was their routine, she took the ticket from her grandma and disappeared into the kitchen.

"Say, ma'am, could I ask you a question?" said Gritzmacher in a friendly tone.

Katherine could feel the three boys' eyes on the strangers as she headed back toward the Staties. Anger began to well up inside her gut. "What's on your mind?" quizzed Katherine, arms extended bracing herself on the bar.

"What is on my mind is that Roger here doesn't think you gave us the whole story about last night. I tried to tell him that I thought you were straightforward with us earlier this afternoon, but maybe we should just run through your story one more time. He just needs some convincing." The agent looked at Katherine with narrowed eyes as he tilted his head.

"I told you that two guys from Tennessee had the medal, they had a few drinks too many, and left. Beyond that I don't know what else to tell you," explained Katherine, crossing her arms across her chest.

Calhoun butted in, "And you never heard the name, Colby Phillips, right?"

"That's right."

"You see...I'm sorry, what did you say your name was?" asked Gritzmacher.

"I didn't say what my name was, but for future reference, it's Katherine."

"You see, Katherine, we stopped at the gas station and Gus said the same thing." Gritzmacher pointed at Calhoun. "Roger told me he didn't believe either of you. He thinks Colby was in here with another guy, and Colby was the one who placed the medal on the bar. My question is why are you protecting him?"

Panic washed over Katherine. Her cheeks turned a deep rose color, and she averted her eyes. "I have no idea what you are talking about." She spun around in a huff and began walking away.

"Wait, come back," Gritzmacher said loudly. "Just one more question."

Katherine paused and half turned around, "What?"

Jay, Robert, and Mark paused their conversation, leaned over the bar, and turned their heads.

"How old is this place?"

Thinking it was an odd question, she replied, "It was built in 1929. Why?"

"It would be a shame if it caught fire. My guess is this place would go up in a hurry," Gritzmacher said with a smirk. "Have you had a State inspection done recently? Maybe I should call the State Health Inspector?"

Katherine's face showed surprise, then fear, then anger. She stormed off without comment.

"You could be charged with lying to a government official and obstruction if we find out you know him or where he is," Gritzmacher threatened loudly enough for all to hear.

Katherine ignored his last comment as Sarah passed through the swinging doors and past her with the food. "Here you go gentlemen," Sarah pleasantly said. She placed the food in front of them, grabbed the condiments tray, put it on the bar, and returned to visit with the boys.

"She's one tough broad," Calhoun commented to his partner and stuffed his mouth with hamburger.

The other one laughed. "She's about to break."

Katherine pretended not to hear and went back to polishing glasses, eyes welled up with tears.

25

Jimmy lay on his side on the couch, while Colby sat in the partially reclined easy chair with his hands in his lap. All the lights were off, and the drapes were pulled. For the time being, they were prisoners for their own good. Walter Cronkite was updating the nation on the Vietnam War, but neither of them was watching it. They were bored. Jimmy knew the war had become highly controversial, but could admit he didn't understand the political, social, and military implications. He was mindful of the fact that a handful of his high school classmates had either been drafted or enlisted. Because of his enrollment at KU, he would be classified as 2S by the Selective Service, meaning he had a student deferment currently and would remain so with the upcoming draft lottery that started December 1st. By his choice, he insulated himself from all the turmoil surrounding the war. While the rest of the country had begun to react in anger with unrest and demonstrations, he was fine living his life coveting the things that were most important to him: family, his classes at KU, and the work required at the farm.

Colby faced the TV but wasn't watching it. Mentally, he had

left the room and become lost in his self-reflective thoughts of the trip, the medal, their predicament. "Turn that down," Colby barked.

Without argument, Jimmy got up and turned the TV down. He sat back down on the couch, rested his forearms on his thighs and looked at Colby.

"You look troubled, Grandpa. What are you thinking about?" Jimmy asked.

"I'm thinking about this damn medal. This isn't how I saw things working out if I ever found it. What if I've been looking at this, and why I want it so bad, all wrong?" Colby's voice shook. He fixed his gaze on the medal in his hand. "Maybe Standing Bear is right. His comment about self-worth hit a chord with me and I think that smudging woke me up." He paused and turned the medal over and over absently. "Maybe the medal *is* bad medicine. Think about it. Kakawita got it from Lewis and Clark and prematurely met his Maker. We found it and got the tar beat out of us. Billy and the other guy had it and who knows what ended up happening to them. Now we have it again, and the damn 'Staties' Gritzmacher and Calhoun are after us. I didn't make a big deal out of it at the time, but I've been having these weird dreams about the medal. Grandma Phillips was even in a couple of them." Colby paused to collect his thoughts. "I am not willing to go to jail or die for it." Colby turned his head to stare at the ceiling. "This maniacal obsession with the medal has been driving me all these years. All the accolades and recognition. I have got a living room full of plaques and crystal awards. I thought finding the medal would give me great satisfaction, proof that I am the best and better than all the rest, but instead I feel hollow on the inside." Colby's words turned somber. "Does this end up in court over ownership? I mean, maybe some judge agrees with the State and we go to jail on trumped up charges of trespassing, or theft, or who knows what they might conjure up." Colby stopped to scratch his head, "Maybe they find a loophole in the official papers we have."

"Slow down, Grandpa," Jimmy said in a calm voice, both hands padding the air. "We're not going to jail. They might try to take it from us, though, if they ever find us. We can wait 'til dark and then head out of town. No one has to know. We'll leave Katherine and Sarah a note and vanish."

Colby sensed Jimmy, foolishly, thought they would be able to escape undetected with the medal. Based on previous experience, Colby explained, "You don't know those two guys, Gritzmacher and Calhoun. They will stop at nothing to get it. I told you I've had a run in with them. They're ruthless. They would follow us all the way back to Kansas. I'm thinking we should repatriate it on the reservation. You have the waiting 'til dark part right, but I say we go west first, then south. We go back to the village." Colby began to talk faster. "Rebury it in one of the holes. That way no one gets it. Then we head home via the west side of the river. Drive as far as we can…spend the night somewhere. In the morning call Ted to bring his grader to cover over the excavation site."

"You would really rebury the medal?' Jimmy asked incredulously. "Just hold on for a second." Jimmy stood, putting his hands in his pockets. "Maybe we should call down to Katherine to see if those agents have come back or what she would suggest. She's helped us out so far. Maybe those two have given up and left town."

"No way they have given up. Not this quickly. But, okay, let's call Katherine and see what she thinks of my plan."

Jimmy got up off of the couch to give Colby a hand getting out of the recliner. They went to the kitchen to look for the phone book. They shuffled through drawers without any luck. Then Jimmy found it under a stack of Sioux Falls Argus Leader newspapers. He found the number for The Caboose. "Grandpa, I think you should be the one to call her and explain to her what you're thinking," he said.

Colby dialed the number; it rang seven or eight times before Sarah picked up. "The Caboose, Sarah speaking." There was an edge to her voice.

"Hi Sarah, this is Colby. Are you alright?" He could sense by her voice inflection something was amiss. He pulled out a kitchen chair so he could sit down extending the coiled phone cord to its limit.

"Not exactly." She sounded angry.

"What's the matter?" asked Colby. Jimmy bent at the waist putting his ear next to the receiver so he could hear, too.

Sarah lowered her voice barely above a whisper, "Those two Special Agents from the State are here, and they are threatening my grandma. They just about made her cry. I don't remember if I've ever seen her like this." Sarah paused. Colby could hear her breathing. "She is really upset. This is terrible. I don't know what to do."

"What do you mean they are threatening her?"

"They were asking how old the bar is and then said how fast it would go up in a fire. Then they threatened to call the Health Inspector. Basically, they want Grandma to give you guys up and tell them where you are. She would never do that." Sarah talked so fast that it became difficult for Colby to understand her. "Obviously, they want the medal. They are so mean. Grandma didn't tell them anything which made them even madder."

Colby rubbed his forehead. His sharp mind received, analyzed, and configured his next move. He spoke in a firm voice. "Okay, here's what I want you to do. Go out there and tell them that I saw their car out front of your bar. I stopped at Gus's and called to give them a message. Tell them the message is that we will meet them outside The Caboose in twenty minutes to talk. Tell them we have the medal."

"Are you sure?" questioned Sarah. "I mean, are you going to give it to them?"

"Not if I can help it. Make it sound as if we are being sincere and plan to give it to them. Pull yourself together and be as cordial as possible. Tell Katherine to stay in the kitchen."

"Okay. I hope you know what you're doing," Sarah said. "Anything else?"

"Just one more thing. Are Jay and Robert around by any chance?"

"Yep. They're here, too. And our friend, Mark, is with them."

"Tell them if this thing goes south, we are going to need back up."

"You got it." Sarah's voice had renewed confidence as if Colby's strength and positive energy had gone through the phone to invigorate her.

"See you soon. Remember, cordial, like no big deal."

"Yep. See you soon."

Colby got up and hung up the phone.

Jimmy took a seat at the kitchen table across from Colby. "You want to tell me what your plan is?"

"When I figure it out, you'll be the first to know," Colby said with a coy wink and a smile. "Let's just say I've got a general outline. First things first, we have to empty the Scout." Colby extended his digits in succession. "Second, we'll have to store our specimen boxes and gear in their garage. Third, we're going to need a full tank of gas. Then we go to The Caboose to spring our trap."

Jimmy had a smirk on his face that complimented his empowered eagerness. "I knew it, Grandpa. I knew you'd have a plan!"

26

Colby poked his head into each room on the first floor to make sure the lights were out before he left the farmhouse. On the way down the back steps, Colby put his hand on the outside of his right pants pocket reassuring himself he still had the medal.

He glanced over his shoulder. "Make sure the door is closed tight." He heard the door close and Jimmy jiggling the handle to affirm the door was securely closed.

Leading the way, he took the short walk to the garage, opened the service door, and flipped on the switch. Immediately he smelled the mildewy dampness that hung in the air. Overhead, the rafters had an assortment of lumber, storm windows, and linoleum remnants. Illuminated by a lone light bulb in the center of the garage, Colby could make out the faint oil stains on the cracked cement floor partially covered by scattered leaves from last fall. Making his way around the front of the truck, he became entangled in the cobwebs that partially covered the four paned square window on the back wall. After he swung open the back door of the Scout, they began working efficiently together, hastily putting the specimen boxes in the far back corner of the garage alongside hanging shovels, rakes, and garden tools. Once they were neatly stacked, Colby pulled out the tarp and covered the boxes. Lastly, they removed all their camping gear piling it in front of the Scout.

"Okay, push the garage door open and I'll back the truck out," said Colby leaning over to put the .38 back in the glove compartment. Once the Scout had backed out Jimmy closed the garage door and hopped in the passenger side. They made their way toward Gus's, progress frustrated by having to slow for cross streets and an unnecessary construction detour. As they arrived at the service station, Gus ambled out to greet them.

"Filler up, Gus." Colby exited his truck. "Catch the windshield, too, please."

"Yessir," responded Gus. "You know, a couple of guys in black suits was looking for ya. Said you had a family emergency of some sort and they needed to help you out."

"Really," Colby chuckled. "That's a good one. Nope, no family emergency. They just made that up to trap you into telling them where we were, or where we were going to be. They're going to find us very shortly," Colby's voice was matter-of-fact. He gave Gus a wink and pointed to Jimmy in the front seat. "Jimmy, you wait there. I've gotta phone call to make."

Colby took the short walk to the pay phone located inside the waiting area. Out of habit, he checked the coin return, but no luck this time. He took a dime out of his pocket and dialed The Caboose.

Fifteen minutes earlier at The Caboose, Sarah had given Gritzmacher and Calhoun the message that Colby would meet them out front in twenty minutes. She had been pleasant with her delivery on the outside, but on the inside, she seethed with anger.

"Thank you, Miss," Gritzmacher politely responded. "That's the first best decision anyone has made in this God forsaken town."

The phone rang and Sarah rushed to the kitchen to pick it up. Her grandma sat in a chair, head in hand, looking old and defeated. Her eyes were red and puffy. Mascara streaked her cheeks. "The Caboose, Sarah speaking."

"Colby again. Tell Jay and his buddies to go to the west side of the bridge and wait there. We'll be there shortly." Colby hung up. Sarah went back to the cash register and quickly scribbled a note to Jay. The note read, 'Colby on his way here. Go to west side of bridge and wait. Be ready to back up Colby on bridge.' She put the note in front of Jay who read the note and responded with a nod of the head. He slid the note over to Robert. They communicated mutual understanding via eye contact.

"You can pay me when you're ready. Thanks for coming in," Sarah smiled and went back to the register to write up the agents' bill. The boys took another long pull of their beer and put two one-dollar bills on the bar.

"Thanks for the beers," said Jay. "We've got to get going."

Mark looked at Jay with a confused look . "But it's Robert's birthday!"

"Time to go," Jay tilted his head toward the door.

Sarah turned around, waving a quick good bye in the direction of the boys as they departed, "Good to see you. See you next time."

She finished adding up the bill and put it in front of Gritzmacher. Through clenched teeth and tightened lips, she did her best to be pleasant. "Thanks for stopping. Hope to see you again soon."

"I told you the old lady was going to crack," Gritzmacher

boasted as he got up from his stool. He was looking at Calhoun but directed his voice at Sarah. "It was just a matter of time before the pressure got to her."

"Copy that," Calhoun said in agreement. Gritzmacher threw a five-dollar bill on the bar and confidently paraded to the door with Calhoun a step behind. Sarah's eyes shot darts at them as they left the relative darkness of the bar to enter the bright sunlight. She hustled to the front window and stood on her tiptoes to see them put on their aviator sunglasses, glancing up and down the street for any sign of Colby or the Scout.

Colby returned to the truck after paying Gus for the gas. He looked at Jimmy and smiled, "Are you ready? Roll down your window and put your seatbelt on. This is where it gets interesting." Jimmy tightened his belt as tight as he could stand.

"On to The Caboose?" Jimmy asked.

"Next stop is The Caboose," Colby answered. "Jimmy, open the ashtray." Without hesitation, he did as he was told. Colby reached into his pocket withdrawing the medal. He held it in the palm of his hand and gave it a kiss. As if handling fine china, he placed it in the ashtray before pushing it shut.

Colby pulled out of the Sinclair station, gave Gus a goodbye wave, and idled at the intersection as two flatbed semi-trucks each hauling a combine from west of the river passed. Evidently, harvest season was well under way with the second cut of alfalfa. At a crawl, he cautiously headed southwest up the street to The Caboose. Windows down, they could feel that the warmth of the day had begun to transition into the cooler twilight. The buildings to their right were casting elongated rectangular shadows across the weathered blacktop. Business owners glanced from behind glass store fronts, locking up for the evening. Townsfolk walking and driving past, splintering in different directions for home. Ahead, two couples were going inside The Caboose for Happy Hour. As they got closer, Colby could see two dark figures loitering in the shadow cast by the bar. The two 'Staties' began to make their way past the parked vehicles toward the street proper. Colby resisted the temptation to run them over and pulled even with the two sinister statuettes standing behind the trunk of their '68 Ford two-door hardtop.

Gritzmacher and Calhoun advanced toward the Scout to crowd in by Jimmy's open window. Gritzmacher skipped introducing himself to Jimmy and got right to the matter at hand. "Evening Dr. Phillips. Nice to see you again. Been a few years since the fun we had in Harris." Gritzmacher's voice dripped with sarcasm. His face transitioned from a wide smile with relaxed eyes to an irritated frown with narrow eyes. "You have something you'd like to turn over to me?"

Jimmy sat silent, eyes forward, arms crossed, refusing to make eye contact. Colby rotated a quarter turn, rested his arm on the top of the steering wheel and leaned back. Relaxed and untroubled, completely dispassionate in the moment. "Yeah. But here's the deal. See, I want to give you the medal, but I don't have it. We left it at our campsite by the village. The truck's empty because we left everything out there. Look for yourself."

Both agents backed away from the Scout just enough to see the cargo area completely empty. Calhoun walked around behind the vehicle to take a closer look. With his stubby hands blocking the glare, he put his face to the rear window and verified the back of the Scout was bare.

"Look, smart ass, I know you have it," Gritzmacher snarled. "Hand it over or consider yourself under arrest for trespassing, confiscation of government property, and obstruction. You want to repeat Harris again? Trust me, this time I won't be playin' around. It will be much worse. How does five to ten at the State Pen in Sioux Falls sound?" Gritzmacher looked at Calhoun who was back at his elbow, "Maybe he wants to die an old man in prison?"

Jimmy's body language remained passive with his elbow resting on the space left by the open window, legs causally flung under the dash, torso angled against the door. His nostrils flared slightly and his left hand made a fist. Colby hoped he'd keep his cool and not take a swing at the glaring Gritzmacher.

"Hey, I'm trying to cooperate here. I don't want any trouble. Just follow me out to the village and you can have it," Colby pleaded.

"Alright, it's against my better judgement, I'm going to trust you. Cross me, and I'll put you and this punk kid behind bars," Gritzmacher said pointing his long slender finger at Colby, then Jimmy in succession.

Colby raised his right hand. "On my honor, but we better get going. It'll be dark soon."

Colby pulled ahead to the corner as the two agents hustled to their car. He saw them pull out as he turned the corner to head west along the railroad tracks toward the bridge. Colby slowed the Scout to be sure Gritzmacher and Calhoun were taking the bait.

A quick look back confirmed they had.

27

The orange sun sat just above the horizon offering its last remaining rays of daylight as they left town, passing combines gobbling up their harvest from the field and a couple of cattle trucks full of meat on the hoof headed east to Redfield, Gritzmacher surmised. The wind blew from the northwest and whitecaps pounded the shore as they neared the bridge. Obediently, the agents stayed tight on Colby's tail following the Scout into the trap Colby had set.

"What's your plan once we get the medal from Phillips?" asked Calhoun.

Gritzmacher thought about it for a second, then replied, "Been thinking. Once we get it, we head back to Pierre and tell them we were unable to get the medal. We'll say that, to the best of our knowledge, Dr. Colby Phillips has it. He was seen with it in the bar, right? The old lady, Katherine was her name, will be our witness. She's scared and doesn't want to cross us. Then we contact JR to pawn it, collect our cash, and live a happy life. How does that sound?"

"Sounds like a plan!" Calhoun said tilting his head back with a laugh. "I like it. But what about Dr. Phillips and the kid? How do we keep them from talking?"

Gritzmacher stared straight ahead then cleared his throat. "Our ace in the hole is the doctored photos of Phillips in, shall we say, a compromised position with that young Indian girl. You think he'd jeopardize his career or his funding? No way. The kid, on the other hand, could be a problem," *he contemplated a possible solution, then turned to Calhoun,* "He would need to be silenced in a manner not to his liking."

Ahead of the state cruiser, Colby's eyes bounced from the road to the rear-view mirror to the fidgeting Jimmy, cracking his knuckles. He turned to look at Colby. "Mind if I ask where we are going?"

"When we get halfway across the bridge, I'm going to stop and let them catch up," Colby answered. "Just sit tight." Colby peered toward the other side of the long bridge for any sign of Jay and his friends. The three-quarter mile long iron superstructure made it tough to see if they were on either shoulder. Although he couldn't see them, he wasn't overly concerned. Colby knew Jay and the boys would emerge if trouble erupted.

Colby could see the tension build in Jimmy as he continued to wriggle in his seat, darting glances at his grandpa, up ahead toward the bridge, and back behind them. Jimmy cleared his throat before he hesitatingly asked, "Aren't you worried about taking them back to the village?"

Colby heard the apprehension in Jimmy's voice and saw the concerned look on his face as they crossed with a thump from the blacktopped pavement onto the concrete roadway of the two-lane bridge. "We're not going to the village," Colby said shaking his head, reaching toward the dashboard to pull on his lights. With his left foot, he hit the silver knob on the floor to turn on his brights. He took his foot off of the gas, coasted, then slammed on the brakes coming to a screeching stop halfway across the bridge. He glanced in the rear-view mirror and smirked.

Colby put the Scout in park with the motor still running, reached in the ashtray and pulled the medal out. He opened the palm of his hand. Jefferson's profile seemed to jump off the face of the somewhat tarnished prize as Jimmy stared at it. "Take a good look at the medal, Jimmy. I'm real proud of the time and effort I, we, put in to find it." Colby stopped. "But this medal belongs, not to us, but to eternity." Colby's voice broke, his emotions getting the best of him. While it pained him to his core to have to do it, he had concluded there could be no other way for him to be free.

Jimmy leaned forward turning to face Colby. Colby watched Jimmy's face transform from the narrow eyes of fright to the big eyes of complete surprise. "WHAT?" he exclaimed with a voice of exasperation. "What are you doing? Are you going to throw it in the river?" He turned to look through the back window then looked at Colby dumbfounded and panicked. "Are you sure you want to do that?"

"No, Jimmy, but that's exactly what I'm going to do." The corners of Colby's mouth drooped, and he shrugged with open palms as if to say, 'There is nothing else I can do.' "It's complicated, Jimmy. Truth is, I've come to realize that I've been a prisoner to the demon of approval all my life. I thought this medal would validate my work, my ego, people's view of me." He paused to check the rear-view mirror, again. "Instead, I think losing it will prove to myself that I don't need it to be whole on the inside." Colby used his index finger to tap his chest. "At the end of the day, I don't really have anything to prove to anyone or myself for that matter. This medal has been nothing but trouble. Standing Bear is right…it's got bad energy, jinxed, or whatever. Obviously,

I've been thinking a lot about this the last couple of days, and I see no other way out of this. The Indians don't want it. It's too risky for us to keep it, and there's no way in hell I'm going to let those two State crooks get it."

Jimmy, wide eyes on a speechless face, turned to look with suspicion in his side rearview mirror at the State car parked behind them. His attention returned to Colby. Jimmy knew he would remember this moment. He felt he was transitioning from an adult-to-child relationship to an adult-to-adult relationship with his grandpa. A metamorphosis he didn't see coming. Instead of looking 'up' to his grandpa he felt he was looking 'at' his grandpa. "But what about the money? You told me it was worth a lot. I thought that was important to you."

"I thought it was," Colby bowed his head, his hand sweeping over his eyes toward his mouth. "It's not anymore. Through all of this," Colby's head swiveled to look at Jimmy, "I finally have figured out that who you are is more important than what you do or what you accumulate." He shrugged, looking through the window at the bridge's massive iron beams. "I don't expect you to understand now, but hopefully someday what I've said will make sense to you. I'm doing this for *me* and no one else. I owe it to myself to unburden myself from all that this medal represents." Colby looked square into Jimmy's eyes, "I know who I am, and it's not determined by this medal."

Colby swallowed hard before he resumed speaking, "Make sure your seatbelt is as tight as you can get it. After I toss it in, we are going to hightail it onto the reservation and try to lose them. They are going to want to rough us up, arrest us, or worse yet, kill us, if for no other reason than to punish us because they didn't get the medal. We will hide out in Brave Eagle. Hopefully, Standing Bear will find it in his heart to hide us. If it gets ugly in the next few minutes, Jay will come help us out. He and Robert are on the other side of the bridge."

Behind Colby and Jimmy confusion reigned. Seeing the bright brake lights against the darkening evening hit them with a wave of surprise. "What the hell is he doing?" Gritzmacher said incredulously. He slammed on the brakes skidding to a shrieking halt a car length behind the Scout. Gritzmacher turned on his headlights and the spotlight from the driver's side pillar. As he looked through the back window of the Scout, it looked like Colby and Jimmy were in an animated discussion.

The Staties were edgy as they sat in their seats and observed. Gritzmacher leaned forward, straining to see, waiting for a sign or movement, anything that would give a clue as to what the holdup was. "This doesn't feel right. It doesn't feel right at all." Gritzmacher began to grab the door handle, deciding to investigate. Without warning, Colby emerged from the truck, looking back as he circled around the front of the truck to the edge of the bridge.

Gritzmacher screamed at Calhoun, "Get the shot gun out of the trunk. Phillips is up to something." Gritzmacher turned off the car, exited, and hastily went around to the front of it while Calhoun quickly went to the trunk to grab the shot gun. He returned to the side of the car and bent on one knee with the loaded shotgun to his shoulder in a ready position.

"Not a step closer or I'll throw the medal in the river," Colby yelled as the wind whistled around the steel girders.

"Okay. Okay. Stand down, Roger," pleaded Gritzmacher at the top of his lungs.

"Tell him to put the gun back in the trunk and then come up to the front of your car. Do it NOW!" Colby hollered.

"Do it, Roger." Calhoun quickly got up and spun around to

return the shotgun to the trunk. He promptly took his place alongside Gritzmacher.

"Okay, that's done, just as you wanted. Now don't do anything rash. Let's just talk for a minute," Gritzmacher pleaded.

Colby's hair blew over his forehead as he skittishly slid closer to the edge.

"No talking." Colby glanced down at the bustling river crashing into the concrete bridge abutment, then back at Gritzmacher. Second thoughts were beginning to creep back into his mind. *I'm about to throw away tens, or hundreds, of thousands of dollars. The money isn't worth it. Hell, maybe jail for both of us. Jimmy's future? Will it totally free me if I throw it in? How to reconcile an irreconcilable situation? No alternative. It must be done. Bastards!* He opened his palm for a last look.

"What do you want? I can help you in so many ways," said Gritzmacher, arms outstretched, inviting a compromise. "C'mon Dr. Phillips, we can work this out."

"I want you to see this," Colby calmly hollered as he opened his hand and dangled the medal in Gritzmacher and Calhoun's direction. The bright lights from the headlights hit the medal giving it a spiritual aura.

The tease irked Gritzmacher. "You sonofabitch. We see the medal. Now hand it over."

"Now you see it," Colby yelled, trembling as he reached over the silver railing and dropped the medal into the dark chasm above the murky river churning sixty feet below. As the medal left his hand, unlike the loss of his treasured wife and daughter, he felt liberated. Free at last. He looked back with a heart full of joyous fury, pointing a finger at both crooked agents. "And now you don't!"

The medal and its history were gone. From President Thomas Jefferson to Robert Scot to Johann Reich to Lewis and Clark to Kakawita to Standing Bear and lastly, Dr. Colby Phillips. From horse and buggy days to the days of men walking on the moon. History woven across the continent and through centuries. Once admired and treasured, now a footnote. It had been carried over 2,000 miles, been traded for, killed over, dug up, and now the medal had found its eternal resting place. Over 160 years of history fluttering to the bottom of the Missouri River, entombed in a foot of muddy silt.

Colby dashed around the truck and hopped in. The door shut with a loud clunk and he punched the accelerator to the floor. His tires howled and smoke came off the pavement as they sped west with the three quarter-moon rising behind them.

Gritzmacher and Calhoun stood stunned, then raced around and got in the car. Gritzmacher killed the spotlight and lit the cherry as he gunned the big one hundred and fifty horse engine in a frantic attempt to catch up to Colby and Jimmy. "'Bout time Phillips finds out who's boss in these parts. Thinks he can get away with this…"

Calhoun unclipped his speakerphone from the dash. "Central this is fifty-nine. In pursuit of two male…" With a backhanded swat, Gritzmacher hit the speakerphone so hard it shot out of Calhoun's hand, ricocheted off the back seat, and came to rest on the floor behind them. "What the…"

"Hell no, Roger. We're off the radar on this one." He stared at his partner, eyebrows raised, daring him to retrieve the speakerphone. The color disappeared from Calhoun's face and his eyes widened, but he said nothing. He knew better than to cross his partner when challenged. The speakerphone would stay right where it had landed. Gritzmacher ran the back of his hand over his lips then pounded the steering wheel with his fist, happy to do harm. "This is personal now. Phillips has no idea what is comin' his way. He wants to play it cute? I'll give him cute. You and that punk kid are mine, Phillips!"

28

Colby passed Jay and the boys going about sixty. He eased off the gas and turned southwest following the path that Sarah had taken when they went to meet Standing Bear. The souped-up Ford closed rapidly. The headlights of the old Scout danced in staccato fashion over the rough road. In the fields to their right, combines were finishing for the day, their headlights looking like the glowing eyeballs of pre-historic creatures. Solitary diesel semis patiently waited for the work to be done and the harvested feed loaded into them. To their left, the darkness was interrupted by the whitecaps on the river and the streetlights of Painted Rock in the distance. Open pastures with occasional fencing were all that lay between them and the shale bluffs that towered above the flowing waters.

Gritzmacher caught up to Colby and followed him from less than a car length behind. "Hang on! I'm going to try to put him in the ditch," Gritzmacher shouted to Calhoun. Gritzmacher buried the accelerator and bumped Colby's rear bumper. "Take that!"

The Scout lurched forward upon impact. Jimmy threw his hands against the dashboard to stop his forward momentum. Colby stiffened his arms on the steering wheel to brace himself. Colby screamed as his ribs absorbed the blow. Jimmy's neck whiplashed against the top of his seat, which slammed his back teeth together sending a piercing dagger of pain through his temples. Colby began to swerve across the center line to negate another clean shot at being rammed. Unfortunately, Gritzmacher had timed the erratic veering and hit them from behind again. The Scout pulled to the right, hit the soft shoulder of the road, and started for the ditch. Undaunted, Colby regained control and pulled the Scout back to the highway. He swung wide to navigate a sharp corner. Gritzmacher followed his track and stayed right on his bumper.

Special Agent Gritzmacher was not going to lose this battle. He pushed the gas pedal maneuvering hard to the left to pull up even with the Scout. He jerked the steering wheel to his right and smashed into Colby and Jimmy. Their truck was pushed sideways through the ditch knocking over a wooden fence post and slid into the adjacent pasture. A cloud of dust enveloped the Scout as it came to a stop.

"Are you alright?" Colby coughed sending a jolt of pain through his body.

"Yeah I'm okay. You okay?" Jimmy's voice carried profound worry.

"I'm fine," Colby answered fanning the dust away from his face.

"What the hell are they doing?"

"I'd say they are trying to kill us."

The red taillights from the Galaxy 500 were stationary by the side of the road twenty yards ahead. Out of the dust and blackness came Gritzmacher and Calhoun arms and legs chugging in a sprint.

"Here they come. Hang on," shouted Colby. Just as the staties had closed the distance to about ten yards, Colby gunned it sending dirt and grass flying. Gritzmacher jumped out of the way to avoid being hit as the truck bounded through the ditch again and onto the road. Both pivoted, raced back to the car, and renewed their pursuit.

The four-cylinder engine in the International Harvester didn't have enough to outrun the finely tuned six-cylinder engine of the Ford. Gritzmacher caught up to them in less than a mile as the pot holed road began to get hilly. On the crest of the next knoll, Colby could see a combine headed their way. It was lumbering along taking up three-quarters of the road. With the speed of the chase, they would pass each other in less than ten seconds by Colby's estimation. He began to straddle the center line in hopes of blocking Gritzmacher's view.

The Ford pressed on. Undeterred, the crazed agent rammed them again from behind. Harder this time.

The wheels of the Scout went airborne returning to the pavement with a piercing thud as the rear bumper skidded into the ditch. Colby and Jimmy both let out a loud yelp when their heads hit the ceiling of the Scout. Colby wrestled back control of the swaying vehicle and gave it more gas. The distance between him and the combine narrowed quickly.

"I've got to time this right," Colby said, checking his rearview mirror. He returned to driving the center line and began to slow down.

"Why are you slowing down?" asked Jimmy, his voice an octave higher than before.

The combine approached. Colby saw the space he needed. "Ever hear of a sucker punch?" He began to ease back into his lane.

Calhoun was surprised to see the Harvester slow down. "I think he's giving up."

"I'm going to try to sideswipe them into the ditch again just to make sure. This time when they're in the field, get the shotgun. Shoot them if they try to get away," Gritzmacher instructed.

"Ten-four. With pleasure."

Gritzmacher hit the gas and yanked the steering wheel hard to the left and crossed the centerline.

Colby saw what was about to happen and crushed the brake pedal into the floor with both feet leaving a thirty-foot skid mark as they fishtailed to a stop. The combine driver hit his horn and brakes at the same time, but it was too late.

"DAMNIT!" Gritzmacher exclaimed while turning hard to the left to avoid the oncoming combine. Their car flew off the pavement, down through the steep ditch, and hit the embankment of the pasture doing fifty. The combination of speed and impact cartwheeled the Ford across the prairie like a tumbleweed in a windstorm, their bodies subjected to traumatic forces.

After four complete glass shattering and parts flying revolutions, the Galaxy 500 came to a stop right side up with half of it extended over the edge of the soft shale bluff. The car looked like the loser in the demolition derby with the roof flattened, the sides crumpled, and the taillights blinking. From the opposite side of the road, Colby and Jimmy looked at each other with mouths agape. Suddenly, with a thunderous roar, the bluff gave way; the car and its occupants cascaded twenty-five feet into the river.

The combine came to a stop thirty yards down the road. The driver came running back with a terrified look on his face. Colby and Jimmy staggered from the truck and hurried over near the edge of the soft, abrupt bank. Colby stared into the choppy waters and saw no sign of the car. The river had claimed it and its passengers, along with tons of soil. There was nothing Colby could do, even if he wanted to. Which, after what the agents had put him through, he didn't. He stood with his hand on his hips, weak kneed, "I really thought they were going to kill us," Colby turned to see Jimmy a few feet behind him, eyes staring straight ahead, unfocused. He put his arm around Jimmy's shoulder, "All I have to say is, those bastards got what they had comin' to them. I'm just relieved it wasn't us."

"I don't know what to say. I've never been so scared in all my life," Jimmy's face was white. Colby drew him close.

Jay, Robert, and Mark pulled in behind the battered Scout just as Colby and Jimmy walked back across the pasture toward the road.

The combine driver met Colby and Jimmy behind Jay's truck. His chest heaved as he tried to catch his breath, his eyes darting between Colby standing next to him and Jay's face in the side mirror. "What the hell just happened? Did you see? I couldn't do anything. Christ sake, what was I supposed to do?" The stocky middle-aged man bent at the waist to rest his hands on his knees, looking like he could vomit. He started to walk toward Jay then spun back, "I tried to stop but the Ford didn't give me any time. Was that a cop?"

Colby leaned forward and looked him in the eye. "Calm down...just take a breath. What's your name?"

"Oh, I'm Stephen Running Dog."

"I'm Colby." He placed a reassuring hand on his shoulder. "I doubt there'd be a cop out here, but that doesn't matter. It's not your fault. That guy was driving way too fast for these roads," Colby said attempting to mitigate Running Dog's anxiety. "On top of that, they tried to pass us in a no passing zone. He just about ran us off the road. Just reckless," Colby scoffed, shaking his head. "Car musta been stolen." Colby scanned up and down the long winding road in both directions, appraising the situation.

He turned to Running Dog, "You got a CB in your rig?"

"Yeah, why?"

"I want to get our story out to the authorities before they start asking questions. The last thing any of us need is law enforcement breathing down our necks, right?"

"Well, yes sir, I guess that's right."

"Ok, here's what I want you to do. This is going to make things easier for both of us." Colby locked his eyes on the combine driver. "Get on your CB, get the Tribal Sheriff to come out. Tell him that you saw a car driving erratically in and out of both lanes. He almost hit you head on and just about ran us off the road. It looked to you like the driver lost control and went over the bluff into the river. Nothing more, nothing less. When the Sheriff questions us that's what we are going to say because it's the truth. Ok? Can you do that?"

The driver shook his head to confirm, "Okay. Yeah I can do it. I sure don't want no trouble."

"There won't be any. You were in a tough spot. There wasn't anything you could have done to avoid him." Colby turned to go and spoke over his shoulder. "Alright then, let the Sheriff know we'll be waiting."

As the sun disappeared behind the horizon, the lights of the Tribal squad car came out of the black and pulled up nose to nose with the Scout. The young Sheriff Dennis Owl was cordial as he introduced himself to Colby and Jimmy. He seemed to know everyone else. Colby watched, nodding at Owl's meticulous attention to detail. Owl surveyed the area with a large handheld floodlight from multiple angles, followed the tire tracks and car parts to the edge of the shale bluff, then returned. Colby and Running Dog gave him their statement which he precisely jotted down on an official form.

"Okay, I think that should just about do it for tonight. Seems pretty straight forward," Owl said with a satisfied look on his face. "I'll be back at first light with another officer to get some pictures and measurements. Since we can't ID the car or its occupants, I'll put out an APB and see what comes up. I know where to find you both if I need you. For now, you're free to go."

Pleasantries and appreciations were exchanged before Running Dog and Owl departed.

Colby passed by the cab of Jay's truck, headed to the Scout. "I imagine The Caboose is still open. You all look like you could use a beer," Colby proposed. "I know I could." Nods and verbal agreement in unison.

Colby and Jimmy piled into the Scout before heading back to Painted Rock and better times. With Jimmy at the wheel, Colby leaned his head back and closed his eyes. A *humph* emanated from his voice box, his lips creasing a smile. *What happens on the reservation stays on the reservation, indeed.*

29

Jimmy heard a loud car horn. His head felt in a vise, his mouth as parched as the Sahara Desert. It felt like his stomach was in his throat, and he might have only rented last night's burger at The Caboose. Wisps of Sarah's hair lay on his face smelling of second-hand smoke and beer. Another blast from the car horn echoed between his ears. Even with his eyes closed, the room seemed painfully bright, like there was a 100-watt light bulb shining right above his head. Jimmy could hear the cheery morning newsman on the TV. Pinned in between the back of the sofa and Sarah, his perspiration-soaked shirt uncomfortable on his skin, he tried to piece together the night before. He rubbed his dry eyes, reluctant to open them.

Desperately trying to get his bearings, his eyes swept Jay and Robert's apartment before settling on the ceiling. Jimmy recalled coming back to Painted Rock from the reservation and going to The Caboose for a beer. Jay, Robert, and Mark were there. Katherine closed early, and they all stayed to clean up while continuing to drink. *We did shots. When will I learn? Grandpa left early. Where did he go?* It was starting to come back to him. *Jay and Robert must be at work already.* He noticed the slivers in his hand and remembered tripping on his way up the back stairs. The car horn blared for the third time longer than the previous two. *Grandpa making a point.*

Jimmy whispered and nudged Sarah, "Sarah, Sarah. I need to get up."

Barely audible, Sarah said, "Huh. What time is it?"

"No idea. I have to get up."

"Go ahead. I need sleep."

Jimmy stiffly, but carefully, climbed over Sarah and knelt beside her. Softly, he spoke, "My grandpa is out back. I'm sure he wants to get out of town before people start asking any more questions. I've got to go." Although her hair was a tangled mess, her face expressed an inner peace. He pushed Sarah's hair away from her face and kissed her on the cheek.

"Go where?" She itched her nose.

"Back to Kansas."

Sarah opened her tired eyes. She rolled from her side to lie on her back and propped her head up on one of the sofa pillows. "Please don't go. Can't you stay just one more day?" She reached out to caress the side of his face.

"I wish I could. Believe me, I wish that with all my heart and with all my soul. I will call you first chance I get. Maybe I could come up on a weekend this fall."

Her face went from sadness to pleading in an instant. "I want to come with you. I want to be with you."

"I want to be with you, too," he said with his voice cracking. He had heard goodbyes were hard, but now he was beginning to understand how hard they really were. "Let's not make this any harder on either of us. It has to be like this, at least for now. I promise to call you." Jimmy leaned forward and kissed her lips.

He pulled away. They stared momentarily into each other's eyes before she leaned in for twisted tongues and lips to complement their active hands.

The car horn shattered the moment. They reluctantly broke off the embrace. "Thank your grandma for me," Jimmy said as he headed for the door. "I can't wait to come back."

"Just go." Sarah said, rolling over and burying her head in the pillow. Spontaneously, she rolled back over and shouted, "I love you!" Jimmy turned at the top of the stairs to go back in but stopped with his hand on the doorknob. Still wallowing in an emotional pool of feelings, he started to answer, but he couldn't. Cognitively he wanted to say he loved her, too, but he didn't know what he should feel before he said that.

Colby leaned out of his window hollering, "C'mon, we gotta go!"

Jimmy wheeled back around, head throbbing, and sauntered down the stairs to get in the passenger side of the Scout. "Sorry, Grandpa. It was a late night. I think I might have drank too much."

Colby gave Jimmy a half smile. "It happens. Katherine was nice enough to let me sleep in the easy chair again last night. I figured I had to let you hang out with Sarah your last night in town. We need to get back to the garage and pack up our stuff. Time to move on."

"Yeah, I figured."

Colby guided the truck through town. Shops were opening as the town was beginning to come to life. They passed moms hustling their kids to the last day of summer school, a mailman intently walking his route, and an elderly couple out walking their dog. Soon they pulled into the driveway of the farmhouse. Jimmy got out to open the garage door allowing Colby into the garage. No sense in carrying things farther than they needed to be. It took them about thirty minutes, but they got all their personal belongings and specimen boxes stuffed into the back of the Scout. Colby backed out and Jimmy closed the garage door. Before getting back in the truck, Jimmy took 360 degrees of mental snapshots. He never wanted to forget this place. Nor did he ever want to forget Sarah.

They took a left at Gus's and headed east. Jimmy put his visor down to limit the blinding rays of morning. The wind through the triangular valance window felt refreshing as he observed that the town didn't seem quite as vibrant or as energized as when they'd rolled into it full of optimism and hope. Jimmy figured life would go on for Painted Rock much the same as it had before they arrived. *Life will never be the same for me, though.* The sun blanketed the fertile fields as they approached the crest of the steep hill that separated them from Painted Rock and the rest of their lives. Jimmy began to get choked up thinking he might not ever see Sarah again. God, how he missed her already!

"Stop the truck!" Jimmy exclaimed.

"What? What happened?" Colby pulled to the side of the road and put the Scout in park. "What is it?"

"I have to go back," Jimmy said looking at his grandpa mournfully.

"I can't believe you let me get this far," Colby said with a chuckle. "You know, Jimmy, if this had happened at any other time, I would be lecturing you on staying in school and staying focused on getting your degree. However," Colby paused as his chest swelled with pride, "in this case, after what we have been through and seeing how you and Sarah took at each other…" His voice trailed off as he put the truck in gear and began to turn around. "The way you look at each other reminds me of when I was courting your grandmother."

"Thanks for understanding."

"I do. Believe me, I do," Colby said smiling at Jimmy.

Colby hit the horn signaling their return as they pulled in behind Jay and Robert's apartment.

"I'll have your dad send you some clothes when I get back," Colby said throwing the Scout in park.

"Could I borrow some money? I'll pay you back. Just 'til I get a job," Jimmy pleaded.

"Of course, Jimmy," Colby said. He pulled two twenty dollar bills out of his wallet.

"Love you, Grandpa."

"Okay, Jimmy. Love you, too. Hey," Colby grabbed Jimmy's arm with a solid grip as he turned to open the door. "Listen," Colby said with keen eyes and a soft voice, "there's a lesson in all of what we've been through for you. Think about it. Up to you to figure it out."

Jimmy stared at Colby, taken back by the timing of his advice. "Okay, Grandpa. Yeah, a lot has happened. Let me give it some thought."

Sarah appeared at the doorway with a surprised look on her face. She threw open the door and walked down the creaky wooden steps, her face morphing into a puzzled expression. "Did you forget something?" She stood apart from the Scout, talking through the window with her arms crossed, waiting.

Jimmy hesitated but with firm conviction got out of the truck taking one last look at Colby through the open door before closing it. With a renewed spring in his step, he went to Sarah. "I sure did." He tenderly placed his hands on her cheeks and guided her waiting mouth toward his. Their embrace tightened, her breasts firmly against his body. Jimmy spoke softly, "I want you Sarah. I want you in my life." A beam of happiness radiated across Sarah's face before she stood on her tip-toes to whisper in Jimmy's ear. A grin burst open Jimmy's face. He took Sarah's hand exclaiming, "Let's go!" They scrambled up the steps pausing at the top to wave goodbye.

Colby leaned out of the window with a big smile and shouted, "You best take care of each other!"

Fate had conspired for happiness in Jimmy's world which made the grandpa in Colby happy. Colby rolled out of the alley, turned on Grand Street to head east, passing by Gus's one last time. With emotions vacillating between relief, joy, and contentment, he drove without looking in his rearview mirror. Passing the old rodeo grounds, he felt good that, in the end, he was the one who'd gotten to dictate the medal's fate. This turned out to be particularly cathartic for him. Colby reasoned that, by breaking the medal's spell, he had freed himself from the shackles of its allure. He chuckled out loud as he pondered how the search for the medal, along with the love he'd so desperately chased within his prison prairie, had controlled a major portion of his personal and professional life. *Live and learn, I guess.* Glancing to his right for one last glimpse of the Missouri River, Colby reflected that he had come to Painted Rock with high expectations for the dig but, with the realization and reconciliation of his inner conflict, left with a better definition of who he was. He felt remade, seeing himself in a whole different light, comfortable in his own skin.

Climbing the last hill out of town, the open window let in the fresh morning air filled with the scent of alfalfa. Dean Martin's, "Everybody Loves Somebody" poured out of the radio, and the open road seemed more open than ever before. Colby turned up the volume and sang along, tapping his fingers on the steering wheel as he headed back to Kansas to begin anew.

Behind him, thunder roared, lightning bolts seared the ground, and straight-line winds traveled the plains toward Painted Rock.

EPILOGUE

The early sun pierced the morning sky. The soft sound of doves cooing floated through an open window as the tired craftsman moved through his well-lit shop with resolve. Wanting to keep things tidy, he placed the silver sulphide back on the shelf next to his hammer and rasp. Barking Coyote removed his denim apron, ignoring the strong chemical smell, and hung it on the hook next to the kiln by the door. The duplicate had turned out much better than anticipated, leaving his mood the sum of pleased plus satisfied. Really a piece the skilled silversmith could handle despite the short amount of time he had. He knew who to call.

"Hello, Stedgeman's…"

"Is JR there?"

"Speaking."

Barking Coyote sat down in his chair and took the loupes off his head. "I have a very rare Thomas Jefferson Peace Medal in my possession that I'd like to sell."

"Is that right? Huh." There was a pause. "Who is this?"

"I'd rather not say. I'm calling you because a customer of mine that works for the State said he had done business with you before. He gave me your number awhile back. Are you interested?"

"I suppose I might be. I'd have to see it to tell you if I would buy it or not, you know. Where are you calling from and how do you know it's authentic?"

"I'm about six hours away from Billings. I know it's authentic because it came out of the ground within the last couple of days. Look, I have no intention of wasting my time or your time."

"You gotta give me a little more than that. How do I know you're not with law enforcement or a state or federal agency?"

"On my family's honor, I am not with any agency or law enforcement." Barking Coyote flipped the medal over on his desk. Then flipped it back. "I will tease you a little, though, by telling you it has both halves still joined together and a crease on Jefferson's face."

The pause on the other end was a little longer this time. "How soon can we meet?"

"I was hoping you would say that." He smiled. This, too, was going better than expected. "I'll meet you, today, in Timber Butte. It's about half-way for both of us. There's a small diner on the east side. Ricky's Diner. Meet me there at noon. Sit at the counter. Order the daily special with no fries and a TaB. I'll find you."

"See you then." The phone line went dead.

Barking Coyote hung up the phone and put the actual Thomas Jefferson Peace Medal in his safe, securing the counterfeit in one of his small jewelry boxes. He let out a giddy chuckle as he hit the light switch and locked the door behind him. A hastily called Tribal Council meeting led by his father would start in a couple of minutes. Checking his watch as he hustled down the stairs clutching the small jewelry box, he thought today could be the best day of his life. *Quick thinking is going to get me paid.*

In a hurried walk up the hill, Barking Coyote passed under the basketball hoop before rounding the corner of his father's house. He smelled the fire first, then saw the smoke wafting out the top of the tepee before entering through the tent flap.

"Sorry I'm late..."

ACKNOWLEDGMENTS

This book had its genesis while our family lived in South Dakota and subsequently blossomed on my return travels once we moved out of state. It matured as my dad and I drove back in July of 2019. I don't know what gave me the idea that I could write a book. I just started to bang away on my keyboard and couldn't stop. Like my buddy Dan said after an early read, "I don't know where all those words came from." Then the pandemic hit—quarantine, isolation… *What else do I have to do?* Along the way, I hit a fair number of speed bumps but wasn't smart enough to quit. Fortunately for me, I had many more voices encouraging and teaching me, people who liked the bones of my story.

Kim Suhr of Red Oak Writing was prominent in each of those categories. Add patience, flexibility, and kindness to her attributes. I will be forever grateful for the tactful manner in which she took this lump of clay and helped to mold it into the shape of a writer. It was really fun to work with her.

The willingness of my advanced readers is deeply appreciated: Lisa Lickel, Kim Suhr, Amanda Waters, Lee Whittlesey, and Lauren Guelig. Thanks to Sue and Greg for their early reads and suggestions; Erin's help with the prison psychologist scene; my mom and dad for their edits and suggestions throughout the project (best teachers and editors ever); and my brother, Steve, for his review and corrections of my manuscript.

Dave, a talented writer and super creative cousin of mine, opened my eyes to character and narrative possibilities. He also turned me on to literature that enhanced my story, along with my writing style. We spent a lot of time over the last couple years discussing my project, his projects, and writing in general.

Thank you to Christa, my wife, for her patience when I would go into my office early and not come out 'till late, and for the times when she would be talking and I zoned out thinking about the book. I know you forgive me. The Master Editor came through, clutch. No surprise there.

Finally, Shannon and her talented team at Ten16 Press helped me run through the tape to get this book published. I thank you all.

I started with a story and ended up writing a book.

ABOUT THE AUTHOR

Pete Sheild is a graduate of the University of Wisconsin and Marquette University School of Dentistry. He is a member of the Wisconsin Writers Association and Red Oak Writing. His first book, Sermons From Thy Father, chronicles his father's journey into the ministry and contains sermons from his first church in Redfield, South Dakota. Retired from dentistry, Pete now enjoys fishing, family time, and writing. He and his wife, Christa, live in Oconomowoc, Wisconsin.

CPSIA information can be obtained
at www.ICGtesting.com
Printed in the USA
LVHW022104011121
702169LV00006B/22